In Praise of
Roots of the Banyan Tree

Vivid, compelling and beautifully told, this story of a half Palestinian Christian, half Lebanese Muslim girl growing up during the Lebanese Civil War deftly interweaves the special complexities of Middle Eastern life and identity with the crushes and excitement of any girl's adolescence. Perfect for mother-daughter book clubs and for classrooms, *Roots of the Banyan Tree* is also perfect for young people, period. I feel sure it will find its way into the hands - and hearts - of many readers. Highly recommended.

—**Gish Jen**, author of *Thank You, Mr. Nixon* and *The Resisters*

Kathryn Silver-Hajo's Noor Haddad al-Husayni is a wonderful heroine—open, honest and just discovering herself as a woman and political being. With straightforward simplicity, *Roots of the Banyan Tree* tells a complex yet universal coming-of-age story of a young person struggling to find a place not only in the wider world but within her own family.

—**Stewart O'Nan**, author of *City of Secrets*

Roots of the Banyan Tree transports us to 1970s Beirut during the Civil War where we find ourselves on Hamra Street walking past restaurants and people in bell bottoms, giving contemporary Beirutis a special brand of nostalgia, a peek into a place that is no longer recognizable. The story describes love and friendship as they bloom in the volatile streets or between the branches of a banyan tree of Beirut, or in New York, where the protagonist is forced to go to flee the war. Written for a western audience but also appealing to young adults everywhere, this story takes the reader on an adventure through the eyes of a young, observant protagonist who confronts monumental challenges with courage and determination.

—**Rima Rantisi**, founding editor,
Rusted Radishes: Beirut Literary and Art Journal

A coming-of-age story that brings to life the pathos and humor of adolescence, set against the backdrop of Beirut and New York in the 1970s. Any young reader who has experienced the emotional turbulence of living in between cultures will recognize themselves in Noor, the charming protagonist.

—**Elias Muhanna**, Associate Professor, Comparative Literature and History, Brown University

Roots of the Banyan Tree

FLOWERSONG
PRESS

a novel

KATHRYN SILVER-HAJO

FLOWERSONG
PRESS

FlowerSong Press
Copyright © 2023 by Kathryn Silver-Hajo
ISBN: 978-1-953447-47-0

Published by FlowerSong Press
in the United States of America.
www.flowersongpress.com

Cover Photo by Aiham Dib
Cover/Collage Art by Lorette Luzajic
Cover Design by Maya Sariahmed
Special Thanks to Alia Haju
Set in Garamond

NOTICE: SCHOOLS AND BUSINESSES
FlowerSong Press offers copies of this book at quantity discount with bulk
purchase for educational, business, or sales promotional use. For information,
please email the Publisher at info@flowersongpress.com.

*For Nasser, Bassil, and Naseem whose unflagging
love and support enabled these pages to take flight*

*To the people of Lebanon, Palestine and everywhere
lives have been changed by war, bigotry, and
racism and in memory of those who didn't make it*

"Your children are not your children. They are the sons and daughters of Life's longing for itself."

—Gibran Khalil Gibran

Also by
Kathryn Silver-Hajo

Wolfsong: Stories

table of contents

Roots of the Banyan Tree

I am Noor
Noor Haddad al-Husayni
I use my mother's family name, Haddad
along with my father's—al-Husayni
I started doing this in high school
though no one else in Lebanon does
and it's not my legal name
I do it as a reminder of all that is behind a name
of things concealed and others revealed

Romance and Rounds
of Fighting

Spring 1975

1.

Springtime is the best time in Beirut. The streets come alive again after the harshness of a chilly, rainy winter. Warm evenings entice couples to stroll arm-in-arm or share outdoor drinks with friends before the scorching heat of summer sets in. The fragrance of sweet spices and frying onions mingles with the sea air and jasmine, all doing their part to mask the odors of exhaust-spewing vehicles, and uncollected garbage.

It was a day like that when I was waiting for the bus after school in the Snoubra neighborhood, welcoming the warmth of the sun on my face. I went to one of the few co-ed English-language private schools and ours had a lower school and an upper school. Even though I was still in eighth grade, I had a crush on a boy in the upper school named Ra'ad. Whenever I saw him in the corridors he'd give me long, lingering looks. Everyone knew he was a big flirt, but I was flattered anyway. When I saw him approaching that day, I ignored him, tossing my hair over my shoulder like the older girls.

Suddenly there was a *ta'-ta'-ta'* of gunfire close enough to make me jump. Fear chilled down my neck. I glanced in all directions, unsure where to run, and before I knew what was happening, Ra'ad was yelling *get down*, pulling me to the ground. The hair was standing up on my arms and legs, and I could feel Ra'ad trembling. I crawled away from the street and he followed behind. We sat with our backs against the school building, panting. I could see other kids who'd run for cover, huddled behind cars, next to walls, some crying, some too stunned to move. I slid away from Ra'ad, embarrassed that our shoulders were touching.

I hadn't heard of any battles in Beirut since a few years before when guerrilla groups had clashed with the army, and then we only learned about it from the news. Now it was right nearby. The shooting seemed to come out of nowhere and it was impossible to judge how close it was, if we were in danger, if we could be hit by a stray bullet. I pulled my knees up to my chest, lowered my head. We stayed like that, pressed against the hard wall, not knowing if we could trust the electric silence that followed the gunfire. When I finally checked my watch it showed we'd been there for more than half an hour.

"What do you think happened to the bus?"

Ra'ad shrugged. Some teachers had run out and were pulling students back to the school.

"Let's make a run for it," he said, getting to his feet.

"No! It's not safe." I doubted my legs would even carry me to the corner. "We should go in too."

"But what if we get stuck here? Let's just go!" he said, grabbing my hand.

I didn't like the idea of being stuck inside the school either—not knowing when we could leave, or even call home to let them know I was safe, so I stood up, bowing my head low. As he pulled me along, a crazy thrill mixed with fear in my belly, like being in the wobbly bucket at the top of the Ferris wheel at Raouche when I was little, looking over all of Beirut and the sea. Ra'ad's daring somehow reassured me, as if nothing could happen to us as long as we stuck together, kept moving.

We ran downhill, laughing from nerves and excitement, bumping into each other, across Hamra Street, cars honking at us, the smell of roasting nuts in the air. We passed the old guy with his leathery face selling fish on a wooden cart, yelling *Samak! Samak!* and on down to Bliss Street where students in bellbottoms and miniskirts strolled with books against their chests and under their arms. Professors smoked their pipes, while eating lunch at Restaurant Faisal across from the arched gate of AUB—the American University of Beirut, where Baba taught. Everyone in the area seemed oblivious, as if the staccato reports had blended seamlessly with the cacophony of the City, and was nothing out of the ordinary.

I suddenly noticed we were still holding hands and I pulled away, afraid someone would see us. Ra'ad gestured towards the entrance of the university.

"Let's go in. We'll be safe in there."

"But don't we need an ID?"

He smiled. "You only need one if you think you do."

At first, I was taken aback. It had never occurred to me that I had such a choice. I'd simply been given my ID and I'd never questioned it before.

The guard was busy giving directions to a young student and we slipped through the gate unnoticed. I was nervous that we'd run into Baba or one of his colleagues who knew me, but Ra'ad led me straight through the campus and into the thicket of vertical roots of an exuberant old banyan tree.

There was no room to sit, and standing in that narrow space, my arm brushed against his. He asked if I was OK and I nodded, realized I was shaking. He put his arm around me and pulled me up against him. He was so close I could feel his breath, warm on my cheek. His skin smelled of smoke and cologne, his eyes dark as Turkish coffee. It was like he was looking into me—refusing to turn away. My cheeks were burning, but I kept staring into his eyes, not wanting to lose the feeling.

His long brown hair fell softly against his neck and I reached up to touch it. He had a cigarette tucked behind his ear and he wore a white shirt with a wide collar, revealing a little of his smooth chest. He cupped my head in his hand and pulled me towards him until his lips barely touched mine, but then he pressed his mouth hard against mine. His lips were warm and firm and soft and salty all at once. It was even better than I'd imagined when I was alone in my room at night.

Ra'ad.

Even his name means thunder.

I ran down the steep stone staircase that led all the way downhill to the Corniche al-Manara, counting—and then losing count—like when I was a little girl. I jumped off near our apartment building, just a couple of blocks before reaching the Corniche and the sea. I could still feel the press of Ra'ad's lips, his body against mine, but my excitement was tinged with the lingering fear and uncertainty of what had happened earlier. Recently my parents had been fretting over the news, talking about how the government seemed determined to crush any attempt by poor people to improve their circumstances, especially if they were Muslim. I was used to political talk at the dinner table and I still remembered when violence had erupted in Beirut a few years back, but we'd made it through then, and now I was older and not as frightened as I had been then. I hoped today's clash was just an isolated incident and soon summer would come, with trips to the mountains and the beach.

I couldn't wait to tell my best friend, Layla, about Ra'ad. She already had a boyfriend and it was finally my turn, so that weekend I put on my best bellbottoms and platform shoes and met Layla at her family's apartment. Now that I was fourteen, my parents let me go out with her, as long as her older brother, Elie, was with us, so he escorted us to Hamra Street, winked and put his finger to his lips before leaving us on our own. Hamra was crowded with people. Traditional Arabic music was blaring from one coffee shop, Abba blasting from another, as if we were walking between two different worlds. Women strolled by in wide-leg pantsuits and chunky heels, their long straight hair parted down the middle, eyes dramatically accented with mascara and kohl. Men with long sideburns and hair sat in sidewalk cafes in the warm sunshine, wearing Ray Bans, sipping Turkish coffee, gesturing with Marlboros gripped between two fingers, wide-lapelled shirts open to reveal a gold chain with a cross or a tiny gold Quran. They watched the women pass by, leaning in to each other to whisper comments, try to catch an eye.

I told Layla how Ra'ad touched the inside of my ear with his tongue, how we slipped out through the gate and the guard with the long, curled mustache yelled, "*Shayaateen!* Devils! Get home before I call your parents!" wagging his thick, hairy finger at us.

"Noor's first kiss," she said, pouting out her lips like a movie star, her eyes glittering with mischief.

"Maybe it wasn't," I said, nudging her with my shoulder. I knew how unconvincing I sounded and Layla arched her eyebrows at me.

"*Khalas*," I said, wishing she would share my secret without making me feel like a kid. I suppose being two years older she wanted to emphasize how mature she was.

There was a beggar huddled on the sidewalk practically beneath the skirts of the shoppers breezing by her, her head and body draped in worn black cloth, a grime-covered baby asleep in her lap. She was holding up one hand, her eyes half closed, chanting over and over, "*Allah ykhalleeki. Allah ya'teeki ya rub. Allah yehmi wlaadik*," pleading with passersby to help. I pulled a few coins out of my pocket and dropped them into her hand.

"Poor woman," I said to Layla. "Everybody ignores her. I guess they figure she's Palestinian so they can't be bothered." Being half Palestinian myself I knew what it was like to have people look down on you.

Layla lifted one shoulder. "Or maybe she makes them feel guilty."

For sure *I* felt guilty, knowing that I'd be going home to a big flat with plenty to eat and nice clothes and she probably went back to a refugee camp at night to sleep in a shack with no running water or electricity.

"Hey, watch it!" A voice jolted me out of my thoughts. We jumped back from the edge of the street, startled to see a boy about to pass by on a noisy scooter, wearing plastic *shibshib* sandals, one hand up in the air balancing a round tray with a brass *rakweh* of coffee and five or six little cups, on his way to a delivery.

The gunfire came out of nowhere. One bullet struck the back of the scooter, right in front of us. We heard the metallic *zinggg!* of the bullet ricocheting off the fender, tipping the scooter over, sending the boy, *rakweh*, and cups flying to the ground, shards of the cups seemingly suspended in mid-air for an instant, coffee spraying onto our shoes, its aroma filling our nostrils.

We screamed and fell to the ground next to the boy, our heads close to the filth of the blacktop. My arms and legs were shaking violently and I fully expected to see them covered in blood, but there was none. People were hysterical, running for cover, dropping to the sidewalk. I could smell the boy's sweat mingled with the oily odor of his scooter, the cardamom in the coffee. There were people lying all around us, some sobbing, some praying. A woman cried out on the opposite side of the street and we saw a little boy on the ground, blood flowing from his head into the gutter. I stared, too shocked to move. Was he dead? This innocent child. How could this be happening?

The woman was bent over him screaming for help, trying to gather up his body. His arms and legs were twitching, but his eyes were closed. I wanted to run to them, but suddenly saliva came into my mouth and I bent over the curb, retching. Then, more gunfire a short distance away and Layla was trying to pull me up.

An ambulance wailed up the street, but people were crowded around the boy and the paramedics couldn't get through. They yelled at the crowd to disburse and someone fired a shot into the air to make them move. More screaming, everyone running. I was still bending down and I feared I'd be trampled, but Layla yanked me up and we ran, too. I turned back and saw the paramedics lifting the boy onto a stretcher, holding the mother back as she tried to throw herself onto her son.

We hurried towards home and I grabbed Layla's arm and pulled her close. We were both shaking hard. Within minutes, the ambulance sped down Hamra Street, the crowds vanished, and all the stores were closed and shuttered. We couldn't believe this was the same street that had been alive with clinking dishes, chatter and laughter minutes before. Now there was a somber, dark feeling, as if danger and death might be lurking around any corner. We held onto each other as we walked silent and shivering, wishing her brother was there to take us home.

Layla squeezed my arm and said, "Maybe we should keep this between us."

"But we could've been killed. And what if our parents heard the gunfire?"

"Do you really want to upset them? Besides," she said, "they might never let us go out alone to Hamra anymore."

I didn't know what to do. It was the second time in a week I'd heard gunfire and this time a child had been struck right next to me. I couldn't shake the image of his little body twitching, of his mother desperate to save him. That bullet came out of nowhere. It could have torn through Layla or me just like that.

At home I went straight to my room after kissing Momma on both cheeks, willing the tears to stay back. She didn't say anything, so it seemed she hadn't heard about the incident.

"I have so much homework," I said. "I have to go study."

"At least have a snack, *hayaati*."

Momma tried to lure me to the kitchen but I lied and said Layla and I had gotten a sandwich.

In truth I had no appetite after what we'd seen. I couldn't stop thinking about the little boy, wondered if he was even alive, how his mother would bear it if he died. I had a powerful urge to run to Momma and tell her everything that had happened, to feel her warm hands on my face, comforting me. Instead, I lay on my bed, staring out the window, thinking about the last few days, trying to make sense of it.

I didn't want Momma to know how much danger we'd been in, didn't want to worry her. I also knew that if I told her what happened, she'd know Elie hadn't been with us and she'd probably never trust me or let me go out alone again. Having the freedom to explore Beirut with my friend was a new privilege and I wasn't about to jeopardize it even though I was too shaken to go anywhere for the moment, too confused about what was happening.

There had always been a lot of political factions in Lebanon—everyone knew that. Some were religious, but a lot of them were just trying to fight for their rights and force the government to treat them more fairly. But now, all these groups and factions were starting to be armed. I worried that being Palestinian Christian from Momma's side and Lebanese Muslim from Baba's could put me in danger in ways I dreaded to even think about. When I was younger, we never worried about such things. I was just *Noor*. People rarely asked what religion or background you came from without some reason, but now these attributes were being used to incite hatred and violence.

I went to the drawer, pulled out my government-issued ID card and studied it. An old black-and-white photo of me with my hair pulled back in a ponytail, an awkward, toothy smile. Official stamps, dates, and signatures littered the document. On the left side, all the "facts" of my identity:

Name: Noor al-Husayni

Father's name: Rasheed ʿAli al-Husayni

Mother's maiden name: Nadine Daoud Haddad

Date of Birth: January 24, 1961

Place of Birth: Tyre, Lebanon

Denomination: Shiʿa

All the facts. Except for one thing. *Denomination:* Shiʿa.

The truth is, Baba wasn't religious—he considered himself a leftist and would never say he was Shiʿa if someone asked. He thought it was an offensive question, so he'd deflect it with a chuckle and say, *I'm a Buddhist*, which somehow fit his open, accepting, big-hearted way. He spent a lot of time inside his head—*the thinker*, Momma liked to call him. Completing the effect, he had a fine, round belly like Buddha.

But there it was in black and white.

The law required that you declare a religion and it automatically had to be your father's and that in turn had to be his father's—and on and on. As for the mother, her religion—or lack of it—and her nationality, had nothing to do with anything. Looking at my ID you'd never know I was half Palestinian Christian. Basically, you were stuck with whatever that document declared—no matter what you might actually believe. People might judge you because of it, not let their son or daughter marry you, give you special treatment, restrict which government posts you could take. They decided who you were because of it.

I thought about Ra'ad saying *you only need an ID if you think you do*. If only that were true. I thought of his warm breath when he whispered in my ear inside the banyan tree. *Ammoorah*, he'd called me – little moon. I was mesmerized by this exciting new relationship—a secret shared only with Layla. Being alone with a boy wasn't allowed—especially at my age, so there was no way my family could know about it, and I had to be careful. I remembered the danger and fear I felt that day, but also the thrill of kissing him—and it made me wish he was there with me, his eyes tracing my face and body, helping me forget everything else.

I went into the living room and put my hand on the huge old brass key that hung on the wall from a long, thin piece of cloth. It was nearly four inches long—the key to my great-grandfather's home in Palestine, where Momma lived until the 1948 war drove them out. I asked her to remind me what the house was like, even though she'd told me many times.

"From Jiddo's stone house in Shefa 'Amr, you could see the mountains and valleys of the Galilee stretching all the way out to the horizon. In summer, the breeze came through and kept it cool. There were olive trees all around and we'd harvest the olives together—Jiddo, Momma, Baba, my two brothers, my sister, and me—the same way the family had for generations."

They'd take some of the olives to a place where they'd press them into thick, green oil. I could almost see my great-grandfather's gnarled hands picking olives one by one—a traditional white headdress on his head and wearing a long, loose *gelabiyyah* robe.

Momma described how every Easter they'd roast a whole lamb and lots of relatives would come. The table would be piled with delicious dishes like *maqloobah* and *musakhkhan*, homemade *ma'mool* cookies stuffed with dates, platters of fresh fruits. Sometimes in the summer they'd drive to the shore so they could swim in the sea. She said it was a lot like the beach in Baba's hometown, Tyre, which was just a few miles north of the Israeli border. I imagined her crammed into the back seat of their little Citroen with her brothers and sister, singing songs on the way to the beach, hanging part way out the window, the wind whipping her hair back.

Momma was eleven when the soldiers came. They only had time to pack a few clothes, a little food.

I passed the key between my two hands, hefting its solid weight, so unlike the little keys I was used to. "But why is it so huge?"

Momma laughed. "I have no idea, really. Maybe it's so we have something big enough to hang on our wall to remember our old house in Palestine."

"I'm sorry, Momma. Maybe someday we can go visit."

"*Inshallah, habeebti.* I hope so. For now, I want you to have the key. Keep it close so you never forget."

Gripping the oversized key in my hand, I could almost feel it entering the lock with a satisfying clunk, a final puzzle piece snapping precisely into position.

A few days later, I was at school and my Classical Arabic teacher asked me to discuss a passage in a difficult ancient text because he knew I was very good at it. At the end of the hour, my classmate Cybelle walked past my desk and muttered, "Who cares? French is better anyway. I hate this class."

Not sure if I was somehow being insulted or she was just complaining, I shrugged and said, "It's our heritage after all, so even if it's hard I guess we should learn it."

"Maybe it's your heritage, but it's not mine."

"Really?" I said, puzzled, thinking maybe she wasn't originally Lebanese.

"My parents say we Maronite Christians are Phoenician, not Arab, so I can't be bothered."

I knew very well that there had been a thriving Phoenician civilization in the area thousands of years earlier, but it seemed absurd that any modern person would call themselves Phoenician now—yet Cybelle seemed deadly serious.

After school, Layla and I met to get a shawarma sandwich and I greeted her saying, "Hello, my Phoenician friend."

She stood up very tall with her arms straight at her sides, imitating the little blue-green Phoenician figurines our parents had in our living rooms. "Where did that come from?"

When I told her about Cybelle she said, "Maybe she belongs in a museum with the other relics, then."

"Do you think there's any truth to it?"

"Sure. Her ass is Phoenician! And so is your left nostril."

I was relieved by Layla's reaction especially since she was also from a Maronite family. But even though Cybelle's declaration seemed ridiculous to me, I couldn't help feeling put down and different. I'd been raised to think that being Arab was something to be proud of, and even though I knew prejudice existed, it had always seemed separate from me, something that ignorant adults wielded like weapons—especially now. But to have a girl my own age talk that way to me was confusing and although it made me angry, it also got me thinking again about my complicated background, what it meant to be all these things. I was so glad to have friends that didn't think that way at all, like Layla. Even Ra'ad, whose family were Sunni Muslims, hadn't mentioned the subject, and as far as I knew it didn't matter to him that we came from different backgrounds. A lot of families wouldn't accept you marrying someone from a different religion or sect, but it was way too soon to be thinking about things like that with Ra'ad. Even so, it made me wonder. *What would happen if we did get serious?*

2.

One Saturday in early April my parents invited a few friends over.

"Momma says I should be more optimistic, stop expecting the worst, so what better way than having a party? Some good music, a little dancing to raise spirits," Baba said, wiggling his hips and shaking his shoulders, making me laugh in a way only Baba could.

I knew Layla was coming with her parents and I couldn't wait for her to arrive, but when the bell rang it was just my parents' friend Yusuf. He'd brought his wooden *naay* flute, along with a bottle of scotch and a friend named Antoine. Later I found out they were both journalists like Momma's father—my *jiddo*—had been, back in Palestine.

Baba kissed Yusuf three times on the cheeks, all the while glaring at Antoine over Yusuf's shoulder.

Yusuf said, "You guys know each other from AUB, no? From waaay back when you were students?"

Baba frowned and said, "Yes, yes," and his neck got blotchy so I knew he wasn't happy.

It wasn't like him. He was usually the one joking around, making people feel welcome, with his open face and smiling eyes that seemed to have lights shining in them. I even thought his Buddha's belly was comforting. He wasn't fat, just robust, in a way that let you know he loved life and food and people, so I knew right away he didn't like Antoine. He excused himself, saying he was going to get glasses.

When Antoine saw me, he put his hand over his mouth and his eyes widened.

"You must be Noor—so grown up!" He shook his head as if in disbelief. "*Mon Dieu*, where does the time go?" he said wistfully.

I wondered who this stranger was, acting like he knew me and speaking half in French.

"I knew your parents, years ago." He pressed his hand to his cheek and spoke slowly like he was remembering. "I've been in America a long time. Too long—and I see nothing has waited for me."

He leaned toward me, expecting me to kiss his cheeks. I didn't want to be rude, but I didn't know him and I could see Baba didn't like him, so I held my hand out stiffly and said, "*Tsharrafna.*" I could see he was puzzled by my formality. He was very handsome, with sandy hair and blue eyes and I felt shy.

"You look just like your mother," he said.

I nodded politely and went to find my parents. I was just outside the kitchen door when I heard Baba say in a low voice to Momma—in English, "Guess what the cat dragged in?"

I peeked in, long enough to see Momma's face. It was pale and her mouth was slightly open. For a minute she seemed frozen in that position, looking beyond Baba towards the door. Finally, she lifted her hand and smoothed the hair above her ear, then clapped down the glass she held in her other hand.

"*Khalas*, Rasheed, enough," she said, scolding. "He's our guest. Go out and be civil. I'll be right there."

As usual, Momma was taking charge of the situation. Sometimes I got the sense that it was a relief for Baba not having to be the one making all the decisions. I never could see why some wives would just do whatever their husbands told them to and I knew even then that in that way I'd be like Momma when I got married.

Baba set down glasses and ice next to the scotch, waved his hand and said, "Help yourselves," rather than serving them like he usually would. He poured himself a double—or maybe even a triple. Momma hated when he drank like that and when she finally came out with wine for herself and Pepsi for me, she gave him a stern look, the two vertical lines in her forehead deepening for a fraction of a second.

I was relieved when Momma's aunt Soraya and uncle Emil came in. They had raised her since both her parents had died when she was little and I called them *Sitto* and *Jiddo* as if they were my own grandparents.

Sitto pinched both of my cheeks and said, "*Amar inti!* Pretty as the moon. You're a photocopy of your mother."

"True," Jiddo said, "but you like to study just like Baba, isn't that right, clever girl? Someday she'll make us all proud," he said winking at Momma, who frowned at him.

"Ah—and I don't like to study *ya'ni?*" she said, exasperated.

Jiddo shrugged and waved her comment away with a flick of his wrist. Momma had been a perfect student at AUB and now she worked as a top editor at a journal that covered current events in Lebanon so her nose was always in books too, but she was convinced that her uncle had always thought of her as a housewife since she'd married and had me so soon after graduating.

They all sat down and Yusuf started to play the *naay* flute. The melancholy sound conjured the desert, even though I'd never been to a desert, and I imagined a lone figure in a long robe, resting against a dune, playing to the moon while the sand shifted like ghosts in the breeze.

The doorbell jolted me out of my dream state. This time it was Layla, finally, with her parents. Janine was with them too. Layla's mother handed a bouquet of roses to Momma. Janine had been my nanny when I was little and I hadn't seen her in years. She planted three firm kisses on my cheeks to show how much she'd missed me and pressed something into my hand. When I opened it I saw that it was a good luck charm—made of blue evil eye beads and a horseshoe charm.

I kissed her cheek and said, "*Shukran*, Auntie. Why did you trouble yourself?"

"This will keep you safe from prying eyes."

It made me smile even though I'm not superstitious. I figured that with everything that was going on in Beirut we could use a little good luck.

Jiddo got the *darbakkeh* drum from the corner and rubbed the taut skin to soften it. He held it under his arm, rapping the head with his fingers, making it talk. *Dum takki takki takk dum takki takk!* Baba downed his scotch, snapped his fingers and moved his shoulders back and forth, beckoning to Momma to dance with him. She resisted, staying in her chair. He frowned and his shoulders dropped, but he poured himself another glass and pretty soon he was up again—as if determined to have a good time. He convinced Layla's mother to get up and the two of them moved their feet and hips to the rhythm, hands making slow circles in the air. I glanced across the room at Antoine, this mysterious stranger who made my parents so uncomfortable and I wondered what he was doing there.

Baba and Layla's mother beckoned to the others to get up and it wasn't long before *Sitto* joined them, as did Antoine and even Layla. Antoine went over to Momma and put his hands out to her, trying to get her to join, his hair flopping over one eye. He moved his slim hips like a belly dancer and most everyone was clapping and encouraging him except Momma. She turned away, her face red. Baba was clenching and unclenching his fist. I don't think anyone else noticed. They were too busy convincing Momma to join. They all went over and tugged on her arms and hands until she got up.

Antoine winked at me and said, *"Yalla!"* but I folded my arms across my chest and refused to get up. He seemed disappointed, but he turned and joined the rest. Momma was a really good dancer and pretty soon they all made a circle around her and snapped their fingers until she relented. She moved her arms and legs effortlessly, as if they were long, flowing ribbons and her hips were the engine driving them with slow, graceful thrusts. She was wearing a traditional long, black Palestinian dress for the occasion, with a vee-neck and draping sleeves like wings. The front and seams had delicate green, blue, red and yellow embroidery and there were two braided strings tied at the neck.

She looked pretty and young with her hair wound up into a bun so you could see her long neck, her slim body moving under her dress in a way that embarrassed me. I didn't want to admit that my own mother could actually be sexy.

When the song ended, they all collapsed back into their chairs. I saw Baba look at Momma. She picked up her wine glass and took a long sip.

She lowered it and glanced across the room at Antoine and then at Baba who was frowning. Antoine had a faint smile on his face as if he was amused by how uncomfortable they both seemed. That in turn made me uncomfortable even though I wasn't sure what was going on, so I got up a little too quickly and my arm bumped my Pepsi, spilling it on the rug. Layla followed me into the kitchen and helped me get a dishtowel.

"Hey, *Imm al-'aj'ah*, you ok?"

I told her not to call me clumsy and said I was fine.

"I'm just bored with this party. Let's go to my room."

Layla wasn't convinced, because it wasn't boring at all, but she helped me clean up the mess and we went to my room and sat on the bed. I had posters all over the walls. Goldie Hawn in *Sugarland Express*, Al Pacino in *Dog Day Afternoon*, David Cassidy with his dramatic eyes. Layla opened her purse and pulled out a bag. She had an impish look in her eyes so I knew she was up to something. She pulled out two square plastic boxes. Each had six colors of eye shadow, a lipstick, blush and mascara. One for her and one for me. I said Momma would kill me if I went out wearing makeup.

"You don't go out wearing it, you put it on in the bathroom at school," she said in a tone that meant—*isn't that obvious?*

It thrilled me seeing all the colors—mauves, browns, and purples and I couldn't wait to try them. I felt guilty though, because I didn't like lying.

"It's not lying, it's just not telling. There's a difference," Layla insisted. She went over to the mirror and beckoned to me.

"No, we can't. What if someone comes in?"

"No one is coming. They've even forgotten we exist!"

There was no winning against Layla's logic, so I let her put two different shades of eye shadow on me, brush pink blush on my cheeks and spread the brownish lipstick on my lips. I stared at myself in the mirror. I couldn't believe how glamorous I looked—my eyes huge and dark, the lipstick making my lips seem plumper than they were already. I imagined Ra'ad kissing them and telling me how sexy they were. I was still staring into the mirror while Layla made up her own face. She smacked me on the butt and slit her eyes at me.

"Naughty Noor. What are you thinking? Tell me now!" Layla had an uncanny way of reading my thoughts.

"Nothing, I swear!"

"You're thinking how Ra'ad would like to kiss those lips, aren't you?"

I know my face must have been red as a radish right then and I didn't know what to say so I just started giggling. Layla made a fist and kissed the gap where her thumb wrapped around her index finger, rolled her eyes up and fluttered her eyelashes.

"*Khalas*, Layla, stop," I said, smacking her arm. "It's not like that with us."

"Really? What is it like then?"

"I'm not going tell you," I said.

"I'm just teasing you."

"Sometimes you overdo it. Can't you stop joking around and just talk to me?"

Layla sat next to me on the bed, hugged me and kissed my forehead. "Sorry, *habeebti*. Of course, you can always talk to me."

We sat like that for a while, quietly hugging. She felt warm and soft and I loved being close to her without worrying what it meant and what might happen next, like I did with Ra'ad.

"Layla? When you're with Kareem do you talk? Or do you just fool around?"

She pulled her mouth to one side and considered my question.

"I don't know. Mostly fool around I guess." She tipped her head down impishly. "Sometimes we talk when I don't feel like fooling around."

"Is that all they want? There's so much on my mind I'm dying to talk to him about, to find out how he thinks about everything, but I get the feeling he's more into *ya'ni—that*." I hesitated, embarrassed by the way this sounded. "Kissing I mean."

"And you don't like – that?"

"Of course I do. It's just…confusing. Sometimes I wonder if that's all he thinks about. I don't know if I can be with someone like that."

"Noor. You're only fourteen! It's not like you're going to marry him. He's just helping you get some practice."

I pushed her arm. "*Akh*, I hate you sometimes, Layla. C'mon, let's listen to some music."

I put a tape into my brand-new cassette player that sat alongside my beloved phonograph—The Captain and Tenille singing *Love Will Keep Us Together*. I think we must have rewound it three times while singing along holding a hairbrush and a comb as if they were mics, jerking our heads like rock stars. Layla went wild on "air drums" and I pounded the "keyboard." After that, we flopped back onto my bed.

"I love you, Layla. Don't ever go away."

"I'm not going anywhere. Lebanon is the best place in the world." She flashed her crooked smile and added, "Even if it is exploding."

I cringed. "Layla, how can you joke like that?"

"I don't know, I guess I just think it will all be fine."

"Don't you ever feel scared?"

She shrugged. "Sometimes, but I try not to think about it too much."

I didn't understand how anyone could not be thinking about it all the time.

"Can I ask you something?"

"You just did."

"Funny. I'm just wondering if, *ya'ni*, anyone in your family is in the Phalange?"

"What? No? What are you talking about?"

"I don't know. I'm just trying to figure out what makes people want to join a militia and even kill people for their cause."

"Noor, that's, I don't know. People that do that are different from us."

"Different? Isn't your family Maronite? Isn't the Phalange mostly Maronite?"

Layla snorted.

"What's funny? Isn't it true?"

"That's like saying I have a bowl of fruit and an apple is a fruit, so all the fruit in the bowl must be apples. Your Momma is Palestinian. Is she in a PLO militia?"

"No, but—"

"So lots of Maronites are just like your family and mine. They want peace, they believe in fairness. They don't like the Phalange any better than the other militias."

"But what about the ones that do? They're the ones that scare me."

"I know, me too. I do have one uncle— *'ammo* Naji—who says he's glad someone is finally doing something to get the PLO and Palestinians out of Lebanon. He thinks they're a stain on the country and doesn't like their allies in the Lebanese National Movement either, but most of my family doesn't think that way at all."

"Well, at least it's only him. Momma says she hates the way some of the PLO guys zoom around in jeeps acting macho and arrogant—that it hurts ordinary Palestinians just trying to live their lives. But to want to kick out all the Palestinians—that's just wrong."

Layla curled her lips up like a duck. "I think the problem is corrupt leaders. People are just like sheep. If their leaders say go that way they go that way. It's easier than figuring things out for yourself."

I considered this for a while. "But not everyone's like that, Layla. Some people *do* think for themselves and care about being fair and doing the right thing."

"Of course. Now all we have to do is figure out what the right thing is!"

We heard noise in the corridor and my heart jumped, remembering I still had makeup on. I grabbed my water glass and tissues, rubbing it off as quickly as I could. Layla giggled while she wiped hers off and I told her to be quiet. Her mother knocked on the door and told her it was time to go.

"OK, Momma, I'll be right there."

We pushed our heads into the pillow to muffle our laughter.

Out in the living room, where everyone was saying their goodbyes, Antoine came over to say good night and kiss my cheeks. I was still confused about him so I gave him air kisses instead.

"I'm so glad I had a chance to finally meet you before I go back to New York."

"New *York*?" I said, intrigued to meet someone who actually lived in that city.

"*Ay*," he said with a chuckle. "Next to Beirut it's the best city in the world! I hope someday you'll all come visit."

I had no intention of ever visiting this stranger, even if he did live in New York, so I smiled vaguely and went to join the others. I was hugging Janine when I noticed that Momma was about to come to the door from the living room when Antoine approached her. I could see he was holding something and his hand brushed hers as he slipped a piece of paper into her palm. She glanced around nervously and put it in her pocket. *What was he doing? Passing her a note?* I was furious.

Later, when I was in bed, I heard my parents talking in their bedroom. I couldn't hear much but I could tell they were upset. Baba was speaking gruffly and Momma sounded like she was crying. There was too much noise outside, though, and I couldn't hear clearly. It was upsetting to hear them so angry with each other.

I thought of Raʻad, wished he was there to talk to, be with. It was always Layla I went to when I needed support, but this time I wanted him there to touch me in that way he had that made me giddy—that would make me forget the strangeness of the evening.

In the morning, I could see my parents were still agitated and when they went out for a walk I thought about Antoine passing something to Momma. I wondered what he wanted, if he was flirting with her. I ran into their bedroom, my heart beating fast, and opened the closet. I felt inside the pockets of her clothes, but they were empty.

Things changed after that. Momma started staying late at work more and more often, Baba was drinking more than ever. It was as if whatever was upending the country was upending our family with it. I ached for those nights when we'd all play backgammon together or read in the living room, or Momma would sing while Baba played the guitar or he'd rub her shoulders and they'd kiss when they thought I couldn't see.

There was one evening when Baba had a faculty meeting and I heard Momma talking on the phone in a low voice. I couldn't make out what she was saying, but I suspected it was Antoine. Questions swirled in my brain. *What would they be talking about? Why had be come back? Could they be having an affair? If he lived in America how could that be?* In any case, I couldn't believe Momma would do that to Baba. Whatever it was, I knew I didn't trust Antoine. I didn't like the way he looked at Momma and how agitated Baba became around him.

When I was younger, life had been so much simpler. People managed to live their lives without killing each other, our family was happy together, I could walk to school and visit my friends without fearing for my life. Now it all was falling apart and there was nothing I could do about it. Sometimes this big mess was all I could think about, other times it made me so angry I just needed to forget about it. One day at school that was how I was feeling—needing to forget about it all.

It was between classes and Raʿad had seen me walking with no one nearby. He raised his eyebrows at me and inclined his head to one side, gesturing down the hallway.

"Follow me," he mouthed.

My heart was pounding, but I followed when I was sure no one saw us. Those days it was still nearly impossible to be alone, but Raʿad had his ways. He led me to an empty classroom that had the lights out and we slipped inside like two thieves. I was so nervous I was shaking. The room smelled of chalk, cleaning fluid, a hint of old sneakers.

"What if we get caught?"

"Trust me," Raʿad said with a wink.

We sat in a corner of the room and he took my hand.

"I miss you, Noor. Where have you been?"

He misses me. The thought of it thrilled me and warmth spread through my body.

"I've been here all the time. Where have you been?"

"Around. I was starting to think you were avoiding me." He traced my profile with his finger.

"Never," I said, as flirtatiously as my not-quite-fifteen-year-old self could manage. I felt very daring, but scared too. If someone discovered us I could get into serious trouble with my teachers and my family, but I decided to stay anyway.

He pulled me towards him and kissed my lips, touched my tongue with the tip of his. It startled me and I jumped, my cheeks reddening. I put my finger to his lips, wondered if all boys were this bold when they were alone with a girl. I was pretty sure they weren't. I liked it and didn't at the same time. He pulled my finger into his mouth and held it there for a second, turning my cheeks even hotter than they were already. I could smell my sweat and I hoped he didn't notice. Being with Raʿad made me feel like I was the most special girl in the world, but meeting like this was too risky.

I smoothed my clothes and gave him a quick kiss on his cheek. "We'd better go."

3.

April 13, 1975. I'll never forget the date. I was walking home from school in the afternoon and there was a strange feeling in the air like an electric charge that made the tiny hairs on my arms stand up painfully. All I could tell from what people were saying was that there had been some kind of attack on a bus. I heard the words *Palestinians, 'Ayn Rummaneh*, and *Phalange* but I couldn't catch all the details. I ran home as fast as I could and into the kitchen where my parents were listening to the radio. They shut it off as soon as I walked in.

"Why did you turn it off?" I said, furious. "I know what happened," I lied. "Everyone is talking."

My parents' faces were grim.

"I have a radio in my room. I can go listen by myself."

I fumed out of the kitchen, and at first Momma came after me and I thought she was going to scold me, but then she stopped.

"OK, Noor. You'll find out soon enough. Better that we are together."

Baba sighed and rubbed his forehead, hesitating, then reluctantly turned the knob of the radio. The room exploded with the news. That morning, Phalange leader Pierre Gemayel was at a church in the 'Ayn Rummaneh section of Beirut when an unmarked car sped past, firing weapons, killing Gemayel's bodyguard and two others. Later that day, a bus returning from a pro-Palestinian demonstration passed through the same neighborhood. Phalange militiamen ambushed the bus, spraying the passengers with bullets, killing dozens of unarmed men, women and children.

I sat next to my parents at the kitchen table with the radio between us, struggling not to show any emotion. I didn't want to give them any reason to shut off the radio even though I had started to feel nauseous and shaky. I couldn't stop thinking of all those people trapped inside the bus, defenseless.

In the early evening, the windows of our flat were open and we started hearing automatic weapons fire coming from somewhere beyond our neighborhood. Near, far, near, far. Then, deeper sounds, like thunder.

A shiver rippled along my arms. *What if our house was hit? Would we all die in an instant? Be burned up? Buried in rubble?*

"Artillery," Baba said angrily. "Big men with their big guns. *Allah ysaa'idna*—God help us."

The sounds echoed through the neighborhood and my parents rushed to close the windows. Even though they said it wasn't as close as it sounded, we went out to the corridor where our neighbors from across the hallway had already set up a crate as a makeshift table and were sitting on a mat playing cards and drinking tea in the light of a kerosene lamp. They weren't taking any chances. Their baby was asleep in Shereen's lap, seemingly oblivious to the chaos reigning outside.

We kissed each other joylessly and Daoud gestured to a second mat. "*Tfadallu*," he said. "Another round of fighting it seems. What a disaster."

"Such a terrible day this has been," Momma said, brushing away tears.

"We can only hope it's just another round of fighting," Baba said bitterly.

Shereen stared at him and rocked her baby, pulling it close to her bosom.

"What else would it be, *hajj*?" she said, addressing Baba respectfully.

"I'd say, hope for the best, prepare for the worst."

Momma, noticing how distraught Shereen was, touched Baba's elbow.

"*Khalas*. Enough talk for now. Let's play some cards."

Momma and Baba played *tarneeb* with Shereen and Daoud, but I could tell no one was enjoying the game. It was just a way of keeping busy. I didn't feel like playing so I sat and stared at the lantern and it occurred to me that there had been no electricity for most of the day even before we heard gunfire. A moth had somehow found its way into the corridor and was madly fluttering around the lantern as if it, too, had been frightened by the thundering booms.

I must have fallen asleep because the next thing I knew I was in my bed. The bare light bulb that hung by a cord from the ceiling was shining brightly, so electricity must have been restored during the night. I'd barely opened my eyes when dread washed over me, the previous day's events still more feeling than memory, the morning sky out my window a grim gray hint of the day to come. Images and memories filtered gradually through my aching head and I wished I could shut them out, sleep. There was a faint odor of smoke in the air wafting through my open window.

When I went to the bathroom my parents were already awake and they said I was to stay home. The streets were too dangerous, too unstable. Clashes had continued throughout the night and although there was a lull first thing in the morning, that electric charge feel was in the air more than ever and there was hardly anyone in the streets.

None of us could eat the cheeses and *labneh* Momma put on the breakfast table. We drank Turkish coffee without sugar instead, its bitterness jabbing at my stomach. Baba had bought the morning paper and he didn't even try to hide it from me when I came into the kitchen. Black-and-white images captured what words failed to convey. Bodies laid out on stretchers. The small bus, emptied of corpses, standing in its place, tires flat, windows a lattice of bullet holes, two blue eyes painted on the hood for luck.

"There were children—" I began, then choked on the words. Momma snapped up the newspaper and thrust it into the trash.

"*Khalas*. We know what happened," she said, pulling me close. I pushed my face against her neck, my throat closing up when I pictured rescuers running with stretchers carrying children, limp and convulsing like the boy I'd seen on Hamra that day with Layla. A hot tingle crept up the back of my neck, and I had to run to the bathroom to vomit. As I sat in front of the toilet retching, the staccato sounds of renewed gunfire resounded like a fireworks display gone wrong, and a solemn realization began forming in my head.

Baba was right. This is more than just rounds of fighting, more than clashes here and there. This feels more like war.

Momma and Baba sat on the living room sofa all morning, trying to call friends and family, the sound of the rotary dial buzzing like a fly, but it was hard to get a phone line and even when they did, the calls didn't go through. Everyone in the city must have been trying to call loved ones. Momma was especially worried about Janine and I knew she wouldn't relax until she could speak with her. When she finally got through in the late afternoon she sounded tense and when she hung up she was pale. I sat next to her.

"What is it Momma? Is Janine ok?"

"Well, yes, but she was supposed to be on that bus. She was at the demo and at the end she was talking with a friend and she missed it."

Baba was nervously fidgeting with the worry beads that had been his dad's. He never used to play with them, but lately he'd picked up the habit, almost obsessively.

"*Hamdilla 'ala salaamitha.* Thank God she's safe! Can you imagine if she'd been on it? Are you sure she's ok?"

"She's OK. Mostly she feels guilty that she was spared. She kept saying *I'm an old woman. It should have been me, not those poor babies.*"

It reminded me of how I had felt when the little boy on Hamra street was injured. Even though I'm young, he was so much younger, so innocent. I wanted to go visit Janine right then, throw my arms around her, but my parents insisted we had to wait until there was a ceasefire. I thought of how she and Momma used to sing a favorite Palestinian song, *Wayn 'a-Ramallah* when we went on road trips. I wondered if the passengers on the bus had been singing, clapping, and chatting as the bus wound its way toward Beirut a little too fast, muffler huffing, worry beads clanking against the rearview mirror as they descended, unknowingly, into hell. I couldn't believe that if it hadn't been for Janine's absent-mindedness, she might be dead now.

That night, I fell into an uneasy, sweat-drenched sleep. I dreamed that my parents and I were strolling along the Corniche, the moist, salty air on our faces. A skinny old man was pushing a wooden cart with hot, puffed up *ka'ak* loaves, dangling like huge elongated ears from a wooden rod.

Momma got me one and I was about to bite into it when a bus with sharks' teeth and lion's claws came straight at us. Baba yelled and pushed us to the side just as the bus hit the cart and exploded.

There were tender rounds of *ka'ak* lying everywhere, but now they were human ears and smoke and dust filled the air. Antoine appeared through the haze, but I couldn't see Baba anywhere. I screamed his name but he didn't answer.

I startled awake, nausea kneading at my belly. Once I came back to myself I sobbed into the pillow, rocked by the strange grief a dream can bring, even though I knew Baba was snoring away in his cozy bed just down the corridor.

Escalation

Fall 1975

4.

For the rest of that school year and into the next—my first year of high school—my parents drove me—when it was open. That fall was worse than ever with political infighting at a fever pitch. Demands for better working conditions and equitable power-sharing in government were being drowned out by more irrational rivalries and hostilities and too many factions and militias were armed and angry. Street battles, sniping and fierce shelling had become part of the regular rhythm of our lives, replacing the laughter, honking horns, music, and petty bickering that used to be commonplace in Beirut. My parents weren't taking any chances. I missed riding the bus with friends, missed seeing Ra'ad, but it did seem safer.

There was a day in October when Baba had a meeting at the University at pickup time and Momma had a doctor's appointment, so I had no choice but to take the bus. When I saw Ra'ad in one of the back rows by himself, I knew heat was rising into my cheeks. At school, we could never be by ourselves and I definitely couldn't invite him home. I sat across the aisle from him and tried to act casual, but he slid into the seat next to me and held my hand. I could smell his cologne and the warm, smoky scent of his body. I was nervous someone would see us and it would get back to our parents somehow, but as luck would have it, there was a popular kid from school sitting up front. He had brought his guitar and was singing *One of These Nights* and no one seemed to be paying any attention to us, so we sat as close as we dared, pretending to have a normal conversation. Ra'ad's voice was deep and manly and when he leaned close to me and said, "You have the most beautiful eyes I've ever seen," it sent a shiver through me.

"Liar," I said, giggling, even though I loved hearing him say it. I told him he was the best kisser in the world and he raised one eyebrow at me and said, "How would you know?"

He asked me to meet him after school the next day. He wanted to show me a special place he had found. I felt a nervous thrill when he asked me. Other than our first kiss inside the banyan tree and last spring when we'd snuck into a classroom for five minutes, I'd never been alone with Ra'ad.

That night I couldn't fall asleep. I kept thinking about meeting him, wondered if I should call it off. The streets were more dangerous than ever, and it was scary not knowing what he had in mind. I thought of Momma warning me about boys—instructing me never to be alone with one because you never know what he might push for. If I lost my virginity, she had said, no man would want to marry me anymore. I knew for sure I wouldn't let him get that far, but I wasn't really sure how far was *too* far. If I obeyed Momma and stayed home, I would avoid the whole problem, but I decided I wasn't going to miss this chance to be with Ra'ad, so I'd have to figure it out for myself. I wished Layla was there to help me think it through, although Layla had told me how she let Kareem put his hands under her shirt, stroking her breasts through her bra. He'd even slipped them just under her waistband—before she smacked his hand away. *Whatever you do, Noor*, she'd said. *Never let a boy touch you down there, ever.* I knew I didn't want things to go that far anyway, but I really wasn't sure what I did want. I was confused and excited and nervous and I couldn't wait to see him.

I had to lie. It was the only way to be alone with Ra'ad – to hold him, kiss him again, so I told Baba I was going to Layla's house to work on a project. Not only that, but I had to promise him I was getting a ride with Layla's mom, since you never knew when two militias would come face to face or have a dispute, and a gun battle might break out anywhere, anytime. Sometimes, even a traffic accident would end with bullets flying if the drivers were from rival parties or clans or religions.

He smiled and said, "Good for you, *hayaati*, working hard on your studies. I'm so proud of you, but please be careful."

His words made me feel ashamed, but I could never admit the truth. Being alone with a boy was out of the question, even in a liberal family like mine. So I just thanked him and asked him to pick me up two hours late.

I remembered a day a few weeks before when a friend gave me a ride home from school early. I was about to get out when I saw a car pull up near our house and Momma got out. I couldn't be sure, but the driver looked like Antoine, even though I'd assumed he was back in America. I hid behind the wall of our building and I heard Momma talking as she got out of the car.

"You know I can't, so what does it matter?" She paused to listen to the person in the car and then said, "I have to go. *Yalla* bye." She closed the door firmly and walked toward the house. I could see she was unhappy from the way she turned abruptly from the car and strode toward the house, giving a quick glance around before going inside. I couldn't be sure what that was all about, but I was convinced something was going on that Momma was hiding and I hated it. Now here I was lying about a boy.

I met Ra'ad a few blocks away from our school and he took me to a deserted apartment building nearby. It was pock-marked from bullets and some of the rear balconies still had striped awnings that were tattered and weather-beaten. It hadn't been occupied yet by squatters like so many abandoned buildings in those days. At least no one would find us there. The day was warm but with a hint of the coming winter in the angle of the sun and the dryness of the air. Ra'ad led me to an old sofa on a ground floor patio. I felt a jolt of fear. What if he forced me? I thought of Momma's words, of Layla's.

He put his arm around my shoulder, gently urging me. "*Yalla, Noonoo,* sit with me."

I tried to be calm. He was my boyfriend, wasn't he? Of course he wouldn't make me do anything I didn't want, so we cuddled and kissed for a while, but then his hands started creeping up toward my chest and I felt nervous again. I pushed his hands away but he didn't stop, so I told him, "*Khalas,*" and moved over.

"Ah, c'mon Noor, what's going to happen?"

I didn't want to reject him—and I was suddenly afraid he might want to leave, so I pushed him again, but playfully this time and said, "Nothing's going to happen!"

He pushed his lips out in a pout and I kissed him quickly and held his hand. I was surprised that he didn't seem angry.

"Why don't you take the bus anymore? Afraid I won't be able to control myself and I'll start nibbling on your ears in front of everybody?"

I pushed him again and said, "After *'Ayn Rummaneh* and all the clashes, my parents won't let me."

"Too bad," he said, nudging me with his body. "Think of all the fun we could have while Georgie plays his guitar!" He raked his long, wavy hair back with his fingers, and gave a habitual pat to the cigarette pack in his breast pocket.

"Aren't you ever serious?"

He put his hands on my shoulders and turned me so I was staring right into his eyes.

"I can be very serious," he said, pulling me against his chest and kissing me hard.

That hadn't been what I meant by serious, of course. Even sitting there in each other's arms on that warm fall day, full of desire, we could hear booming in the distance. There was always a clash somewhere—sometimes closer, sometimes farther away. It seemed there was no peace from that sound, no time to just relax and be kids again. Whatever else I was doing, part of my mind was always dwelling on those battles, but Ra'ad never wanted to talk about it.

"But seriously, oh lovely one, I seriously think you should get your parents to let you take the bus again."

I couldn't help smiling, even though he was teasing me.

"I mean, bullets could hit your parents' car as easily as they could hit the bus right?" He was grinning and I felt my back stiffen.

"Not funny."

For me thinking about bullets hitting a bus brought only one thing to mind.

"Oh, c'mon Noonoo. I didn't mean anything by it. It's just that anything could happen to any of us at any time. We both know that. Is it really so bad to want to enjoy life and be happy while we can?" He frowned and seemed sad for a minute but recovered quickly and tried to get close to me again, but I held back.

"No one likes it, Ra'ad, but avoiding it won't make it go away."

"True, but talking about it won't make it any better either."

He did sort of have a point and I was starting to realize that no matter how much we talked we would probably never think the same way about things. But I'd grown up in a family that was always talking about politics and religion and social issues, so it was strange for me to be with someone who could just ignore it all—even with tensions in the city so high; that I could like him so much but somehow not like him at the same time. I sighed and glanced at my watch.

"Sorry if I made you mad," he said. "We can go if you want."

I circled my pinky around his. "No. I'm not mad. It's just, I don't know. Forget about it."

I remembered Layla joking about not taking the relationship too seriously, just having fun, but for me to want to be in a relationship it had to be more than just fun. But I also knew that if I wanted to be with him, I couldn't force him to be something he wasn't.

He lifted my hair off my neck and kissed under my ear. I relaxed against him. His hands felt good on my body, like he was an expert at all of this. He even avoided going near my breasts this time, drawing circles on my shoulders and back instead. I breathed in his slightly sweaty smell and kissed his Adam's apple. I wondered how many girls he'd kissed even though he was only sixteen. I wondered if he loved me, or if I even loved him.

On the ride home with Baba, I was quiet, deep in thought. How could I feel so good with Ra'ad, but so ambivalent at the same time? Even though part of me wished I could just enjoy life like he did, the truth was it made me feel guilty having a good time when people were dying just because of their backgrounds.

Baba squeezed my shoulder. "What is it, Najnouj? Everything ok?"

Suddenly I was afraid that he somehow knew I hadn't been at school. I was probably imagining it, but I was embarrassed, so I tried to change the subject.

"It's all so confusing, Baba. I just want everything to be the way it was."

"I know, 'ayni. Me too, but the war won't last forever." I loved the sound of Baba's voice, soft and calm like a hug.

"It's not just the war."

He seemed puzzled. "What then?"

"It's you and Momma. I know something's wrong!"

He pressed his lips together. I thought about Momma getting out of the car with the man who I thought was Antoine. I wanted to tell him, but instead I said, "She's never around anymore and we haven't even had a good meal in like three weeks, Baba."

He touched my hand and for one second I thought he might talk to me, might actually tell me what was going on, but instead he sighed again and cursed Beirut traffic, and Lebanese drivers.

"*Brothers of whores*," he said under his breath, as if I might not hear if he whispered it.

I could see him going back into his own thoughts. I knew that look all too well, knew there was no use pressing him.

Baba made us *hummus* for dinner and he fried *awarma* and pine nuts to go on top. I arranged radishes, tomatoes, cucumbers, scallions and green olives on a plate and heated up platter-size Arabic bread loaves over the gas flame. The smell of fatty lamb and nuts frying made my mouth water and he poured it on top of the *hummus*, melted fat and all. We both ignored the fact that Momma wasn't there and ate like two starving people, without saying a word.

I licked my fingers and told him, "Baba, this is the most delicious dinner I've ever tasted." He smiled a big, goofy smile, like a little boy who just got a 100% on his math test.

After dinner, I went up to my room. I put in my *Imagine* cassette and hummed along with it while I did my homework. *Imagine there's no country. It isn't hard to do…* I loved his voice. *Nothing to kill or die for, and no religion too.* It was as if he was singing to me. I sighed and mumbled, "*Yareet.* I wish."

When Momma came home, I switched off the music. She came into my room and said, "Good evening, *hayaati*," trying hard to sound cheerful. I kissed the air next to her cheeks. "What is it Noor?"

"Nothing. *Wala shii.*"

"Why are you talking like that?"

"Like what?"

A year before, Momma would never have accepted me talking to her like that. She wouldn't have slapped me the way some parents do, but she would've slit her eyes at me and taken away some privilege, like allowing me to go to Hamra with Layla—not that anyone was doing that those days. I knew she felt guilty about spending less time at home with us.

She had a strange mix of sternness and sadness on her face. I tried to avoid her eyes, wondering which emotion would win out, almost hoping she would yell at me. At least that way I could react, yell back, make her get into an argument. When I was younger, I dreaded it when Momma gave me that stern look, when she yelled at me, but I was older now and I was aching for a confrontation.

"Noor! I am your mother and I won't tolerate you talking to me this way."

This was what I had been waiting for. I crossed my arms and said, "OK, how am I supposed to talk to you? You are hardly ever home. You never cook any more. You—"

"Noor, you know perfectly well why I have to work so hard. You know I have to work double to make up for the staff that left for Europe or the States because of the war."

"What about *us*? Don't we count? Why does it have to be you that makes up for those cowards?"

"This is war time. You can't blame people for doing what they can to keep their families safe—and of course you count! More than anything." Now sadness won out on her face. "Don't you think your father and I have thought about how to get you away from all this madness? Every time I go to and from work I'm worried. Worried for you, for me, for Baba, worried for everyone, but we don't have a home or relatives in Europe or America. And to be honest, as scared as I am sometimes, I'm also proud to be playing a part. It's important to keep publishing. Keep getting news out for people. At least I can do that much. Otherwise they've already won."

I turned away. "Who's *they*? Otherwise, *who's* already won?" Even though I was still angry at Momma and I felt there was another angle to the story I was curious to hear what she thought.

"I mean the right wing, I mean the parties who don't want to give up any power, don't care about real democracy. Who only care about getting richer and more powerful. Look, I know a lot of people in the national movement and on the left have made mistakes and done terrible things, too, but before all this violence they had a good cause. They still have a good cause and your father and I are part of that cause and we deserve a chance to make things better."

"Of course! I know that, but what about our family? It just seems like sometimes you care more about everyone else than us."

"Noor!" She pointed her finger at me but then let her arm drop to her side. "You know that's not true and even though things are very tough right now I'm still your mother. We can continue this discussion when you are ready to speak to me with respect!"

She told me to stay in my room and she walked noisily down the corridor toward the kitchen. It seemed silly to me since I had already chosen to be in my room, but I knew she was angry and feeling guilty about not paying more attention to Baba and me. I knew she was frightened of what was happening in the country and that it was hard for her to admit it. I also knew I had made my point and I didn't want to push my luck.

I could hear them talking in the kitchen in low voices, so I cracked open my door, snuck out of my room and down the corridor. I stood out of sight behind the bathroom door. The corridor was still filled with the smell of fried meat and pine nuts, making me hungry again. I had to strain to hear what Baba was saying.

"You've always been the strong one, Nadine. You can't just fall apart on us. Especially for Noor's sake. She needs you more than ever."

"I'm falling apart? Working is the only way I know to *keep* from falling apart. You're the one running to the liquor cabinet every five minutes!"

Baba was quiet for a minute and then he said, "I guess we all have our ways of coping, but who is picking her up every day? Who makes sure dinner is on the table most days?"

"I know, Rasheed, I know. I just feel so helpless. At least at work I feel like I'm contributing in some small way."

"You are contributing in an important way, Nadine, and you know I admire that, but you have to admit, Noor does have a point. Don't you think family comes first?"

"So what do you want me to do? Stay at home and be a good housewife?"

"You know that's not what I want, but there could be some balance. And what about Antoine?"

"What about him?"

"What is he doing? Why is he even in the picture?"

"He's trying to help, Rasheed. If you'd only recognize that."

"Oh, I'm sure he is!"

There was a loud explosion in the distance followed by lots of machine gun fire and my stomach clenched but I heard footsteps approaching the bathroom, so I hurried back to my room as silently as I could and eased the door closed. I threw myself onto my bed and kicked at the tangled bed sheets. Both their voices were tense and angry in spite of trying to be quiet.

Outside my open window, somewhere beyond knowing, was the constant roiling of mortar shells, like thunder at sea. It had become a nightly ritual and somehow I had started to welcome it. It seemed fitting that the whole world should be raging.

5.

By late fall the war had become blatantly sectarian and competing militias took over the fancy hotels in downtown Beirut. They battled each other from the rooftops and abandoned rooms, and rocket and artillery fire thundered through the city from the front lines nonstop, our heads throbbing day and night.

One evening I was in my room doing homework. Baba was reading in the living room and Momma was editing an article for the weekly journal, *Beirut al-Aan*, at the kitchen table. I heard an eerie whistling sound outside and before I realized what it was, there was a powerful explosion—a mortar shell slamming into the ground nearby. The lights went out and I heard screaming and glass shattering from everywhere at once—inside our apartment, outside in the street.

I ran out into the hallway from my room, sliding my hands along the dark wall, hearing the panic in my own voice. "Momma, Baba, where are you? I can't see."

Momma came to me with a kerosene lantern, and we ran to the living room with our heads down to where Baba was standing, broken glass all around him.

"Rasheed get away from the window—watch the glass!" she yelled, shining the light for him.

When Baba was next to us in the corridor, I could see by the weak glow of the lantern that blood was seeping through his white shirt.

"Baba, your arm!" I screamed.

He twisted it up to see and put his hand on the round of my head. "*Baseeta, habeebti*," he said. "It's nothing."

He was trying to sound calm but I heard a catch in his throat when he spoke that made me even more frightened than I was already. Momma took the blue silk scarf from around her neck and wound it around Baba's arm to create a bandage. I gasped when I thought of blood staining the soft fabric, but she didn't hesitate.

We were all huddled on the ground, barely able to see, using our slippers to push away broken glass when another shell landed, shaking the building, reverberating through my body. Another landed right after. I screamed and grabbed Baba's uninjured arm and he squeezed my shoulder but didn't say a word.

"*Yalla*, let's go!" Momma said. "Hurry."

I was glad she was taking charge and seemed to know what to do, even though I knew she must be holding back her own fear. They each held one of my hands and we crept towards the front door of the apartment with our heads down in the semi-darkness, out into the corridor where there were no windows to shatter.

Daoud and Rasheeda, who lived across from us, were there, and some neighbors from upstairs had come down, too, afraid of being on a higher floor during shelling. Someone had lit a candle and brought a battery-operated radio to try to see if there was any news. Rasheeda was trying to comfort her panicked baby, but it seemed to me that she was as terrified as the child, nervously patting its back—rocking it roughly from side to side.

We sat with our backs against the walls of the corridor and I leaned against Momma. She put her arm around me and I felt her trembling.

"It's OK, Momma," I whispered, having no idea if it really was OK.

I knew she was afraid too and I wondered if she was remembering being a little girl in Palestine when the fighting got close to their house. I wrapped my arms around her and put my foot against Baba's.

Our other neighbors who lived upstairs came down, too, with cheese and olives to share when a strong blast shook the building and they dropped to the floor, the bread they were holding scattering. After a few minutes I grabbed the lantern and ran back into our apartment to get some more—Momma yelling all the while that it was too dangerous, but I went anyway. There were twelve of us including the baby—adults, children, teens. We ate as if we were starving, savoring every bite. The saltiness of the cheese. The pungency of the olives. The comfort of the bread.

The next hour felt more like five or six, never knowing when the next shell would hit. What if one struck the building—hard enough to make the roof collapse, or the wall shatter around us?

Would chunks of concrete cut us or be buried in our skin? What would we do? What if we got separated? What about the baby?

I shivered, stared at the candle flame that conjured a sheltering cave of light around us. I thought of Ra'ad, wondered if he was safe, if he was thinking about me, too. I imagined his arms around me, that it was just him and me alone in the candlelight, him admitting he was scared too, but it would be OK, we'd get through it together. I thought of him pulling me close inside the banyan tree and it made me smile. That day I had thought the gunfire was just a random incident. I had no idea what was coming—no idea what it might mean for Ra'ad and me, for all of us.

Baba interrupted my musing by singing a silly popular song and Momma made fun of the words, exaggerating the lilting Lebanese accent, and replacing it with a strong Palestinian one.

Daoud went across the corridor and got his guitar against his wife's objections and everyone sang together.

After that, Baba started telling Abu Abed jokes—the "clean ones," as he said. In one, Abu Abed was telling his friend about the time he was chased by a lion. Abu Abed kept evading the lion by climbing a tree, a wall, a ladder, etc. Each time, Abu Abed's friend would say it was impossible, because lions can climb – trees, walls, ladders, etc. Finally, Abu Abed threw up his hands and said, "Fine! He ate me, ok?" Baba made us laugh and laugh and eventually we all felt calmer, so we decided to go back inside. We set up the kerosene lantern, swept the glass and tried to get a little sleep. We decided it would be safer to wait until morning to tape up the plastic sheets that we'd bought at a local, well-stocked shop for just such occasions. So we put mosquitos coils in all the rooms to keep away the bugs and went to bed, exhausted.

In the shelter of my own bed, I hugged my pillow, closed my eyes, and imagined Ra'ad hugging me, our lips pressed together in the darkened classroom, how exciting it had been, how risky. Maybe he was lying in his bed thinking about me too, thinking about that day in the classroom. I slept imagining him next to me.

In the morning, my parents said we needed to get out of town. Momma said it would be crazy to stay here now so we covered the broken windows with plastic sheets and headed out, glad we'd had the foresight to buy these recently, although who wants to feel good about planning sensibly for having their windows blown out by an artillery blast?

Momma and Baba had arranged to meet Layla's parents at their summer place in the mountain town of Deir al-Qamar, where the plan was for us to stay until things settled down a bit. Schools couldn't stay open for the moment anyway so I wouldn't be missing anything, although I brought my books along so I could study. At least that was one thing I had some control over.

Layla rode with us, along with Janine, who called to ask if we could give her a ride to her friend's home in the village of Beit ad-Din, since it was close to Deir al-Qamar. I sat between them in the back seat of the car. On the way, we stopped by the *lahhaam* to get meat and chicken, the greengrocer to get fruits and vegetables and Baba went to the *furn* and brought back half a dozen bags of hot, steaming Arabic bread.

"Rasheed, are we moving in?" Momma said.

He shrugged and piled bags between our feet, along with the biggest jar of olives I'd ever seen, and a five-kilo bag of oranges with leaves still attached. The smell of fresh baked bread filled the car.

As we drove out of the city, I wished I had found a way to see Ra'ad before we left. I hadn't seen him since before the recent clashes. School was closed more and more often now and since Momma and Baba surely wouldn't let me bring him home, I rarely saw him. My parents didn't even know he existed. All I could do now was hope he was fine, since it was increasingly difficult to get a phone line and there was no other way to get in touch. I think Janine sensed that I was sad and she held my hand with her sturdy, leathery one and I rested my head on her shoulder.

The road wound around the mountain like a long, lazy snake, and every few minutes we got a new view of Ras Beirut in the distance below, like a great lion's head stretching out into the Mediterranean, the sun catching on the glass of its office buildings and hotels and on the whitecaps of the sea beyond, the light skipping along the water as we moved.

"Look, *habeebti*," Janine said, gesturing with a bony finger. "From up here it's a paradise."

Having Janine next to me seemed to allow all the fear, anger and anxiety I'd been suppressing to come to the surface and I swallowed hard to avoid crying. She stroked my head and whispered, "shsh" in my ear like a secret, like I was still little, but coming from her I didn't mind. She took care of me from the time I was two, when Momma started her editing job, until I entered kindergarten. It had made Momma happy having a Palestinian nanny for me. It was a way she could help someone from her country and she treated Janine like an older sister or an aunt. Her face was still the same, a tattoo on her chin and sad, gray eyes—the ones that used to look right into me when I was little, somehow knowing how to read my moods.

As we came around each bend, one village after another appeared in the valley—old stone houses with red tile roofs emerged as if growing out of the earth, clusters of tall evergreen trees with long, bare trunks and clumps of green perched on top. On one steep curve, I slid into Layla. She grabbed my arm and pointed.

An olive-colored Army tank blocked half the road, the treads having chewed up the earth behind it, the gun turret aimed straight at our car. We all stiffened. The Lebanese Army didn't much like Palestinians (Momma, Janine and half of me). Or leftists (Baba and Momma). Janine slid her white headscarf off so they wouldn't know she was a Palestinian Muslim. I pulled my ID card out and stared at it.

Shi'a.

The word sat on a line by itself. My mind raced. A lot of soldiers were Muslim, weren't they? And at least some were Shi'a Muslim. I slid my ID back into my pocket with a clammy hand. Baba talked fast. He knew an officer in the Army. They'd gone to school together. He pulled a card, tattered and wrinkled from his wallet and handed it to the soldier along with his own ID card.

"Call him," Baba said confidently, tapping his chest as if to say, we're OK, we're good guys.

The soldier frowned at the card, glared at Momma, Janine, Layla and me. He handed the card back and waved us on with the muzzle of his rifle. We were all silent. You could smell the sweat.

Once we were driving again, Janine patted Baba on the shoulder. "*Shukran, ya Hajj.* Good work. Thank God for our safety!"

Hearing her soothing voice, I realized that if she'd said a word at the checkpoint, her Palestinian accent would have given her away for sure, but now that we were on our own again it made us all relax. Janine could make you feel better in any situation. I noticed Layla twisting her hair around her index finger and chewing on it. A nervous habit.

"That was scary," she whispered.

I squeezed her hand. "Did you see the way they aim their guns at you like they're playing with toys?"

We continued up the mountain in silence, with only the sounds of our own breathing, the straining of the engine. Above the valley, a hawk drifted on the wind, wings spread wide. We passed a Bedouin family selling cactus fruit by the side of the road. Some things never changed. As the car rounded a steep curve, my ears blocked up as if stuffed with cotton. It wouldn't be too much longer before we'd be in the beautiful, peaceful village of Deir al-Qamar, perched high up above a valley. We'd be safe there.

Suddenly, Baba hit the brakes and said, "Shit!" loudly, in English. Straight ahead was another checkpoint—but this time, Phalange. He had taken an alternate road to avoid checkpoints, but this was clearly not our day. For a minute, I thought he might turn around and make a run for it, but he knew it was too late for that. I couldn't believe it. We got out of the mud only to end up in quicksand?

I knew my parents were afraid of the Phalange militia and the Phalange didn't much like Palestinians (Momma, Janine, and half of me) or Muslims (Baba and Janine and half of me) or leftists (Baba and Momma and possibly me). I swallowed hard and dry. Knowing that most Phalangists were Maronite Christians my mind seized on the idea that it might help that Layla's ID indicated "Maronite," but I recoiled at my own thoughts, shocked by how fear was making me think in the very way I'd always rejected, how easy it was to get swept up by sectarian thinking.

Janine and Layla were both pressed up against me. I heard Layla's breathing and smelled Janine's stale, old person's breath. Momma turned back and told us sternly, "Not a word. Let Baba do the talking."

This time he used his university credentials.

"My good friend, Dean George Khoury, can vouch for me," he said.

The militiaman demanded all our IDs and told Baba to get out of the car. He held his rifle high across his chest like a barricade. I wanted to yell, *Get that gun away from my father!* Instead, I cracked my neck to both sides and dug my fingernails into my palms. Momma gave me a fierce look, as if she could read my thoughts.

They talked for a long time, and finally Baba got back in the car and the soldier told him "*Rooh!* Go!" with an upward sweep of his chin.

"Well?" said Momma. "What did you tell him?"

Baba said he had taken some of Dean Khoury's cards on a recent visit to the Engineering Department. He'd never even shaken hands with him. How had he thought of that?

We never made it to Deir al-Qamar. There was one more checkpoint—this one for the Druze Progressive Socialist Party. They peered suspiciously into the car, but by that time we were all more hungry and cranky than scared. Baba actually was friends with a deputy of the Party head, so we got off with a sidelong glance from the militiaman, whose enormous mustache obscured his mouth when he spoke. He insisted that we turn back immediately since clashes had broken out near Deir al-Qamar. He looked into the car, winked at me, patted Baba on the shoulder, and told us "*Allah ma ʿkum*—God be with you."

Baba drove a short way and then pulled over by the side of the road. He held the steering wheel with both hands and put his head down.

Momma squeezed his hand. "You tried your best, Rasheed."

He shrugged her off. "Don't you see? If we can't be safe up here, where can we be?"

It worried me hearing him talk like this. He was usually the calm one, but I knew he was right. The mountains had always been a refuge. Cloaked in clouds, shaded by cedars and umbrella pine. Indifferent to what went on in the lively, chaotic, polluted city below. Indifferent to rivalries, to cruelty, even to love, but now these slopes were catching on fire.

"We'll find a way," Momma said firmly. "I've been through worse and survived, and I know we'll survive this too."

So, shaken, defeated, and with no escape, we headed back to the heat and tension of a city without electricity or running water, with reeking garbage beginning to pile up on street corners, to our apartment with the windows blown out and no refrigeration, lugging sacks of meat and vegetables, with no idea of what we'd face next.

"We should have gone to Tyre," Baba said when we arrived home. "Sometimes I think I'm too stubborn for my own good."

"But we could still go, couldn't we?" I said, hopeful.

I loved going to the south, seeing the cousins I only saw on rare occasions, going to the beautiful beaches and cafes in Tyre, but even though it was safer than Beirut at the time, Baba avoided going because his family was religious and they didn't like his leftist tendencies. It was impossible to go there and not stay with his parents, but he'd always felt pressured by them to become more observant. They weren't the strictest Muslims, but his mother wore the hijab, and even I had heard his father admonishing him for not praying.

"Not this time." Baba gave a discouraged shrug. "I'm going to see about getting the windows replaced—thanks to those enterprising guys who've been accommodating the recent spike in demand."

6.

It had been raining for days, the kind of rain that invades your bones. Rain that makes you weep. That makes you want to give up.

Not until after the retaliation did we hear about the killing of four young Phalangists. Four young men, that is. That's what the war did to us. Made us all labels, symbols. Questions. Do you smoke Gitanes or Marlboro? Display a semicircle or triangle? Say *Bandora* or *Banadoora*? All bones are porous, blood red, tears salty. But the smell of fear at the wrong checkpoint. A dead giveaway.

They called it Black Saturday. Because you have to call it something, don't you? When three hundred people or more, who we will simply call Muslim, are stopped, identified, and cut down where they stand? Because if you say, *It was Saturday December 6, 1975 and it was cold and my nanny who had a green tattoo on her chin and a gravelly voice and strong, warm hands was one of the hundreds and it was the worst day of my life even though nothing actually happened to me, nobody put a pistol into the soft flesh of my belly, while they called me swine and filth*, would it be enough?

Baba expertly maneuvered through sandbagged, deserted roads, around massive, water-filled potholes, past barely standing buildings whose walls seemed comprised more of bullet and shell holes than of concrete, ultimately arriving at Sabra refugee camp where Janine had lived. By the time we got there, it seemed that every resident of the camp was out in the muddy roadways assembling for the funeral procession. Palestinian flags, posters of Arafat, banners for the different militias hung damply from the electric wires that crisscrossed from building to building. Flyers with Janine's smiling face were pasted on nearly every building and shop. Janine's body lay within a simple, flower-covered coffin draped in a Palestinian flag. We shuffled along with the crowds of mourners who created a boisterous, almost joyful grief, with their loud cries and weeping, prayers, and embraces. PLO military vehicles led the procession, firing automatic weapons into the air as they rolled slowly through the narrow streets. I was heartbroken but also grateful to see so many people honoring Janine, remembering her, sharing their love and memories as if the entire camp was her family.

I couldn't believe she was gone. Janine with her leathery skin, who wore her white scarf tied loosely at her neck. When I was little she'd dress me up in my favorite clothes even if we weren't going out. She made the best *mana'eesh* for breakfast, fragrant wild thyme sizzling on the baking dough and she'd sneak me sips of strong, sweet tea. I could still feel the firm touch of her hands on my head, lathering my hair up with shampoo, pouring warm water to rinse it away, her hoarse voice as she sang me lullabies with her rural accent, the *Qaf's* pronounced like *Gaf's*.

Black Saturday and Janine's death made me realize that in the midst of a sectarian war, revealing your identity—at least that part of your identity that was visible to the world—could determine if you live or die. How could I be truly myself, the carefree girl I used to be, the one who never had to think about such things? I wasn't even sure I *knew* what it meant to be me anymore, to be just Noor. In those days, fear and paranoia seemed to be what was defining us.

School soon reopened—yet again—and I was sitting next to Baba in the front of the car on the way. I unfolded my ID card and put it on my lap. I remembered the day Ra'ad and I slipped into the AUB campus with no IDs at all and him saying, *You only need one if you think you need one.*

I held the card up where Baba could see it and pointed at the line that designated religion. "Isn't it true that any one of us could die just because of what it says on this paper?"

Baba pulled forward as if he'd been punched. "God forbid, *hayaati!* Why are you saying such things?"

"Because it's true, isn't it? It happened to Janine, so why not me? Why not you?"

Baba put his hand on mine. "It's impossible to say for sure, Noor." He reached back and tugged the longish hair at the back of his neck. "But your Momma and I will do everything in our power to keep us all safe, especially you, *habeebti.* We couldn't bear it if anything happened to you.

I was grateful to him for being honest. He didn't always say what was on his mind, but when he did, he spoke the truth. It was like talking to a friend.

"So what can we do, Baba? We have to do something."

He paused for a long while and both of us stared out at the pelting winter rain, the storm clouds that seemed like they would last forever. I switched on the radio, searching for some music and there it was again. *You may say I'm a dreamer but I'm not the only one.* It was like it was chasing me, teasing me. *And the world will live as one.*

"There's a protest and some meetings planned at the University. Some ideas will come out of it for sure. I don't see why you couldn't come if you want to."

"For sure!"

Baba lent me his Rolleiflex camera for the demo. I loved everything about it. Its boxy shape that reminded me of old-fashioned cameras, the double lens, the viewfinder that popped up to frame the scene, the winder on the side for advancing the film, the leathery smell of the smooth, brown case. As soon as I put my hands on it, I was mesmerized. With the Rollei in my hands, I could imagine all the thoughts in my head finding expression through pictures. A week or so before the demo, I started snapping photos of everything I could see in our neighborhood. A cascade of purple bougainvillea on a neighbor's wall. A dog—gray from filth—sunbathing on the sidewalk, tail tucked between angled hind legs. Layla making a kissy face. The blood-orange sun melting into the sea, viewed from the far end of our veranda. A couple strolling on the Corniche during a lull in the fighting and a break in the clouds. A building scarred by gaping mortar shell holes and thousands of smaller bullet marks. An armored personnel carrier grinding down the street, flying the Lebanese flag. Momma covering her mouth with her hand, a twisted strand of hair across one eye. Baba squinching up his face grotesquely. Nothing escaped my lens. I snapped picture after picture, used up roll after roll, prompting Baba to pinch my cheek one day and say, "My dear, you're going to have to get a job just to pay for all this film."

"Of course I will! I'll work at *Abu Khodr* making *shawarma* sandwiches after school."

I must have sounded very serious, because Baba laughed out loud—an uncommon event in those somber days. "Yes, sure you will *habeebti!*"

The next day he brought two bags home with him: one with six rolls of film and the other with a *shawarma* sandwich in it. I wrapped my arms around his middle.

"*Shukran, Baba*. Thank you, thank you, thank you." I grabbed up the yellow and black film rolls in both hands and kissed them as if they were gold ingots.

The demo turned out to be the only one of its kind. The organizers had planned it without the knowledge of the administration. Even inside the campus it was considered too risky to have a big group gathered in one place. It only lasted about a half hour, but it is a half hour I'll never forget. My parents both went. Momma wore bell-bottomed jeans and an embroidered peasant blouse, hair wound up in a bun. She brought a Palestinian flag with her and seemed to be as excited as I was to be doing something other than hiding out at home or work, avoiding clashes and artillery shells, moping and being bored. For once, Baba seemed to be the nervous one, almost refusing to let me go at the last minute.

"It'll be fine, Baba. Anyway, I have to use all that film on something," I said, smiling sweetly.

Momma piped in saying, "Rasheed, I'll bet the AUB campus is the safest place in Beirut right now. *Yalla*, let's go." She tugged at his sleeve and they smiled at each other for a moment before we headed out the door. I hadn't seen them like that in a long time and I felt my face flush with pleasure.

The demo was mostly students, and a few professors. It wasn't really a demonstration in the true sense. More a coming together of people angry and frustrated with the sectarian battles raging in our streets, seizing the chance to vent their feelings. I took as many pictures as I could. A few people held up signs, with slogans like, "NO SECTARIAN WAR" and "WE ARE ONE PEOPLE." Others pumped their fists, and chanted, still others waved flags of nationalist and leftist political parties. Someone flashed a "V" sign. I even got a perfect shot of Momma waving her flag.

It didn't take long for the campus police to come down and break it up, but before that happened something changed in me. Instead of the endless frustration and boredom of having to stay home, dwelling on my grief and anger, having to decide whether it was worse to switch the news on or switch it off, always be worried and anxious, here we were joined with others for that short time, all expressing what was on our minds – and just for a few minutes refusing to worry about what could happen to us.

Since the beginning of the war I had believed that there must be something other than violence or passivity. Something better. Something people could choose – that *I* could choose. The demo convinced me that no matter what happened I wasn't going to let fear hold me back—that from then on I would be part of that something better. I just had to figure out what it was, and I was pretty sure I'd have a camera in my hands when I did figure it out.

After that day at AUB, something lifted in me. I realized that I'd been spending all my mental energy worrying. Worrying about my parents, about Antoine, about a mortar shell landing on our building and killing us, about friends getting injured, about Ra'ad and me, about my future, about how the war would end, about prejudice and hatred, about what it would be like if the extreme right-wing took full control. I decided that no matter what anybody said or did, I was going to be in charge of my own life. I'd be the one to decide for myself how to feel and live and think, and I wasn't going to be afraid any more.

I knew something else, too. I had to convince Baba to give me the Rollei.

I don't remember exactly when the idea started forming. School was closed often in those days, so I had a lot of time at home to ponder our strange and dangerous new reality. The reality of war and fear and boredom and death. I was angry that some people were using religion, sect and nationality as excuses to hold on to their power. Thousands of people had already died because of what my English teacher called the *accident* of their birth. If only everyone thought like John Lennon. *Nothing to kill or die for…no religion too.* The lyrics seemed permanently stuck my head—like a mental broken record, mirroring the way I thought about life. Not that I was really against religion. I just believed it's something that should be practiced in private and never used to harm you, to judge you.

From there, I got to thinking that if a person doesn't know what religion you are, they can't very well use it against you. After Janine's death, I was more convinced than ever that it was nobody's business what religion or sect I was or wasn't and I decided to refuse to share that information with anyone unless it was a matter of life or death.

I was excited to get back to school to share my ideas. Between classes I stopped everyone I knew, and tried to be as persuasive and provocative as possible. Basically, I'd ask them a few simple questions.

"We're being killed because of religion, right?" Most people didn't argue with that.

"And how do they know our religion?" I tried to sound like Baba when he was being a philosopher—how could you argue with simple logic?

"From our ID cards!" Some shrugs, some nods. "We hand them over at checkpoints like we're sheep." A few more nods. "So why do we do that? I say it's time to stop."

By the end of the day there were four of us—the usual suspects. Layla, me and two friends from school. Not as many as I'd hoped for, but it was a start. I asked Ra'ad, but he just grinned maddeningly and said it wasn't his thing. I was starting to seriously question why I was still with him.

When Momma came to pick me up, I told her some friends were coming over to do homework, which was partly true. I closed the door of my room and everyone sat down and pulled their ID cards out of their backpacks. I opened the desk drawer, got out two black markers.

"*Yalla*. Let's get to work." I opened my ID and pulled it out of its plastic sleeve.

There it was. Shi'a.

Those black letters on the page that could define me and change the course of my life if I let them. I felt a jolt of fear and excitement, but the others were hesitant. I knew I had to act quickly, so I pulled the cap off one of the pens and pressed the black point onto the paper. I was shaking as I drew a thick, wavy black line across the word Shi'a and just like that— it vanished.

Someone gasped and we all stared at that shocking, uncompromising line. I made a fist and pumped it toward the sky like a triumphant boxer and had to keep myself from screaming. Layla grabbed one of the pens and the others fought over the remaining one.

The mothers found out by accident. I hadn't really thought about if and when I would tell Momma, but after our other friends left, Layla's mother came to pick her up. Layla was closing up her backpack and she tripped over the shoes I had left by the door and her ID card tumbled out—right at Momma's feet. Layla and I both lunged toward it but we were too late. Momma was already reaching to pick it up. As she held it out to Layla, everyone could clearly see the thick, black line. Layla and I froze.

Layla's mother cocked her head to one side questioningly. Momma squinted at me. I could see she had a pretty good idea of what we'd been up to when we were supposed to be doing homework. I felt myself wilting like a flower exposed to glaring sunlight. Momma had a way of doing that when she disapproved of something.

Layla's mother took the ID card in her hands. "What's this?" she said. "What happened to your ID?" she said in a concerned voice. She studied the black line, puzzled. Layla's mom was a nice lady, but nowhere near as sharp as Momma, who took hold of my arm and said sternly, "What have you done, Noor? Show me your ID right now."

I had no choice but to get it from my room and show it to her. Momma directed us all to the living room, the lines in her forehead forming deep grooves. She took both our ID cards and placed them flat on the coffee table, exposing our crimes to daylight.

"Whose idea was this?" Momma asked, her eyes fixed on mine.

I opened my mouth but Layla jumped in before I could speak. "We all agreed. We decided together."

Even though this was half true, we both knew it was really my idea – that I'd convinced everyone. It meant a lot to me that Layla was trying to protect me, but it made me feel ashamed too.

I pinched her elbow to stop her. "It was me. I came up with it."

"But why?" Layla's mother asked, still puzzled.

Momma shook her head. "I should never have let you go to that demo. That's what this is about isn't it? You want to show how grown up you are? By breaking the law?"

Heat rose in my cheeks, shame turning to anger now. "They're the ones breaking the law! They take our ID cards and humiliate us—or worse. Someone has to do something—why not me?" I wondered if she, too, was remembering when she told me how important it was to her to keep working, not to *let them win*.

"And what about your friends? Did you think about how much trouble they could be in because of you?"

Momma always knew how to get to me. I still believed we had done the right thing, but I didn't want to get anyone else in trouble. I hadn't thought of it that way when I came up with the plan, but now I realized it would be on my shoulders if anything happened.

Layla answered Momma before I had a chance to respond. "It's OK, Auntie. It's not her fault. We all want to do something to fight back."

"But not like this," Layla's mother said, clearly distraught. "What are we going to do now?"

"We'll have to try to replace them – say they got lost," Momma said. "Don't worry, Marie, we'll find a way to make this right."

Even as she was talking I knew it wouldn't be that easy. This was wartime. Some government offices were shut down and even when they were open I doubted they'd be in a big hurry to replace some foolish girls' ID cards. I did feel bad about Layla and the others, but I wasn't the least bit sorry about it for myself. I couldn't wait for the first time I'd wave my ID in the face of some *fascist bastard*, as Baba would say.

I dreaded him coming home. I knew I'd feel guilty again when he gave me his worried, weary look, his shoulders dropping and a question on his face. He wouldn't be angry like Momma, just concerned. Then he'd pour himself a big glass of scotch, like he was doing more and more often those days and go silently into the living room to watch the news.

As I predicted, there was no easy way to replace the ID cards. We filled out applications, but the official who processed them was suspicious of why all four of us had lost our IDs. We had a story ready for him about how they'd been taken away at a checkpoint and not given back, but he pulled his glasses down his nose, his eyes were telling us, *Really? Do I look stupid?* He instructed us to leave the applications.

"We'll see," he said. "*Inshallah bukra.* God willing, tomorrow."

It's never promising when someone says *inshallah*, especially in a government office, and tomorrow could be, well, any time after today. We had no choice but to wait and hope for the best. After that, I tried to avoid checkpoints whenever possible, but one day Baba and I were driving home from school and the Lebanese Army had set one up right on the road. There were sandbags on both sides of the street and Lebanese flags flying. There were two soldiers in fatigues, carrying rifles across their chests. My stomach tightened. So far, I had never had to show my tampered-with ID. Baba spoke with a much sterner voice than usual.

"Don't open your mouth. I'll do the talking—and don't get your ID out unless I tell you!"

Baba pulled the car slowly up to the checkpoint and stopped. He cranked the window down and one of the soldiers leaned on the doorframe, peering into the car. The muzzle of his gun poked inside, the oily, metallic odor of it mixing with the cigarette he was smoking. I stared straight out the front of the car and sat on my hands to try to stop them from trembling.

"*Yalla*," he said so loud it made me jump. I couldn't help turning towards him. He had a thick, brown mustache and eyes that said, *Don't mess with me*. He put his hand inside the car and gestured impatiently with his fingers for us to give him our papers. Baba gave him his own ID and I kept my hands under my thighs. He took Baba's ID, flicked his cigarette to the ground and pushed his head farther into the car.

"*Yalla*," he yelled at me, reaching his hand across Baba's chest toward me.

Baba nodded. As I reached to pull it out of my backpack I was queasy and lightheaded, like I might faint. I thought about Momma, about Layla and our other friends. I kept thinking, *Please don't let anything happen. Please don't let anything happen*, but another part of me was excited. This was the moment I'd been waiting for. My hands shook as I passed the ID card to Baba to give the soldier.

He unfolded the ID card, his eyes flicking between me and the document.

"*Shoo ha?*" he said, twisting the fingers of his free hand up rapidly, in a *what the hell?* gesture. He called the other soldier over and they both put their heads inside the car and stared at me. The second one was young— no more than twenty. He had a soft face with fine stubble on his chin, gentle eyes. He smiled at me and said something I couldn't hear. I looked down, heart beating fast.

The first soldier said, "My compatriot says of course you are Shi'a, because the Shi'a are always breaking the rules."

He poked his gun into the car again and this time I jumped, remembering that terrible Saturday when so many people were shot at checkpoints, including Janine. A chill spiked through my insides, as I realized I could die right then—that Baba could die because of me, depending on the mood of these soldiers. How could I have thought I could have any power against them? My arms and legs were numb, like in a dream when you can't move.

"What do you have to say for yourself?"

"I—I," I stammered.

Baba took my hand and squeezed. Then he put his hand to his heart and said to the soldier, "God bless. It was just a silly prank some kids at school did." His tone was respectful but relaxed. "She's just a child," he added, turning the palms of both hands up to the sky.

I was grateful that Baba had stayed so calm, but I resented being called a "child," and I pulled my shoulders back and my head up proudly. I wanted so badly to confront them, to tell them to go to hell, to say that nobody had a right to judge me—that they didn't even know me, but I kept quiet.

The older soldier turned to the younger one. I saw the young one wink at him and gesture as if to say, *just let it go.*

The older one turned back to us, slowly folded the ID and threw it back into the car. "Be careful who you give this to. Next time you might not get away with it." His voice was edged with menace. He inclined his head sharply to the left and said roughly, "*Rooh!*"

When we were out of sight of the checkpoint, I started sobbing.

"I'm sorry, Baba. I'm sorry. I guess this ID thing was a bad idea."

Now that the fear had subsided, it was replaced by humiliation. I had just recently vowed not to be afraid anymore and here I was bawling like a baby. He pulled over to the side of the road, wiped my tears. His eyes were red too. He put his arms around me and his round belly and the soft wool of his sweater felt soothing against me, but part of me wanted to pull away. I was still angry that he'd called me a child, angry that I'd had to back down and I cracked my neck in irritation. I had imagined the scene completely differently. I'd seen myself boldly presenting my ID at a checkpoint and when the soldiers questioned me, calmly telling them, "*You want to know who I am? I am Noor. Noor Haddad al-Husayni. Don't ask me my religion, my sect, my ethnicity. Because you have no right to.*"

But those are precisely the words I hadn't dared to speak and now I could see that concealing your identity could be just as dangerous as revealing it. It made the soldiers furious that they didn't have full control, that they'd been tricked. So what could you do? Try to pretend to be what will get you into the least trouble at any moment? Act neutral? Stay in hiding?

Baba squeezed my shoulder. "Sorry? *You're* sorry?" Baba said, "They're the ones who should be sorry! You are very brave, *hayaati*. To be honest, I'd like to do the same thing, but we're going to have to be very careful. Let's start by not telling Momma what happened, if that's OK with you."

Relieved, I hugged and kissed him over and over. I loved the way his bristly, black mustache felt on my face. I could never be mad at Baba for more than a second or two.

"*Khalas*, you're getting my face all wet," he joked with me, wiping his cheeks with his sleeve.

"Did you see his face when he saw your ID?"

"The Godfather, only with a thicker mustache!"

Baba twisted his face into a scowl like Marlon Brando's Don Corleone and said, "I'm gonna make him an offer he can't refuse." I hadn't been allowed to see *The Godfather*, but Baba loved to imitate Corleone, so I knew exactly what he meant and we both laughed the rest of the way home. Before I got out of the car, I gave him another kiss on the cheek.

"I love you, Baba."

He put his hands over both my ears and kissed my head. It felt good, but by the time I got out of the car, my mind was already speeding ahead to what I'd do the next time. I knew there was a good chance that Baba wouldn't be there to bail me out.

7.

A couple weeks later, school opened again and during a free period I went to meet with my History teacher. Afterwards I was walking down a quiet corridor. Most students were having lunch outside or their parents had driven them home to eat if they lived close enough. As I walked past a darkened room, I remembered the day Ra'ad and I had snuck into an empty classroom to be alone. My back and legs tingled when I remembered how he had pulled me towards him so boldly. I remembered the strange mix of smells that day—of chalk and dirty sneakers, body odor and cleaning fluid. I checked to be sure the corridor was empty and then turned the door handle. There was a scuffle and I froze, turning just my eyes in the direction of the noise. I immediately recognized Ra'ad's shape with another figure next to him. As my eyes adjusted to the darkness of the room I realized it was Cybelle. Ra'ad jumped up. I bolted for the door, tripping over a chair leg as I went.

"Noor, wait." Ra'ad's voice was hoarse.

At that moment I knew what it meant to hate someone. I wanted to rip his eyes out, to pick up a chair and smash both of them with it. I couldn't believe he would do that. I couldn't believe he would do it with Cybelle of all people. Cybelle who thought she was superior to me because I was an Arab and she was supposedly "Phoenician."

"I hate you! You disgusting pig!"

I blurted this out, not even thinking that someone might hear, not caring at that moment. I just wanted to get away from that scene. I ran down the corridor pushing down the pain in my throat, barely able to breathe.

I wanted so badly to be with Layla, to tell her what had happened, but with tensions overflowing in the city, I wasn't allowed to walk by myself even when school was open, even with a lull in the violence. Most people avoided walking in the streets and if they had no choice, they hurried to their destinations, with their heads down.

When I got home, I closed the door and lay on my bed, so angry I couldn't even cry. I thought about everything that had happened with Ra'ad, all the sweet things he had said to me, the gentle way he caressed my body, the urgent way he kissed me. I tried to think what had gone wrong. I remembered the times I had gotten annoyed with him and pulled away. Maybe he thought I didn't like him, maybe he felt rejected, maybe I should have been nicer to him. Then, the image of him wrapped around Cybelle came back and I pounded at the mattress, screamed into my pillow.

"Stupid donkey! How dare you! You disgust me."

On the weekend, my parents had to go to the Coop for supplies, and I convinced them to take me to visit with Layla while they were shopping.

Layla scoffed when I suggested it might be my fault. "*Khara 'alay*," she said, as crude as an old fisherman, not holding back her contempt for Ra'ad. Her reaction was so decisive, it reassured me, but I was still uncertain.

"But don't you think if I'd been nicer to him—"

"Like what, Noor? Like letting him do things you aren't ready to do?"

"Not that, but like not pestering him to talk about the war and everything."

Layla frowned and thought for a moment. "OK, there were things about him that bothered you, right?"

"True, but—"

"Did that make you want to run off and smooch with someone else?"

"No, but—"

"No, but nothing, Noor. Forget him."

"Easy for you to say."

"He doesn't deserve you, Noor. From the beginning there was something—I don't know—something I didn't trust about him."

"So, why didn't you tell me that? You tell me now when it's too late?"

"It's not that easy, *habeebti*. I wasn't sure of anything. It was just a feeling."

When Layla said this, I thought of how uncomfortable I'd been when I was alone with Ra'ad at the abandoned building and I had to keep avoiding his hands. Then there was the time he convinced me to go with him into the closet of an empty classroom. I'd stayed even though I knew it would be much worse for a girl to be caught with a boy than the other way around in those days. And of course he knew that, too, but he never hesitated or seemed to notice when I was nervous. Those things did bother me, but I'd been too smitten to admit it.

I had to wonder if he'd ever cared for me as a person at all. Whenever I'd bring up anything that mattered to me he'd change the subject and now he'd gone with another girl without even breaking up with me. And not just any girl, but the very one who had treated me so scornfully. I couldn't help wondering if Ra'ad wanted to be with Cybelle *because* she was Maronite. Maybe he also thought he was better than me because he was Sunni Muslim and I was Shi'a, that it elevated him if he was with a Maronite. I couldn't believe I was thinking that way, but the war made *everyone* think that way—that you weren't a human being first—you were your sect or your political affiliation first of all—and maybe last of all.

I went around with an ache in my belly for weeks and even knowing he was a jerk didn't make it easier. Every time I saw him coming down the corridor I'd avoid him, or turn my head to the side to give the message that he didn't even deserve to look me in the eye.

What is Lost What is Taken

1975-1976

8.

As 1975 dragged itself dismally into 1976, we began what was to be the harshest winter I can remember. There were weeks when there was a cold rain for days on end, there was mud and garbage everywhere, and often, the nauseating, cloying smell of death in the air. The fighting was worse than ever—so bad I started losing track of all the incidents.

But on January 18th, six days before my fifteenth birthday, a thousand Muslims and Palestinians were murdered in the Karantina section of Beirut. *A thousand.* Two days later, Palestinian militias attacked the Southern town of Damour and slaughtered hundreds of Christians. I vowed never to celebrate my birthday again.

My parents made me stay home for a month after that, and insisted on driving me to and from school when it was open—which was more and more infrequent. The days were long and lonely and I thought I'd lose my mind, so I picked up the Rolleiflex again. Baba wasn't using it anyway, so I'd take close–ups of my parents' faces, use the windows to frame pictures of the street outside, the little snack shop across the street, a car spraying water onto a passerby. One day, both my parents were at work, but school was closed. The doorbell rang and it was Layla.

"What are you *doing* here? *Yalla*, hurry up and get inside."

"I'm dying of boredom. C'mon let's go out."

"*Out?* We can't, Layla. Let's just stay here. I have an idea."

I picked up the Rollei and started snapping pictures of her as if I was paparazzi—kneeling down for a better angle, turning the camera in different directions. Layla loved it. She weaved her fingers into her hair and struck poses like a fashion model, pouffing out her lips and making cat eyes. The film was black and white so it wouldn't show her green eyes and fair hair but it didn't matter. She was gorgeous.

"OK," she said pulling on my arm. "Enough. We're going out. One hour. What could happen?"

Other than Ra'ad, Layla was the only person in the world who could make me do things I knew I shouldn't, because being with her was always an adventure and since she was two years older, some part of me felt like she must be wiser too, even though I knew that wasn't really true. I squeezed my eyes shut and breathed in deeply as if I was about to dive into the sea.

"OK," I said. "One hour."

There were still hours left before my parents would get home. It wasn't raining, but it was chilly and dark from the heavy clouds of winter. I put on a thick, wool turtleneck sweater, zipped up my jacket over it, slung the camera over my shoulder and followed Layla out the door. I shivered. From cold, nerves, the electric feel of the air, the thrill of sneaking out with Layla.

"Where are we going?" I asked.

"You'll see."

We walked up the outdoor steps through the International College and AUB campuses, all the way to Bliss Street. I'd climbed those steps thousands of times, always start to count, then get distracted. There had to be more than a hundred, maybe two, maybe more. It was unsettling going through the school grounds when nobody was walking around, no laughter, no couples stealing a kiss in the bushes. The few people we did see had their collars turned up against the cold and they seemed rushed and nervous. It still felt safe there though, like there was an invisible bubble around the area, protecting it from the madness all around.

When we got to the top, Layla said, "Let's go see my cousin Reem. She has an apartment off campus near the hospital. It's not that far."

I hesitated and she said, "It'll be fine. Come on, we'll run."

"No. No running. We'll attract attention." Somehow I seemed to have an instinct about such things that Layla didn't, but that carefree, daring attitude made it so much fun being with her, as if I was always in a conspiracy when we were together. I think that was part of what had attracted me to Ra'ad too.

As we walked, the sky darkened, threatening rain. I put up the hood of my jacket and took a picture of Layla from behind—of her striding along in front of me and looking over her shoulder to see why I called her, half her face covered with a thick cluster of hair. We turned a corner and there was a smoldering pile of garbage on the sidewalk. Just when we started across the street to avoid it, a bunch of oversized cockroaches scattered in all directions. I screamed and grabbed Layla's arm.

"*Yukkh! Yin'an deenhum,*" she said, cursing "their religion," and we rushed across the street, shrieking.

"Cockroaches don't *have* religion!" I said, squinting one eye and snapping a picture of the garbage pile.

"How do you know? Maybe they worship the god of trash."

"Well, at least they aren't killing anyone for it. I wish they were the worst thing we had to deal with."

"True, but I curse their religion anyway! Let's get out of here."

We went down one street and ended up facing a road that had been blocked by iron crisscrossed barriers. We had to go around it and somehow in the gloom, Layla lost her way.

"I've only gone there once, but I'm sure I'll find it."

"Layla. C'mon we have to go back."

I had an uneasy feeling, the hair standing up on my neck, but I wasn't sure why. Nothing was out of the ordinary—or what had become ordinary to us—but somehow we'd gotten into a tangle of streets and neither of us knew how to go back or forward any more, and no one was around to ask.

The rumble of artillery coming from off to our right had barely registered at first. It could have been a thunderstorm brewing miles away, but as the sounds became steadily louder, punctuated now with staccato retorts of machine gun fire, I realized we had strayed dangerously close to the hotel district and the front lines. My watch confirmed that we had been wandering for almost an hour.

I squeezed Layla's arm. "Stop for a minute. We have to make a plan or we'll walk right into the fighting."

The sky was even darker now and we heard rumbling from off to our left.

"What is that, Layla? Thunder or guns? I can't tell anymore."

"Honestly, I don't know. All I know is I wish we'd stayed home. You were right."

"Well at least it isn't my fault this time."

"True. So glad we have those doctored IDs on us in case anyone stops us." Layla said, trying for a joke to deflect the tension and fear neither of us could avoid, but I could feel her arm trembling against mine. She pulled her scarf around her face, covering everything but her eyes. "Guerrilla or *mhajjabeh*? They'll have to guess."

We leaned against a concrete barrier and I opened my camera, snapped a picture of her like that, green eyes peering out from above the scarf like a cat ready to stalk its prey. I moved the camera around, peering into the viewfinder until I caught the image of a poster across the street—the melancholy face of Kamal Jumblatt next to the logo of the Progressive Socialist Party he headed.

I was suddenly inspired. "Layla, I have an idea."

"What's in that devious mind of yours now?

"You're going to think I'm crazy, but what if we go *toward* the fighting instead of away from it?"

"What? Crazy only? You've completely lost it. The war has scrambled your brains and made an omelet."

I made a conciliatory gesture, realizing there was probably more than a little truth in what she said.

"We're lost anyway, so at least we'd be doing something and to be honest, some days when I'm hiding at home like a coward, I think about going to the front lines, just to see what it's like, to take pictures of the battles, try to understand what they're fighting for. Maybe I could even sell some photos to one of the newspapers. Can you imagine?"

"Noor! Do you know how many snipers are on the hotel roofs? You'd be killed in seconds. I say *you* because *I'm* not going anywhere near there."

"We're already near and besides, aren't you just a little curious? All those young men ready to die for their causes? Using hotel rooms as bunkers. Raiding the kitchens for food."

"Just like a bunch of spoiled children let loose with no parents, but with RPGs instead of squirt guns."

"I'm going."

"You're insane."

"We already established that."

"*Yalla* bye."

"Bye," I said and headed directly toward the unrelenting sounds of combat with camera in hand.

"Noor! Don't leave me alone here." Layla sounded really panicked now.

I waved over my shoulder and kept walking. I dug around in my pocket until I found the good luck charm from Janine and clasped it in my hand. *Why did you have to die? Why does anyone? I promise to do something to honor your memory, Janine. I promise.*

When Layla caught up with me she yanked my arm. "Noor! We're going back—right now."

I pulled away. "I'm not going anywhere, Layla. You go back if you want to but I'm not going to miss this opportunity."

We'd never had a serious argument before and I hardly recognized her, her eyes wild, face red.

Finally, she agreed to walk with me until we could just see the fighters, to hide behind a wall long enough for me to take six pictures and then leave.

"Six, only," she said, gesturing with her fingers, as if there was some magic in the number.

It was only a few more minutes walking before we could see the tall buildings. Adrenaline coursed through me and I was emboldened, fearless. I even imagined myself holding a rifle, running between buildings, heroic, but I knew I'd never be able to kill anyone, that the Rolleiflex was my "weapon." I clasped Layla's hand in mine and crept toward a small enclosure between two buildings where we had a narrow view of the area between the Holiday Inn and Phoenicia Hotel. Even from this distance what I saw shocked me—much more than the black-and-white pictures in the newspaper. The two towering hotels had gaping holes in the walls, huge black char marks where mortars had hit, open frames where windows had been blown out. It was like being on a movie set, except that every hair on my body seemed to be at attention, alert to the danger I was trying to ignore. I made Layla stand behind me.

I felt her breath on my neck as she whispered, "*Allah yehmeena.* God help us. What are we doing here?" I ignored her trembling voice.

Click. A picture of a young man in fatigues with unruly, shoulder-length hair, bandana tied around his forehead sprinting across the sandbagged street, firing the Kalashnikov rifle he held in one hand towards the sky.

Click. A militiamen on an upper floor with a rocket-propelled grenade balanced on his shoulder, pointed out a window hole ready to fire; a curtain, still intact, hanging part way out the window.

Click. A maroon-colored Fiat with the hood smashed in, doors open, tires flat, in the middle of the street, surrounded by rubble.

"*Yalla,* Noor, let's *go!*"

"Three more," I said, determined to document whatever I could with those six photographs and feeling strangely detached from the scene from behind the camera.

Click. A cluster of teenage boys behind a mound of sandbags firing through gaps between the bags.

I was about to take the fifth picture—a sniper on the roof of one of the buildings—when he turned his binoculars in our direction.

"Get down," I yelled at Layla, not sure if he'd seen us or he was just scouting the whole area.

She screamed and ran back in the direction we'd come from, disappearing around the corner of the building behind us.

"Layla, no!"

I glanced up and saw that the sniper was focused elsewhere. I ran after Layla but I couldn't see her and I tripped over a chunk of broken concrete, twisting my ankle badly. There was a heap of rubble and soil, with children's toys, soda bottles, a broken chair piled in it and I fell against it, unable to continue. I heard a noise and realized someone was nearby, must have followed us, perhaps heard Layla scream. A young man in fatigues, with no party insignia that I could see to identify him, approached me almost shyly. For a moment I thought he was going to help me, but instead, as if making a snap decision, he put his hand over my mouth and told me to be quiet. I struggled for air, but my breaths came shallow and painful. I tried to bite his hand but he was pushing too hard on my face. I was about to black out but I knew I had to stay conscious, so I forced myself to breathe slowly through my nose. The smell of his sweat was acrid and foul and nausea rose up.

A surge of adrenaline flooded through me and I kicked him hard, sending a searing pain through my injured ankle. He held my legs down with his knees and pressed my arms down in a vice grip, overpowering me. *Was he going to rape me? Kill me?*

I tried to push back against him again but this time it was as if I was frozen, unable to breathe or move. He was very young, the hair on his face like soft down, almost feminine. Suddenly he shifted his hand and I bit down, screamed at him to get off me. He clamped his palm over my mouth again but my scream had attracted the attention of another man, who ran over.

"What are you doing, man? Are you crazy?" He grabbed the young man and pulled him off me, smacked him on the face. "Shame on you. Leave her alone and get out of here, you donkey!" He pushed the young man, who stumbled to his feet and ran off.

"And you—what are you doing here? Go on—run before you get shot. That way," he said, pointing, and then he, too, disappeared.

I forced myself up, sobbing and gasping for air, but there was no way to run with my injured ankle so I hobbled in the direction he pointed, which was not the way Layla and I had come. I was terrified that I was walking into more danger, but I had no choice but to trust him. After what seemed like a very long time, holding onto anything I could find—the side of a building, a wall, a tree branch serving as a cane—I saw ahead of me a gray expanse that took a few moments to distinguish from the gray of the road, the gray of the sky. I squinted to be sure and there—like a great, unfailing compass to guide me home—the sea stretched solemnly out in front of me.

I avoided walking along the Corniche on the water side because it was deserted and exposed, choosing instead the side of the road closest to the apartment buildings and trees that lined the street. I had ridden down this road many times with my parents on the way to the waterfront and downtown before the war, so I knew exactly where I was. I had never seen it empty like this though—lonely and bare.

I paused and took in a few deep breaths. All I had to do now was keep out of sight and follow the road all the way to Ras Beirut and then up a few streets to our apartment building. If I hadn't been injured, exhausted, and ducking out of sight every time the occasional vehicle passed by, it might have taken me a half an hour or so. As it was, when I finally limped through the front door of our building it was after dark. The electricity was off and I pounded my fists against the glass door of the mute elevator, as if those last two flights of stairs were more than my body and soul could bear.

I suppose it is impossible to expect a fifteen-year-old, even a sensitive, thoughtful one, to understand what goes on inside a parent's heart, but the pain and grief I caused Momma and Baba that day was beyond anything I could have imagined and it will haunt me until my dying day.

That night was long, Momma weeping as if I actually had died, Baba distraught, and me feebly trying to explain myself—that I'd never intended to go downtown.

"We were so bored, sitting home all the time. Layla thought we could visit her cousin, Reem, just for an hour. But we got lost."

Between sobs, Momma pressed me. "But of all the places, Noor. Of all the places."

"I'm sorry, Momma. I never meant..."

Baba had put his hand gently on Momma's shoulder. "Nadine. Let her sleep now. We'll talk in the morning."

When I finally went to bed, I lay sleepless for most of the night. The ice and Panadol they gave me did nearly nothing for the throbbing in my ankle and head and every time I drifted toward sleep, I half-remembered, half-dreamed of being held down, unable to move or breathe and I woke sweatdrenched, gasping for air.

Many nights after that I barely slept, and when I finally did, I'd have a recurring dream that Layla ran off cursing me, saying I'd almost gotten us killed, and I was held down one after another by a group of soldiers from all the different factions, each one taking a turn with me, the sounds of machine guns and artillery in the background. I'd wake up screaming and Momma would come lie next to me, holding me while I sobbed. She'd sing to me the way she had when I was little, to make me sleep, her voice sweet and mellow, her hair soft against my neck.

"Naami, naami, ya zgheereh
Ta neghfah 'al-haseereh
Naami 'al-'attaymeh
Ta tinzaah al ghaymeh..."
"Sleep, little one, sleep.
Fall asleep on your mat
sleep in the darkness
until the clouds move away..."

Sometimes I would sob against her shoulder, always holding back key details of that day. What Layla had told them about our misadventure was bad enough—that we'd been disoriented and strayed close to downtown, that I'd insisted on documenting the snipers, that she'd been unable to change my mind. The last thing I wanted was to add to Momma's dread and fear. She was so distressed I don't think she was even angry. I wanted to beg her forgiveness for being so foolish and swear I'd never do anything to worry her again, but I knew it was a promise I couldn't keep, so even though no part of me felt like a child anymore, I let Momma rock me in her arms like she had when I was little, whispering, "It's all right, *habeebti*, it's all right."

It wasn't all right, though. That young man had taken something away from me—something I couldn't fully explain to myself yet, even though I knew that in some ways I would never be the same. It shocked me that someone—a man—could take away my freedom, my strength, my confidence, in an instant, that he could have such power over me. I thought about Momma's warnings, but I hadn't thought she meant anything like this. What would make a person act like that? Maybe it was one more thing war did to people—made them hard and callous and cruel like wild animals. I thought of how soft his beard was, his feminine appearance. But he was nothing like a girl, not any girl I'd ever known. I didn't think I'd ever tell anyone—even Layla—what happened after she left me.

After an especially difficult night filled with ominous dreams, I woke at dawn with a start—a black shadow rushing at me. I screamed but nobody heard. Was it even out loud? Out the window a steady gray drizzle. More gray drizzle. Would the sun ever shine again? Noise in the kitchen. Pots and dishes clanking. Smell of coffee, painfully good. Parents talking tensely.

"I'm frightened, Rasheed. We have to do something." Momma paused. "We could drive to Damascus—just to get out of here."

"And then what? We have no visas, nowhere to go."

"I don't know, I don't know, but we'll think of something."

I must have fallen back asleep, because the room had brightened slightly when Baba knocked. When I didn't answer he slowly pushed the door open. He sat on the bed next to me and gently put his hand on my shoulder.

"Good morning, *Najnouj*. I brought you a little breakfast."

I slowly sipped the tea he brought, chewed a little white cheese and bread dutifully even though I had no appetite.

I slept on and off for the next few hours and Momma and Baba seemed to understand I needed time to process what had happened even though they didn't know the half of it, that it wasn't witnessing street fighting at close range that had traumatized me so deeply. In a strange way, that had actually energized me.

In the early afternoon, I was startled by Momma's voice calling me from the doorway.

"Layla is here to see you."

"What? No—I don't want to see her."

But it was too late. Momma had let her in and brought her to my room. When she knocked on my door I told her to leave but she took a hesitant step in anyway.

"Noor, I—."

I sat up in bed and pulled the blanket up around my chin. "Just go!"

I sensed her hovering at the door, unsure how to react to my anger.

"I just want to tell you how sorry I am," Layla said, choking on her words. "I thought you were right behind me, but when I turned around you weren't there."

"You left me there. I fell and injured my ankle and I couldn't move. I could have died."

"Noor!" Momma's voice just outside the door startled me with its anger, so different than the soft, reassuring tone she'd used earlier.

"I tried. Believe me," Layla pleaded. "But by the time I ran back I couldn't find you anymore. I was so afraid. I thought we'd both die."

"If it had been me, I never would have left you."

Even as I said this, I knew how cruel and unfair it sounded, although it was true, I probably would have stayed, even if I had died trying to save my best friend.

Momma stopped working late. There was clearly no need to ground me. At first, I even refused to go to school, couldn't bear to walk outside or see anyone, but eventually I started dreading the recurring thoughts and terrors in my own head more than I dreaded facing the outside world and I relented to my parents' urgings, but only if they were with me. If school was open, they would always drop me inside the corridor and be there to pick me up at the end of the day. Otherwise, Momma would usually stay home with me. AUB was often closed, so Baba was home a lot, too. He was working on his manuscript, *Assimilation and Identity Among Arab Migrant Populations in the West*, so if he didn't have classes he'd work from home—often late into the night, sometimes falling asleep on the sofa with his glasses on his nose, papers still on his chest, empty whiskey glass on the table next to him, a cigarette with a two-inch long ash in its tray.

I hoped that if one good thing could come out of my ordeal it would be that we'd feel like a family again. In some ways that was true, but the atmosphere was as tense inside our home as it was in the whole country. My parents argued a lot. Argued about his drinking, about the war, about who would pick me up or drop me at school, about the dangers of staying in Beirut, about never leaving me alone. It all made me feel even worse than I did already. I felt mistrusted and smothered.

One night when I couldn't sleep, I heard them talking in the living room. They probably thought I couldn't hear.

"Rasheed, we have to get her out. We have to find a way."

"Like what? What way?"

"I don't know, but drinking and burying yourself in your book won't solve anything."

"Well, I don't have a magic solution. I wish I did, believe me."

"I have an idea, Rasheed, but I know you're not going to like it. I just hope for Noor's sake you'll keep an open mind."

"I'll keep an open mind but I don't have a good feeling about this."

"I think we should talk to Antoine."

After that, they went into their bedroom and closed the door so I couldn't hear anything more. Talk to Antoine? I hadn't even thought of him recently with everything that was going on. I wondered—and dreaded—what she might be thinking.

The next afternoon, Baba went to the library to do some research for his book and Momma stayed home with me. I was doing homework in my room and I heard her talking on the phone. She had closed the door of the living room where the phone was and I knew it was an overseas call because she had to raise her voice to be heard, even though she was trying to be quiet.

"I don't know what to do. You can't believe how bad it is here."

I was pretty sure she was talking to Antoine, because we didn't know anyone else overseas other than her brother, Amjad, who lived in Qatar with his wife and kids and she had a different tone when she talked to Amjad, like she was trying to reassure him that everything was fine. Now her voice was strained and I could tell she was fighting tears.

"No, no. I don't know. Maybe we could send her there? If only Rasheed would accept."

Then a pause while she listened.

"*La, la, la,* Antoine. It's much too late for that—but Noor," she said lowering her voice. "It's too dangerous for her now." Then I barely heard her say, "Please. Just call him. He agreed to talk to you."

I was shocked to hear her ask him if they could send me there. I would never consent to going to America, especially to be with *him*. I wanted to shout at Momma, to tell her I wasn't going to let her send me away, but I'd have to admit I'd eavesdropped. And I was so tired. Tired and angry and powerless and discouraged. Before that day, I rarely got depressed, even when things were really bad, but at that moment I felt so hopeless, I actually imagined throwing myself into the sea. Somewhere I'd read that drowning isn't so bad. That you succumb to it somehow. And so many people were dying around me, even some I knew.

I thought of Janine, of the little boy on Hamra Street, of all the people who had died at checkpoints, on the bus, in street battles—how their lives were snatched away from them in an instant. Each one of them had a whole life, families who loved them and people they loved, something they were passionate about, a story to tell that was theirs alone. I was overcome by shame. There were thousands of families grieving right now, people who would give anything to bring back their loved ones. How could I even think about throwing my life away just like that?

For a few weeks, I didn't hear anything more about Momma's schemes. At night, when my mind drifted back to that day near the front lines or to other dark thoughts, I'd push them away and instead fantasize about elaborate, daring escape plans. It would be better to run away than be sent away.

I'd make my way to the Syrian border by *servees* taxi, slip across unnoticed, while border agents were busy with cars carrying big families desperate to flee the chaos in Lebanon. Once in Damascus, I'd cover myself with a black veil, vanish into the winding alleyways of the old *sooq*, my back pressed against a wall between a gold merchant and a fruit seller, the aromas of incense and spice competing with the diesel smoke that hung over the city like a pall. I'd hold up my hand and beg like the *miskeeneh* on Hamra Street, poor woman. Was I really all that different from her, anyway?

Another time, I imagined rubbing my clothes in dirt and tearing them, slipping out into the darkness and making my way to Sabra and Shatila refugee camps. I already had the experience of walking long distances through dangerous parts of the city and surviving and in this case, it would just be a little farther. I'd walked through the streets of Sabra camp during Janine's funeral so I had an idea what it was like. I'd need a map and I'd hide behind buildings and dash across streets while the city slept. Once inside, I'd navigate the narrow streets, jumping over the open sewers that snaked along the roads. I'd ask for a tent and a sleeping bag, sign up for UN rations. After all, I was half Palestinian and Momma had been a refugee at one time.

I became obsessed with these fantasies. They helped me push away my anxiety-and-dread-fueled thoughts and offered the possibility of a newly empowered Noor—stealthy, ingenious, living by her wits, fiercely independent.

Every day people came to visit, a neighbor or friend dropping by to chat and drink coffee, play cards or backgammon to pass the time. Nobody bothered with telephones—they'd just drop by and you'd drop whatever you were doing to sit with them. Mostly I'd started avoiding these visits if I could because in my state of mind I found it exhausting to sit with people and be polite, but sometimes I had no choice. Whenever there was a ring or a knock at the door, I found myself wishing it was Layla. I missed her more and more, longed to talk to her about how I was feeling, how I jumped out of my skin every time I heard a noise at night or saw a soldier holding a gun. She was the only person I could imagine talking to about what had really happened after she ran off, but I was still angry with her and too confused to even know where to start if she did come.

Finally, one day she called and I happened to pick up the phone.

"Noor, is that you? I've been trying to get a line all day. Please don't hang up!"

My heart beat fast when I heard her voice, but my joy was still tainted by anger. At first I couldn't even speak. Hearing her voice brought back all the dread of that day, but for all those weeks without her to talk to it had seemed like an organ or a limb was cut from me.

"Noor? Are you there?"

"I'm here."

"Oh thank God. Noor I miss you so much. Please don't be angry." She was crying and I had to fight not to let her hear me sob. She hated crying, thought it was a sign of weakness, so I knew how upset she must be, not even trying to hide it.

"You can't imagine how many times I've replayed that day in my head. Noor, I would change everything if I could. I've been so afraid you'd never speak to me again."

"It's just..."

"I know, I know. I *was* a coward. I was so afraid. I thought the best thing I could do was to run for help but I couldn't find anyone until finally I found an open shop and begged them to let me use the phone but there were no lines."

I listened, needing to believe that she had done everything she could.

"But they gave me directions to get home and I ran so fast that when I got there I could hardly speak."

I stayed quiet, not knowing what to say.

"My parents and your parents drove around for hours searching for you. I was so worried I almost fainted. They said I was hyperventilating and they wanted to take me to the hospital."

"No one told me." I had no idea what Layla had gone through. I was so preoccupied with my own situation, I hadn't even thought about what might have happened to her after she ran, that she'd been frightened and in danger too. I'd been so angry I pushed her away, not wanting to even listen to her.

"It's not a big deal," she said. "They say it happens sometimes when you panic."

I thought of how I'd frozen and been unable to breathe. "Yes. I know."

"All I could think of is how brave you are, Noor. I wish I could be more like you."

"I'm not brave. I think it was just temporary insanity! I've been so frustrated and feeling so helpless since Janine died. I hate sitting at home doing nothing when people are outside dying every day, but I know it was foolish and I feel terrible that I put you in danger too."

"But you were trying to do something good. You risked your life to show what's going on."

"But it was all for nothing. When I tripped, the camera broke."

"You should still try to get the pictures developed. Maybe you can get them published like you wanted."

I thought again of what Momma had said about needing to keep working at the journal and how angry I had been at her at that moment. Layla's words made me realize just how alike Momma and I were, and I smiled at the irony of it.

"Thank you, Layla, my dearest friend. Maybe I will try."

After the phone call with Antoine, Momma seemed less stressed and there were days when we actually did feel like a family again, especially when the clashes were so bad no one could go out, and schools and offices closed. I'd been so discouraged lately I was glad not to have to go out, not to have to face my teachers and classmates with a fake smile.

There was one day in March 1976 when Momma got up early and made a real breakfast: eggs and *fool*, cheeses, *labneh*, *za'tar* in oil, tomatoes, radishes, olives, green onions and sweet tea in small goldrimmed glasses. By the time Baba and I got up, it was all laid out on the kitchen table. It was so colorful it reminded me that springtime was coming, in spite of the chill that lingered in the air. We all sat together at the table and ate.

For the previous two days, we had been hearing gunfire closer than usual. There were snipers on every street and it was too dangerous to go out. After breakfast that morning we listened to the news together until the batteries went dead on the radio. There was no electricity, so we couldn't plug it in or watch TV. It was the first time we'd all been together like this in a long time and I was trying to think of what I could do to keep my parents in the room together. My eyes went to the backgammon board, with its beautiful inlay, the white and black backgammon pieces hidden inside.

"Who wants to play?" I said, bringing the board over to the coffee table. I opened it, revealing the game surface with its elongated triangles.

Baba's eyes lit up. He pulled his shoulders back and sat down, rubbing his *karsh*. "Hell, yeah," he said in English, the corners of his mustache curling up along with his grin. "What about it, Nadine?"

Momma *tcch'd*, signaling *no*. "*Yalla*, you play Noor."

I refused, saying I preferred to watch. Momma sighed, but finally she smiled and sat down opposite Baba and they starting playing. As the game heated up, the lines in Momma's forehead deepened with concentration. Baba's eyes grew fierce as he considered his next move. He rolled one bead after another of his worry beads between his cigarette-stained fingers, the green tassel riding up to one side and then down again. It was a close game all the way and as it approached the end I started dreading the outcome. I cracked my neck to one side and then the other. One of them had to lose and I couldn't bear the thought. I didn't want anything to happen to cause tension between them again so I jumped up and blurted out, "I changed my mind, I want to play."

Baba usually couldn't be ripped away from a game once it started, but he must've read my thoughts because he pushed himself up and said, "*Shukran, 'ayni*. Thank you. You saved me from defeat!"

That day eased into night, the quiet broken every few minutes by gunfire, far, then near, like angry birds calling back and forth. The lonely sound of the *muezzin's* voice from a nearby mosque calling the faithful to evening prayers—clashes or no clashes. Momma lit the lantern and Baba fired up the canister of the gas heater, putting pieces of orange peel on top to make a nice smell in the air. They opened a bottle of red wine and let me have a small glass. I got up and kissed them both. I'd forgotten what it felt like to be happy and that night I let myself believe we could stay that way forever.

9.

One evening when the school year was nearly finished, I was washing the best I could by soaping up and pouring water over myself using a plastic water jug. The tank on the roof had been empty for days so I had to use water we'd stored in the bathtub. When I finished, I was wrapping myself, shivering, in a towel when I heard Momma calling.

"*Yalla habeebti* get dressed and come join us."

I took my time, sensing that this was going to be more than just having a glass of tea and a biscuit. My parents were sitting on the sofa in the living room and Baba gestured for me to sit.

"Noor, I hardly know where to start," he said. "This has been such a dark, difficult time for us all." He paused and tugged the hair at the back of his neck. "Momma and I have been trying to figure out what to do. It's so dangerous now. We can barely walk outside. Everything closed. And after—" He hesitated. "After what happened, *ya'ni*, you—we—"

At this point Momma put her hand on Baba's arm and took over.

"What Baba is trying to say is that we've been exploring ways to get us out of Lebanon for a while until things cool down. At least for the summer, but we don't have a lot of options, Noor—" Now she was the one hesitating and I dreaded what I instinctively knew was coming.

"But, you remember our friend, Antoine – you met him last year?" She coughed as if something was caught in her throat. "He works in New York and he's offered to let us all stay there with him and his sister, Gabbie, until we figure things out."

I hardly knew how to process what they were saying. Things were happening so fast, decisions seeming to have been made without my knowledge.

"You go stay with Antoine if you want. I don't even know him. I'm staying right here—*saamida!*"

I said the word *steadfast* while striking the arm of the chair with my fist for emphasis.

"Noor!" Momma clearly wanted to scold me, but Baba stopped her.

"*Najnouj*, I know you're sorry for what you did—putting yourself and your friend in so much danger, but the fact is, it made Momma and me realize just how easily, how *ya'ni*, just like *that*," he said, snapping his fingers, "something could happen to any one of us, and honestly, if anything did happen to you, *habeebti*, it would be more than either of us could bear or ever forgive ourselves for."

Listening to Baba, his voice heavy with emotion, I bitterly regretted my impulsive decision to go to the hotel district that day. The consequences had tumbled like stones down a mountainside, and this was the worst of all. Yet, even with everything that had happened I couldn't imagine leaving Lebanon—being *forced* to leave.

"*Yalla*," Momma said, "We'll talk more in the morning. Let's get some rest now."

That night I lay in bed, images looming behind my closed eyelids. Janine's lifeless body, the young militiaman pressing down on me, bullet-scarred buildings, piles of burning rubble and trash, boys barely older than me firing weapons from rooftops, out of windows, between sandbags. I concentrated on slowing my breathing, tried to pace it with the distant sound of waves, until I was calmer. I thought about how panicked my parents were, just knowing I'd been near the front lines, how much worse it would be if they knew everything that had happened to me there—and what *might* have happened. I remembered how calm I'd been, watching the action through the viewfinder, how that calm dissolved into panic and terror when I was held down, expecting the worst, somehow saved by a stranger who had a conscience.

When the turmoil in my busy, sleepless mind eased and my anger at my parents ebbed a bit, some private, secluded part of my brain sought to picture what America was like, what kind of a place New York was. I thought of American movies I'd seen: *The Sting, The Way We Were, Young Frankenstein*, but none of them helped me form a picture. I had some vague ideas of blonde people, fancy cars, skyscrapers, easy life, but I couldn't imagine what it would be like to live there. Would people be friendly or hostile? Would I make friends? Would I panic every time someone came up behind me or I heard a loud noise like I'd started doing here?

I knew my parents—especially Momma—were resolute and there was a strange relief in it, even though it tormented me to think of leaving everything and everyone behind and going where it was safe—the way I'd felt when Layla left me at the front lines and sought safety. Yet it made sense, didn't it? Isn't that what we're wired to do? Seek safety? Strange how easily that wiring can be short-circuited in extreme situations.

Many times that restless night, my mind wandered to Raʿad. Even though we'd broken up and I was glad for it, it still bothered me to leave without saying goodbye. I knew he was a jerk, but some part of me still cared for him, if only a little. He was the first boy I'd kissed, after all. I could still remember his hair sliding between my fingers, the soft warmth of his neck when I kissed it, the way his skin smelled of cologne, smoke, and a hint of sweat. The thrill when he pulled my body against his. I thought about Momma's warnings and how I had resisted him even though it felt good being close, how later I'd been forced by someone else. It made me think about the idea of virginity, how protective we are of it, yet I had no doubt it would have been grabbed away from me like an apple yanked off its branch and devoured without a thought, if that second stranger hadn't come along. It was as if I'd already lived a whole lifetime since that first kiss in the banyan tree.

In the morning I asked Baba how he could accept going to stay with Antoine, when he so clearly disliked him. He told me three surprising things. One was that he had spoken with Antoine and was convinced of his good intentions, that he even offered to move out and stay with a friend until we found our own flat. Two was that Antoine was working on securing a temporary editing job for Momma at the newspaper where he worked and he'd hopefully help us secure visas as well. Three was that Baba would stay in Lebanon initially and follow us once he took care of a few logistics. I had more or less resigned myself to leaving Lebanon for the summer, but I was unhappy about Baba staying behind even though he promised it wouldn't be for long.

"That way you'll have everything set up for me and all I'll have to do when I arrive is put my feet up and watch someone else's bad news for a change on one of those nice big, color TVs while you and Momma feed me American hamburgers and *batata* with *Heentz* ketchup."

"For sure, Baba. I'll feed you grapes one at a time, too!"

"Oh—and don't forget the apple pie."

Momma said *good luck with all that*. What she was most looking forward to was electricity 24 hours a day and a hot shower whenever she wanted it. It was good to see how relieved they both seemed to have a plan in place, and part of me was excited about the adventure, but apprehensive, too, about going as Antoine's guests, about Baba not going with us. What if something happened before he could join us?

I spent a wonderful last day with Layla. It was finally spring and on a bright, beautiful day, her family and mine went for a walk on the AUB campus, with its lush greenery and colorful flowers bursting everywhere. You'd never guess there was a hot war going on nearby. We strolled arm in arm, spread out a big cloth and set up a picnic lunch of cheese, olives, hummos, tomatoes and some *kibbeh* Layla's mother had made along with a thermos of steaming Turkish coffee. I pulled Layla close and told her I'd be back before she knew it.

She put her arm around my shoulder and sighed, her head resting on my arm. "Oh, Noor. I will miss you too, too, too much, *habeebti*, but honestly, I am kind of glad you'll be where you'll stay out of trouble!"

"We'll see about that, I'm not so sure I know how," I said, doing my best to smile.

At the airport, I clutched Baba's hand so hard my fingers tingled. He walked with Momma and me to the ticket counter with my carry-on bag slung over his shoulder, one I'd had since I was little. It had an image of a panda bear cub chewing on bamboo and it made me smile to see him carry it. When it was time to board the plane I held on to him as long as I could, my face against his chest.

"I don't want to go, Baba. I wish we could all just stay."

"I know, *Najnouj*, but it's going to be fine. There's a funny thing that happens when you travel somewhere new."

I listened, trying not to cry, for his sake.

"When you start the journey you're thinking about everyone and everything you're leaving behind, but when you arrive at your destination, your mind shifts to all the things and people you're seeing for the first time. It's a kind of magic that happens."

I squeezed him tighter and said, "I will never stop thinking about you, Baba. Not until we're back together again. Not ever."

"*Habeebti*," he said with a sad smile. "It will be very, very soon. Promise." He reached into his pocket, pulled out his worry beads, the ones his father had given him, and said, "Take these, Noor, just a small remembrance. I wish I'd been able to get something nicer."

"This is perfect," I said, clutching the beads. I loved the way the smooth, round stones felt in my hand. I kissed his face over and over again until he pushed me toward Momma with a final wave.

All the Things and People

Summer 1976

10.

I had always dreamed of flying in a plane, but I never thought it would happen like this. I sat silently, with my head against the oval window, temples throbbing, as the Middle East Airlines jet taxied and took off towards the south.

The mountains rose off to the left so close I could have jumped into the village of *Bchamoun* onto one of the balconies. The jet curved out to sea, the blocky buildings growing fainter and smaller in the haze—lines of flapping laundry like tiny, waving flags. Then, the plane tipped right until it reversed direction, skirting the coastline of Ras Beirut—now off to the right. I was desperate to catch a glimpse of my city before it vanished, so before Momma could stop me, I snapped off my seatbelt, pushed past her, and made my way to other side of the aisle. I ignored the stewardess striding towards me, hands waving.

In the few moments I had before I was marched back to my seat, I saw the afternoon sun glancing off the windows of Beirut's buildings—kissing them one by one—bringing alive the pale huddle of concrete towers, which seemed to cling to the red earth as if holding on to life itself. From this distance, although smoke rose in billows and plumes here and there, you couldn't see the scars, hear the weeping, feel the suffering. It was the most beautiful thing I'd ever seen—my city from the air—proud, stocky, steadfast—framed by water on three sides and mountains on one. My chest tightened as I strained to watch the waves pummel the rocky shoreline. That was my last glimpse.

We changed planes in Paris, and during the long flight I drifted off, but was jolted awake over and over again by a loud cough or sneeze, an announcement on the loudspeaker, only to feel a raw wave of grief each time. I tried to stay inside myself, keeping my eyes closed, allowing images of Lebanon to come to me, one on top of another. There was a large envelope inside the panda bag with all the photographs I'd managed to print before I'd left, along with several undeveloped rolls of film. The broken Rolleiflex was in the bag too and I hoped to have it fixed in New York, see if the film inside was salvageable. For now, I'd have to rely on my imagination.

Inside the suspended calm of the airplane with its subdued lighting, muffled engine sounds, reassuring voices of the stewardesses, I wanted so badly to capture all the images that were in my head—and then an idea came to me. I could write them down. Like a poem or an essay or even just words. I had a notebook in my bag and I pulled it out and started writing.

Lebanon

Old men in a coffee shop, smoking hookas

white hattas on their heads

Fried fish and tabbooleh on the beach in Tyre

Red tiled roofs

French perfume

Cigarette smoke

Beggars with outstretched hands

Electricity—on, off, on, off

Arabic coffee brewing with cardamom

Car horns rigged to play "Lara's Theme"

My first kiss in the banyan tree

Janine's hands soaping my head

Militiamen with rifles

Artillery booming like thunder

Taking cover in the hallway

Fear, Exhilaration

Baba with his round belly and weary smile

Layla Layla Layla

Backgammon

The Key

It wasn't the same as photography, but it was a record all the same. Something to hold onto when I was far away, before the images faded like a dissipating fog. Momma knew I was still angry at being forced to leave and she tried to talk to me a few times while I was writing, but I did my best to stay inside my thoughts.

"*Habeebti*," she whispered, "Do you need anything?"

"I'm fine."

She sat back, sipping the glass of champagne the stewardess had offered her in both French and English—but not Arabic of course. A little while later she unwrapped the blanket they gave us and put it over me and finally my mind settled enough to sleep a little before the next interruption.

The Atlantic was seemingly endless and gray, so different from the blue of the Mediterranean in summer, and when the stewardess gave us a last snack, and the plane made a wide circle around the sparkling buildings and bridges of Manhattan, it was as if I had entered a futuristic movie, where everything was vertical and metallic and shiny. I expected to see flying cars at any moment, weaving in between the skyscrapers, swooping by the Empire State Building. Buildings I'd only seen in magazines were suddenly underneath me and I was both terrified and amazed. It confused me to see a huge patch of green, like a forest in the middle of the city and I had no idea what it might be. Like Beirut, Manhattan was surrounded by water, but no mountains loomed, no laundry danced on cords stretched across balconies.

I remembered Baba's words: "*When you arrive at your destination, your mind shifts to all the things and people you're seeing for the first time. It's a kind of magic that happens.*"

It *was* magical—this new city rising into the air towards us, with its towers of shining glass and steel, the sun sparkling off the water all around, long barges approaching the shore. If only Baba had been there to share all these sights with me, I might have felt truly happy.

The row of taxis at JFK airport were like children's toys—gleaming, bright yellow, neatly lined up at the curb. Antoine and his sister Gabbie met us at the arrival gate and helped us get our luggage. I kissed them dutifully but refused Antoine's offer to take my carry-on bag.

"No thank you," I said, gripping the heavy bag to my side.

"As you like, *habeebti*," he said with a shrug.

Momma gave me a look and I knew I'd be walking a very fine line as long as we were in New York accepting Antoine's hospitality, being polite but not more friendly than required. I hoped it would be easier once Baba arrived but for the moment everything seemed strange and awkward.

I watched Momma and Antoine to see how they greeted, waiting for the slightest hint of impropriety, but they kissed on both cheeks as we all do, friendly but nothing more. I was still puzzled about the relationship, but since Baba seemed to have relaxed about Antoine, and Antoine was still planning to live for the summer with his friend Aziz, who was also

Lebanese, I decided to take a wait-and-see approach, especially since I didn't have much choice.

As we drove towards Brooklyn, I couldn't help staring at the meter in the front of the taxi, which showed the distance we were travelling and the dollar amount that jumped up every few seconds. I could tell there would be no bargaining with *this* driver, no stopping to let in more passengers, no Arabic music blaring, no worry beads hanging from the mirror, no evil eye decals on the windshield, no friend of the driver getting in and joking with the passengers, no one asking to stop by the butcher to pick up a kilo of meat on the way home.

I had a pang of longing for our old, beat-up, dusty Mercedes Benz *servees* taxis, which honked their way through Beirut, cruising for additional fares to pick up. It cost only a few Lebanese liras to go just about anywhere— even if it meant putting up with an occasional detour.

The windows were rolled up and locked—AC blasting—and I had to put on a sweater to keep from freezing, so I had no idea what this new place sounded or smelled like. Outside, there were looming metal structures all around and above us. They were rusty, seemed ancient, like they might collapse at any minute, bringing cars or trains crashing down on our heads. I'd been hoping to see skyscrapers, but instead we kept driving by old, dirty brick buildings with rusty iron staircases on the outside.

People looked different than in Lebanon—but not in the way I expected. I suppose I expected everyone to appear the way they did in Hollywood movies—glamorous and carefree, though later I realized how silly this was.

There were lots of Black people—many dressed colorfully, some with afros—both men and women—like I'd seen in magazines. Some Asian people, who walked with their hands behind their backs. Still others were dark and had black hair—like us—but with different features.

One young man, with shoulder-length hair, his shirt a little too unbuttoned, crossed the street in front of us and turned back to stare at me through the window. He was very attractive and I was embarrassed by the attention—especially with Momma, Antoine, and Gabbie sitting right there. To make matters worse, Antoine—who had been talking nonstop with Momma—noticed, and pulled himself upright.

"Who does he think he is? I should put him in his place!"

I scowled at Antoine. What business was it of his?

"Oh, c'mon, Antoine," said Momma, "When you're as pretty as

Noor…" Her voice trailed off as she noticed a heavy-set woman wearing a tight-fitting shirt and Spandex leggings.

"Oh, my *goodness*," she said letting out a guffaw.

"What? So what?" I said, defensive even though I had no connection to this woman or anyone else, for that matter. I was still in a bad mood—uprooted, exhausted and bewildered—and I wanted it to be clear to Momma I wasn't happy without being outright rude.

"Like no one is fat in Lebanon?" I said.

I hated it when she judged people, and since I was already upset, this didn't help. Just seeing all the different kinds of people on the street and all the crazy outfits, I suspected I'd be listening to lots of comments from her. Most people thought she was very open-minded, and in many ways she was—until she didn't approve of something.

"Back home, at least they know how to *cover* it!" she said.

I decided it was best to drop the subject and I distracted myself by looking out the window again. Some people were dressed very messily—with torn jeans and faded t-shirts.

One man—with gray stubble all over his face and filthy pants held up by suspenders—stumbled into the street, almost running into the taxi, so the driver had to slam on the brakes and honk loudly, yelling at him through the closed window. The man held up his middle finger and roared something at the driver. I didn't yet know exactly what that gesture meant, but I knew it was rude and he was clearly angry. I hoped I wouldn't be seeing many people like him when I was out on my own.

A woman in a tight dress with waves of black hair down to her waist, was embracing a man with equally tight bell-bottoms and a paisley shirt. She was leaning up against a building and they were pressed together, kissing as if they didn't know anyone was around them. I couldn't stop staring, my head turning back as we passed, until they were out of sight.

At one point, the driver was waiting to turn onto a different street and a truck sped past with its horn blaring. I screamed and grabbed Momma's arm, heart pounding, my vision suddenly darkening as if I might black out, before I noticed what I was doing and let go. That's when it occurred to me that we hadn't seen a single military truck, or soldier, or even anyone carrying a rifle.

Antoine's apartment was on the fourth floor of a featureless building—brick—like all the buildings in New York seemed to be. It was in a neighborhood called Boerum Hill—though it seemed perfectly flat to me—and there was a nice park nearby. It had three small bedrooms, a living room with a sofa, chair, and TV, a dining room and a kitchen so small the four of us could barely fit in it at the same time. Momma's face dropped when she saw it. Our kitchen in Beirut had a table in it, long counters for preparing, a big gas stove, and a view of the fruit trees on Baba's veranda garden.

Momma glanced from Antoine to Gabbie to me and smiled faintly. "So this is our home away from home." The line in her forehead appeared briefly.

Antoine pulled his shoulders back and grinned. "*Ahlan wa-sahlan!*" he said, welcoming us, not noticing Momma's disappointment that was so obvious to me. "C'mon Noor, you look like you're at a funeral. Smile!"

I wanted to tell Antoine that living in Lebanon at the moment was a bit like being at an ongoing funeral, that I'd been taken away from home against my will, that I really didn't want to be here with strangers in a strange place, so what did I have to smile about? But I kept quiet and I knew Momma was relieved I did.

"Give her time, Antoine," said Gabbie. "Poor kid has been travelling for a whole day, plus it's her first time here! Come," she said, with a warm smile, "I'll show you to your new room."

I couldn't help liking Gabbie, with her short-cropped hair and huge, intelligent eyes. In spite of talking with the same French-infused accent and diction as Antoine, she was down to earth and funny, a little tomboyish and, at five years younger than Antoine, I could almost imagine her as the older sister I didn't have.

Those first days, the *feeling* of Beirut never left me. It throbbed relentlessly in my body, numbing me to everything outside, like having a movie play over and over in my head, as I went through life. I didn't understand how everyone around me couldn't see it, feel it, hear it, care about it and it made me resent everybody and everything in America. The only thing familiar was the hot, humid air, but it didn't hold any of the fragrances of home. It smelled of steel and exhaust, of oily odors coming up through the subway grates. The apartment buildings were featureless rectangles that towered over you, blocking out the sunlight. Once in a while, though, when the wind was blowing just right, you could smell the humid brininess of the East River that separated Brooklyn from Manhattan and if I closed my eyes I could sometimes imagine the salty fragrance of the Mediterranean.

At first, when people would ask me where I was from, I felt proud, but when I said Lebanon they'd give me a blank stare. One day, a few weeks after we arrived, I walked to the Korean grocery store on the corner to get a snack. It reminded me of our *dukkans*, where I used to get a chocolate bar or *man'oosheh* after school.

I walked through the short aisles with their neat cans of tuna, baked beans, packaged doughnuts, dishwashing liquid, most of the labels different from what I was used to, except for a few familiar brands. Out front there were wooden crates of colorful fruits and vegetables just like you'd see back home.

I remembered when I was little, how I loved going to the tiny *dukkan* on our street with Baba for batteries or bread. I'd hold his hand and stare up at the shelves, stacked high with seemingly endless items. Laundry detergent and creamy tahini. Orange Bonjus and Nescafe. KitKat bars and olive oil. Pampers and Marlboros and McVities and Crest. Rayovac, crackers, and Halls cough drops. Pink, pickled turnips. Olives both green and black. Arabic bread and speckled eggs. Pomegranate molasses beside dried red lentils. Chickpeas, broad beans, favas, sweet spice, seven spice, allspice, cloves.

I placed the Pepsi and potato chips on the counter and pulled a handful of coins out of my pocket. I wasn't used to the currency yet and as I fumbled with the coins, I sensed that another customer had approached and was standing next to me.

"You gonna take all day, *goil*? What's the problem?"

The man was so skinny I could see his jawbones through the stubble of his beard, which poked through his skin like gray and white splinters. Fear tingled down my neck and a familiar frozen sensation took over.

The Korean woman behind the counter pointed to the man and said, "You. Wait in line one minute," and then to me, "Sixty-five cents, girlie."

I managed to reach into my pocket for more money, trying to steady my hand so I wouldn't drop the coins on the ground. I hoped the woman would understand my predicament since she was foreign too, might help me out so I could finish and get away from this awful man as quickly as possible. But instead, she sighed and brusquely picked out a quarter, two dimes, three nickels and five pennies from the pile.

The man, now part way behind me, spoke again, his cold, brittle voice sending a shiver down my spine. "Where you from, anyway?"

"L-lebanon," I mumbled without turning back, regretting that I hadn't just ignored him.

"Huh? Oh, Lebanon. I know *awl* about Lebanon," he said.

He stepped forward again, pointing a long, bony finger at me. "I read the Post every morning with my *cawfee* and donut."

It seemed to be taking the woman forever to drop the coins into the till and put my things in a small paper bag.

"The *Mawslems* are killing off the Christians. It's not civilized over there."

I grabbed the bag and was about to leave when anger suddenly rose like a fever up my neck and into my scalp, taking over from the fear that had paralyzed me moments before. "You don't know anything!"

"Hah! So she can *tawk*. You're not a *Mawslem* are you?" he said, as if spitting the words out.

"It is not your business!"

There was no hiding my thick accent. I was still *fresh off the boat*, as Antoine had annoyingly said when he first heard me speaking English. Never mind that this man also had a strange way of speaking—at least to my ears. What Antoine called a *Brooklyn accent*.

I ran out of the store, forcing my legs to propel me away. I kept glancing back, afraid he would follow me, but all I saw was people walking dogs, carrying grocery bags, unaware of what had happened to me. I wondered whether they'd care even if they did know. Maybe they would act the same. For all I knew, they all thought like him. I ran to a nearby park and sat on a bench, shaking and crying, covering my face so no one would notice.

I was wiping my eyes when something brushed against my leg and I was startled to see a tancolored dog with pointed ears. He stood directly in front of me, long tail wagging. It truly seemed like he was trying to comfort me. I didn't know much about dogs and I was a little nervous, so I just held my hand out and he started licking it. I couldn't help smiling. I heard a sharp whistle.

"Brutus! Get over here!"

A very handsome man in a white shirt and jeans rushed toward me with a leash in his hand and there I was, with swollen eyes and mucus running down my face, desperately wishing I could disappear. I dabbed at my eyes and nose with my sleeve. I imagined that my mascara had left dark trails down my cheeks, that I had puffy bags under my eyes.

"I'm so sorry!" he said.

I wasn't sure if he meant because I was crying or because of the dog.

"It's OK," I mumbled, pulling my hair across my mouth. "He's nice."

I half expected him to change his attitude when he heard my accent, but he came over and put the leash on the dog, a friendly smile on his face.

"He's a good boy," he said, patting the dog's head. "You ok?"

"Fine," I said with a wave of my hand, not knowing what to say and wishing he'd just take the dog and go. He seemed like he was in his twenties and he had a warm smile and kind, dark eyes that crinkled at the corners. Somehow, his being so nice to me made me feel even more awkward and ugly than I did already.

"C'mon Brutus," he said patting his own thigh. "Let's go, boy."

But the dog was lying down now, on the grass next to the bench with its snout up, sniffing at the air, clearly not planning to go anywhere. There was a food cart nearby and the black end of his nose twitched from side to side, making me think of a cartoon I'd once seen, where a little gray curl of aroma is wafting into some animal's nostrils.

The dog's owner held both hands up. "Oh Brutus, really?"

I couldn't help smiling, my shoulders relaxing. "Why you call him Brutus? He's so sweet."

"That's why. He's my gentle brute, but I probably should've call him Boss instead, since he *is* the boss as you can see!"

He kept his eyes on mine when he spoke and I looked down, embarrassed, but when I glanced back up again he was still looking at me. I couldn't be sure if he liked me or he was trying to figure me out but either way I hoped he wouldn't ask me where I was from. I probably would have run straight out of the park before I'd tell another person I was Lebanese that day.

Luckily, he didn't, and when Brutus finally got up to follow some other good smells, practically yanking his owner across the grass, the man turned and waved.

"I'm Benjamin, by the way," he said, "Nice talking to you."

I smiled and put my hand up. "*Ana*—I'm Noor," I said, suddenly sad. I had said my name without worrying about what he'd think and now I wondered if I could have told him where I was from and it would have been fine, but now I'd never know.

"Benjamin." I whispered the name. It sounded musical to my ears and I repeated it under my breath. *Benjamin.*

Once I got over the shock of the incident in the convenience store, what stuck with me was not so much the hateful way the man spoke—I didn't really think everyone in America was like him—but what did stay with me was that the only thing he mentioned about Lebanon was the war. I was longing to talk to people about my country, but I didn't really want to talk about war, or who was civilized and who wasn't. I wanted to brag about how you could drive from the beach in Beirut to the snow-topped mountains of Faraya in an hour and a half. How boys walked with their arms draped around each other's shoulders on the streets just because they were buddies. How you could show up at a friend's house without calling and they'd be happy to see you. How everyone talked politics and even if they argued and yelled, five minutes later they'd be joking around again.

I'd always heard America called a "melting pot" and I'd thought this meant that whoever you were you'd just flow in with everyone else, be accepted for who you were, but after my convenience store experience I realized it might not be that simple. In Lebanon, the war had made me worry constantly about my identity, and I'd hoped at least *that* would be different in New York. Yet, here I was again thinking it was best to avoid talking about my background as much as possible.

That night, I shut the lights off and closed the windows so I couldn't hear taxis honking four stories below, or drunk passersby shouting obscenities. I put the pillow over my head, remembering When I concentrated, I could almost smell the sea brine, burning brush, black coffee, lamb roasting on skewers, hot Arabic bread—fresh out of the oven, puffed up like a cushion. I pulled the pillow down into my arms, remembering Ra'ad's warm lips on mine, but then the image of him with Cybelle snuck into my fantasy and I pushed the pillow back, angrily. *I hate you*, I said, squeezing back tears. *Oh Baba, where are you? How will I survive here?* I imagined him laughing softly, nodding in his wise way and saying, "*If you survived Lebanon you can survive anywhere, habeebti!*" After that, I let the night sounds and smells back in, and this time when I clutched the pillow I thought of Benjamin with his smiling eyes and easy manner, the way he let Brutus pull him across the park. "*He is the boss, as you can see*," he'd said, and it made me smile, made me wish I'd found a way to keep talking to him, even though he was much older than me—26 or 27, probably. Maybe I would see him again at the park some time. Some time when my mascara wasn't running down my face.

One Saturday, not long after that strange day when I'd met a truly awful person followed by a truly nice one, Antoine came to the apartment before I was even fully awake and announced that we were all going to Chinatown for dim sum. I had no idea what either Chinatown or dim sum was, but when he said Chinatown was in Manhattan I agreed.

I had always been curious to see that crazy, exciting part of the City and besides, Gabbie was coming and it was always fun being with her. Before dim sum, Antoine wanted to take us up to the gleaming towers of the new World Trade Center, but I'd always dreamed of going to the top of the Empire State Building, so he agreed. Once we were in the elevator, Gabbie squeezed my arm and said, "hold on for dear life!" and I couldn't tell if it was the thrill of finally being there or climbing 102 floors in a few seconds that made me tingly. From up there you could see a cluster of skyscrapers, the river beyond them, wide avenues with endless streams of tiny cars and a million taxis marching along like yellow ants, the verdant green of Central Park in the middle of all that concrete and steel. I thought of the day we arrived, circling Manhattan by air—how I hadn't known there was a colossal park right in the middle of the city.

Once we were back on the ground, the streets were even more crowded than Hamra, and with so many different faces from all over the world— black, brown, Asian, white, even some I thought were Middle Eastern. Couples caressing right in front of everyone. All kinds of crazy hair and clothing, as if we were at the circus, right alongside businessmen in suits and polished shoes. I was pleased that Momma refrained from commenting except once when two shirtless teenagers with mohawks walked by us and she said in Arabic, "They look like a pair of roosters. *Ma ahlaahum.*"

"Momma," I said yanking her sleeve after they'd passed. "What if they speak Arabic?"

"Do roosters speak Arabic?"

I laughed in spite of myself.

What amazed me about Manhattan was that every few blocks you seemed to be in a different neighborhood and Chinatown was unlike anything else I'd seen, with its packed, bustling streets, nearly everyone speaking a language whose sounds were completely new to me. We passed stores that had strong-smelling salted fish, dry ducks hanging from hooks, melons, green vegetables I had no names for—some wrinkled, some long and stringy. There were people bargaining with shopkeepers, arguing, talking loudly. Banners stretched across the streets, painted with bright red characters that looked like people striding along or dancing. It seemed to me that you could buy anything in Chinatown. A bathrobe with a dragon design, silk slippers, pots and pans, fresh fish, toys, an umbrella, magazines, fireworks, a bamboo plant.

When we got to the restaurant, we walked up a small set of dirty concrete stairs and into a big dining area with seemingly hundreds of plain round tables and stiff wooden chairs. I could never have guessed from the outside that there would be so much space. There were mostly Chinese people, but a few, like us, from different backgrounds. I'd had Chinese food a few times in Beirut, but the smells here were different—wonderful. Ginger and garlic and meat and onions and all kinds of things that were unfamiliar, but I was eager to try.

I loved the way the waiters came through every few minutes with trays of different foods, the little dumplings inside lidded bamboo containers reminding me of our *shish barak*, but in seemingly endless varieties, each more delicious than the last. As they circulated through the restaurant with new offerings I insisted on trying each one even though Antoine tried to object at times.

"*Ya* Noor. Better pace yourself, *'ayni*. This is a never-ending story!"

"*Bass*, Antoine, let her enjoy! Didn't you know she has an extra stomach?" Gabbie had a way of finding humor in almost any situation and I loved that about her.

I knew that Baba would have loved this restaurant, all the delicious new tastes, the noisy, casual style. I was sad he still wasn't with us and that night I asked Momma when he was coming.

"Hopefully very soon, *habeebti*. The publisher for his book is based in New York and they're trying to help him secure a visa so he can come do research here, but he's still waiting. Everything is more complicated and time-consuming because things keep shifting on the ground."

"Shifting? What do you mean, shifting?"

She said the government had decided to crack down on the Lebanese National Movement because they were gaining too much ground, the army had split and a lot of soldiers were on the LNM side.

"It's a crisis for the government because they can't count on using the military to control things anymore. They're searching for any way to avoid granting the progressive side more power."

"What are they doing about it?"

"They brought in the Syrian army, which is much larger and more powerful, to 'restore order.' It's hard to know what this will mean in practice."

"So, what's next?"

"I'm sure the government will try to go back to the way things used to be, with the right wing in full control again. It's very bad, but hopefully at least it will mean less blood being spilled."

"*Ya'ni* all that fighting was for nothing?"

"I wouldn't say that, Noor. As you know, the situation is very complicated and it's still too early to know what will happen. There have been dozens of ceasefires so far and none of them held."

"And if Baba doesn't get the visa?"

"*Inshallah* he will soon, *habeebti*. We have to be patient."

I had an uneasy feeling after that conversation. What if things got worse instead of better? What if Baba couldn't get the visa and got stuck? What if we couldn't go back? Everything in Lebanon was so irrational and unpredictable. I knew, too, that my parents—especially Momma—didn't want to take any more chances with my safety. They'd found a way to keep me out of trouble, or so they thought, and I couldn't see them reversing that decision any time soon unless the situation completely resolved and it just didn't make sense to me that bringing foreign troops in to control all the warring factions would work. After all, if they didn't have a problem fighting each other why would they have a problem fighting outsiders?

Even though I knew my parents were doing what they thought was right for me, I was still angry. No matter how bad things were I wanted to be in *my* country with *my* people. Here in the US, I didn't know who I was. It seemed like there was no purpose to my life any more. I don't think Momma had any idea just how angry I was. Every day I wrote in my journal. It was a place I could vent my feelings and try to keep some perspective on what was going on in Lebanon, which was nearly impossible to do in the middle of New York, where not even Gabbie and Antoine talked much about home any more. They preferred to talk about the weekend plans or to gossip about people at work. I wondered if *that's* what the melting pot really meant—you became like everyone else and forgot what you came from. I became obsessed with reading and listening to the news, picking up on any little tidbit I could find about Lebanon, sometimes even writing articles, doing my own analysis just to try to feel less disconnected.

The City and Samantha

11.

One Saturday in late June, Antoine's boss at the *New York Sun*, Bernard, a short, round man with no hair, who drove a Maserati and had a nervous monkey laugh, invited us all to lunch at his brownstone in Manhattan. It was the fanciest place I'd seen in New York so far—three stories high and the floor of the entrance corridor was a mosaic of a boar hunt that Bernard had somehow brought from Sicily.

Antoine wanted me to meet Bernard's daughter, Samantha, who was the same age as I was. When I first saw her I thought, well, here is that typical American girl we always imagine in Lebanon. She had long, straight blonde hair and bored blue eyes that seemed to say, *I am too good for this house, this family, and definitely you.*

I immediately disliked her, but out of habit I reached out to kiss her cheeks. She drew back and shook my hand limply.

"So, do you want a tour of the *Castello*?" she said sarcastically, putting on a very convincing Italian accent.

"Samantha, don't be a brat," her mother, Geraldine, said, wagging her finger. She was like an older Samantha, with squintier eyes and lines around her mouth.

I knew I was blushing, but before I could say anything, Samantha gestured to me to follow her up the broad oak staircase. This house, which seemed like a normal apartment building from the outside, really *was* like a castle or a fort inside, with its dark wood, stained glass windows and iron railings. One side of the house was rounded all the way up like a silo, so on each level there was a semicircular room, with big curved windows. Samantha led me up to the third floor and into one of these rooms where we could see down to the elegant, tree-lined street below, as chic New Yorkers walked by with their dogs.

"Sorry about my parents. They can't help being square," Samantha said. I was shocked that she spoke this way about her parents for no reason that I could tell.

"They seem nice," I mumbled, blushing again.

"Hah! Are you always so polite?" she said. It's way more fun to be rude, y'know."

I had no idea how to answer this strange girl I had just met.

We wound our way back downstairs and Samantha led me around each level, gliding through the corridors in her bare feet like a nymph in one of the mosaics, pointing out sitting rooms, sewing rooms, archways, bathrooms, and libraries with little flicks of her wrist. There was something amusing about this too-skinny girl with her sarcastic expressions and off-handed comments.

Samantha sat next to me at lunch. They served veal *parmigiana*, garlic bread, and salad, with red wine for the adults and Italian *aranciata* for us. She leaned over and whispered into my ear.

"Of course you know everything Italian is better, right?"

Her sarcasm even came through the whisper. I wanted to tell her, *actually, no, everything Lebanese is better,* but I kept quiet, hoping her family wouldn't notice us.

At the end of the visit, Samantha and I exchanged phone numbers and I was surprised to find myself looking forward to the next time I could see her. I realized she was the first person my own age I'd spent time with since we'd arrived in America a month before. She was such an unlikely friend—so different from me in so many ways—skinny and pale, brash and sarcastic—not to mention spoiled, but at the same time, I couldn't help admiring her self-confidence and quick sense of humor. Not to mention that I was in desperate need of distraction, of something to get me out of my own dark thoughts and worries.

On the ride home, Gabbie was up front with Antoine, Momma and I sat in the back. Momma sat forward and said to Antoine, "*Mashallah,* I didn't know it paid so well to own a—how do you call it?"

"Tabloid paper?" Antoine said.

"Yes, yes, but, how beautiful is their house? So nice," Momma said, smiling.

"True," Antoine said. "*Mais,* Bernard's real money is from collecting and dealing in Italian art." He rubbed his thumb and forefinger together.

"They travel there minimum twice a year, sometimes more."

"Good for them. Why not?"

Then, Momma leaned toward Gabbie and spoke quietly, as if I couldn't hear.

"But that girl. Disaster," she said, shaking her head.

I was surprised at how defensive I felt of Samantha. "Why a disaster?"

"Never mind, *habeebti*. This is America after all. Not like Lebanon. Definitely not like Palestine." Momma made a dismissive gesture with her hand.

"That is so rude," I muttered, pushing myself up against the window.

Antoine glanced in the rearview mirror and chuckled.

"OK, guys, *khalas*, ceasefire, please! Nadine, I swear she is fine. This is a good family. So she is a teenager. No big deal. It's good for Noor to have a friend."

In her usual disarming way, Gabbie jumped in. "I wouldn't mind having that corn silk hair of hers. I bet she lets it down from the tower like Rapunzel to bring her boyfriends up."

"Gabbie, please!" Momma said, clearly alarmed that Gabbie would even refer to such a possibility in front of me.

"Don't worry Momma, I won't be letting my hair hang out of the apartment window any time soon, and anyway, who even said she's my friend?"

Momma sighed and Antoine put in a cassette of cheesy Lebanese pop music.

As it turned out, I spent a lot of time with Samantha that summer. Most of her girlfriends were away for the summer, and she was bored. I was bored too, and anxious to get out more, so I suppose you could say we helped each other pass the time. Antoine and Gabbie eventually convinced Momma that she could be trusted to show me around the city, at least nearby areas. I think Momma gave in because she had started the temporary proofreading job Antoine had arranged for her at *The Sun*, where he wrote a regular travel and culture column, and she didn't want me moping around the apartment alone all day. I'd spent enough time doing that in Beirut. But the first time I brought it up, Momma was not happy.

"I'm meeting Samantha tomorrow," I announced a few days after the visit to the *Castello*, trying to act as casual as possible, knowing that Momma would probably say no.

"Meeting *Shamandar*?" she said. "When—and where—and *how*?"

"Her name is Samantha," I said, meeting Momma's frown with my own.

"She is not a beet! And her father is driving her here at 10:00 tomorrow morning and then we're going out."

Momma opened her mouth to speak, but Gabbie jumped in.

"Nadine, I have an idea. I only have to be at the shop tomorrow until 1:00. If it's OK with you, they could have a nice walk, get a sandwich. Then I could meet up with them afterwards. It will be good for Noor to get out of the house, *n'est pas?*"

"Well, true," Momma said, smoothing her hair. "And I suppose if you're here for her that's different."

When Samantha arrived the next morning, I felt like I'd been set free, and as soon as we were out the door and half way down the block, Samantha held my shoulder to steady herself, reached down with her other hand and pulled a tiny pouch out of her sock. She stuck her nose into the pouch and fluttered her eyelashes. I waited, puzzled.

"Oh, yes! Life is good," she said pulling a joint out of the pouch. It looked to me like a cigarette someone had stepped on.

"Did you take that from your parents?"

Samantha opened her mouth, as if dumbfounded by how naïve I was.

"That is a good one, my friend," she said, quickly recovering, "but when I said my parents are squares, I mean they are *squares*!" She drew a box with her fingers. "But this is some really good grass. You're gonna love it."

I had no idea what to say. I had heard about pot, of course, but I didn't actually know anyone who had smoked it, except possibly Raʿad. I had never seen him do it, had just smelled the odd, pungent odor on him once. I had always been against the idea, thinking people who used any kind of drugs were weak or stupid or both. On the other hand, I didn't want Samantha to think *I* was square.

"You never smoked, *did* you?" Her eyes were sparkling.

"I don't take drugs," I said, feeling defensive.

She grabbed my arm and laughed. It struck me that Samantha had her father's monkey laugh, only when she did it, it came out softer and, somehow, cute.

"Sister, grass is not drugs! This here," she said, stroking the joint a little obscenely, "is pure green delight, but if you don't want any, well, *va bene.*"

Why did this have to be the first thing that happened when I went out with Samantha? I had been thinking it would be like the days I used to go with Layla to Hamra Street and we'd enjoy just strolling, looking at cute boys and eating ice cream. I felt a longing for home so powerful I thought I would burst out crying.

To my surprise, Samantha put her hand on my shoulder, pulled on the thin strings of the pouch and replaced it in her sock.

"Hey, it's no big deal, ok? I just thought it would be fun."

"Honestly, I don't mind if you want to—"

"Like I said, no big deal. So what do you want to do? We're free!"

"Thank God! I thought I'd become crazy if I had to stay in that apartment another minute, but I have *no* idea where to go."

"Well, neither do I!"

Here we were, free to do whatever we wanted but neither of us knew the first thing about Brooklyn. We wandered for a little while, sweating in the heat of the humid July day, and every time we'd pass a good-looking guy, Samantha would turn her head coyly and give him sweet eyes. She was even bolder than Layla, but I was too shy to flirt like that, so I'd just smile and giggle.

"Hey, I have an idea," she said. "I do know one place in Brooklyn. One time my parents took us to the Brooklyn Botanic Gardens. It's sort of boring, but cool just to walk around and see stuff."

"What is that?"

"It's this big, fancy garden. You'll see."

We got a map in a small shop and it took us about a half hour to walk there. Samantha was right. It was cool. Actually, it was much better than I expected from her description—but that was Samantha. She didn't get excited about much. I couldn't believe there was something so beautiful this close to where I was living. In Beirut we really didn't have anything like it.

My favorite part was the Japanese garden. Walking over a little arched bridge, we could see hundreds of orange and yellow fish that Samantha explained were goldfish. It made me feel as if we had travelled to Japan. We sat down in a quiet area away from people and Samantha pulled out the joint again and grinned.

"What about just a tiny, little toke?"

"Go ahead, really I don't care."

And it was true, I didn't. I was happy, enjoying exploring this gorgeous place that seemed to materialize magically out of the pavement and brick city.

Samantha lit up the joint and took a couple hits and then offered it to me. I shook my head.

"Really? What's not to like?"

"I don't know. I just don't want to."

Samantha shrugged and smoked by herself, taking a few long, slow drags with her eyes closed. Then she stubbed it out and put what was left of it back in the pouch and lay on her back staring up at the sky. She was wearing a green halter top and the widest bell bottom jeans I'd ever seen, a beaded choker around her neck. The little bag where she hid the joint was next to her on the ground and it had a picture of a Black man with long dreadlocks.

"Who is that?" I asked, tapping the picture.

Samantha burst into monkey laughs and rolled over on her side to face me, her knees bumping into mine.

For the second time that day I felt embarrassed and foolish.

"Sorry, I'm just feeling giggly. But seriously, you *really* don't know Bob Marley?"

I shrugged.

"Well then you're in for a real treat. You're coming to my house next week and we're going to have a Marley-thon. Sister, there is so much you have to learn and so little time, but right now, I'm starving! Let's go get a couple *heroes*!"

"*Heroes?*"

"Let's go. Now! No more questions or I might bust my gut."

She stumbled as she got up and grabbed my arm. Without thinking I put my other hand on her arm, the way I would back home with a friend, but she drew back.

"I'm fine. I'm fine. Just a little, tiny bit high is all."

I woke up early to use the bathroom and the smell of *mana'eesh* baking lured me to the kitchen. I loved it when Momma cooked *mana'eesh*. When she had the time, she'd make her own dough, mix fragrant wild thyme— the *za'tar* she'd brought from Lebanon, with oil, spread it on the dough, and bake it until it sizzled and bubbled, releasing its sublime aroma, reminding me of Janine. I'd take it over a pizza any day of the week. I gave Momma a quick kiss and sat down. She, Gabbie and I sat at the kitchen table, eating *mana'eesh* with the *labneh* Momma made by draining yogurt in a cheesecloth until it was thick and creamy. We sipped sweet black tea from Gabbie's gold-rimmed tea glasses, me still in nightgown and slippers. The sun poured in from the open living room windows. When I closed my eyes and inhaled, I could almost imagine I was back home.

After we'd finished, cleaned up, and dressed, the doorbell rang and Antoine came in.

"Guess what today is?" he said, chirpy.

"The Fourth of July, *duh*," I said, imitating Samantha and then instantly regretting it.

Momma glared at me and I mumbled *sorry*.

Antoine continued, seemingly oblivious to my sarcasm. "*C'est vrai!* But not just *any* July Fourth. This is the *bicentennial!*" he said.

"Why should I care about the Americans and their independence?" I said.

I was eating a tomato and a cluster of seeds squirted out of my mouth.

"Noor!" Momma said. "Don't talk with food in your mouth and don't be rude to Antoine. He is telling you something about history. Don't act ignorant."

Antoine smiled. "Don't worry, Nadine, I can defend myself. The bicentennial is exactly two hundred years since America gained its independence."

I refrained from making a comment about how it was hard to get worked up about two hundred years when we came from a culture that was *thousands* of years old and instead said, "And all we did was invent the alphabet."

"We the *Phoenicians*," Antoine said, dodging a smack on the arm from Gabbie.

"Antoine! *Khalas*," she said.

"Look, Noor," Momma said, "no one is suggesting we go around waving American flags, but it's a historic day here, so at least we should be aware—"

"It's just hard for me to get excited about it when our own country's independence is falling apart."

Antoine shrugged. "Suit yourself. I wasn't making a political point, I was just going to say, the Tall Ships will be sailing on the Hudson and it's a beautiful day. We could go up to the waterfront in Manhattan to see. It will be fun. *Shoo fii-ha?* Why not?"

"We're *Palestinian*," I said, looking at Momma. "Not American. I'm not celebrating *their* independence day."

"We're Palestinian now, are we?" Antoine said.

"I was talking to Momma."

"Noor, I don't like your tone. Now go to your room," Momma said.

"Fine!"

I dressed quickly and pushed my wallet into the pocket of my bell-bottom jeans. Sneaking down the main corridor, I could hear Antoine and Gabbie trying to convince Momma that it was just typical teenage behavior and I'd outgrow it soon enough. Momma replied angrily that *that girl* was a bad influence on me, that American teenagers don't respect their parents and she had half a mind to make me stay home and read for the rest of the summer. I was able to slip down the small hall between the kitchen and front door unnoticed.

I walked to the corner and put my dime in the payphone, dialed the Simmons residence, aka the Castello, to let Samantha know I'd meet her in Manhattan. I decided to walk across the Brooklyn Bridge because the trains scared me with their screeching wheels and sparks, the electrified third rail, the plunge into darkness as if entering hell. Once I reached the upper part of the bridge, I leaned against the railing, taking in the great sweep of the river far below and the shimmering city beyond. With a thrill, I saw that there were hundreds of small boats swaying in the water, reflecting the morning sunlight with almost painful brilliance, realized they must be waiting for the Tall Ships to arrive. I rested my chin on my arms and felt a moment of regret for how unkind I had been to Antoine. Even though he annoyed me, I realized there was nothing to be gained by being rude.

Samantha had agreed to meet me in Greenwich Village, and during the long walk, my mind kept going over the way I had acted with Momma and Antoine. I wasn't sure why I'd gotten so angry. I didn't want to believe that Gabbie was right about my acting out because I was a teenager, or that Momma had a point about Samantha's influence on me, although I couldn't deny that there was at least some truth in what they said. Lately, it was as if I had two personalities. One minute I'd be perfectly fine and the next it was as if I had swallowed a potion that turned me into a crazy person.

But it was more than that. I could see how easy it was to lose yourself in the melting pot, now that I understood its true meaning—everyone melting together into one stew until you forgot what you came from and who you really were. At first, I thought I could be a proud Lebanese-Palestinian girl in America, rather than becoming just another American girl of Lebanese-Palestinian descent. The way Antoine and Gabbie seemed to have melted away from their Lebanese-ness, comfortable and happy in their chosen existence, almost never mentioning home—if they even thought of Lebanon as home any more. That's the real reason I got upset with Antoine. I never heard him talking about what was happening in Lebanon, how our people were suffering. I couldn't tell if it even mattered to him, but he was as excited about somebody else's independence day as if it was his own. Unlike Antoine, I didn't want to be in America in the first place, so why would I celebrate anything about the place? I just wanted to go home—and somehow get through the days until then.

On top of it all there was the stress and uncertainty of not knowing when Baba would join us, *and* my suspicions about Antoine's motives.

I wondered what happened when Momma realized I'd gone out. She didn't like me wandering around alone—especially in Manhattan, which was strictly forbidden. I thought about turning back, but I'd walked nearly an hour and a half already. I wondered if Antoine and Gabbie convinced her to go see the Tall Ships anyway, or if she would be sitting silently with her chin on the knuckles of one hand, tapping her cheek with her index finger, a deep groove in her forehead. I knew it was unrealistic, but I hoped she'd understand, forgive my bad behavior.

When I finally got close to the Village nearly an hour and a half later, people were carrying folding chairs and picnic blankets, preparing to go see the ships. American flags and banners decorated buildings and utility poles. Children chased each other, shrieking every time a cherry bomb exploded nearby—a sound that made me start sweating, my heart pound until I remembered where I was.

Samantha was wearing a denim jumpsuit with the first few buttons undone, her big square sunglasses resting on her head. She sauntered towards me in her chunky platform sandals, as if it was no big deal getting together, even though I knew she'd been waiting for me. I grinned, happy to be meeting my strange American friend on such a beautiful summer day. I wished I could reach out and kiss both her cheeks, but by now I knew that wasn't the way American teenagers greeted each other.

"Ooh, pretzels!" Samantha said, doing a graceful little shimmy as we approached the pretzel cart.

"What are those, anyway?" I said and immediately regretted it, realizing I was showing my ignorance once again, but Samantha just said it was her treat and bought us two of the big, steaming, bready pretzels with mustard on the side. The sight and smell of them reminded me of the *ka'ak* they sold from carts back home, but with chunks of salt instead of sesame seeds. I salivated thinking about it, but when I bit into the pretzel, the taste was nothing like *ka'ak*. I hoped my disappointment didn't show, but Samantha was too busy smearing mustard on her pretzel to notice.

We ended up walking to the waterfront along the Hudson River, wriggling our way through the crowds of people all waiting for a glimpse of the ships. When we found a small patch of grass I collapsed on the ground, exhausted from all the walking. Samantha reached into one of the pockets of her jumpsuit and, expecting her to pull out a joint, I wondered how she could think of smoking with all these people around. Instead, though, she pulled out a small, hand-held cassette player.

"Marley time, Baby. So much better than disco!"

She turned it on and put it close to my ear. I listened intently to the warm, hoarse, sad voice singing *No Woman No Cry*. I closed my eyes, feeling that *I* was about to cry. How had I never heard of Bob Marley before? I put my head on Samantha's lap and she startled me by lifting up a strand of my hair and curling it around her finger absentmindedly.

I ended up watching the Tall Ships parade up the river, after all, just not with Momma, Gabbie, and Antoine. I'd only seen such sailing ships in pictures before, with their swelling sails and towering wooden masts. The whole time, I couldn't help thinking about Momma and how worried she must be and I told Samantha I needed to make a phone call. We walked a few blocks until we found a payphone and I called home.

"Oh my God, Noor. Where have you been? We've been too, too worried." Momma's voice was on the edge of hysterical.

"I'm sorry, Momma. I'm fine. I met Samantha, that's all."

She told me to come home immediately and when I hung up the phone, my hands were shaking.

"You're in trouble, huh, you bad girl?" Samantha said, before she noticed I was upset. "Hey, I'm just kidding. You ok?"

"I'm OK but I have to go."

"Cool, I'll walk you to the train."

"No, no train!"

"OK, I'll walk you to the bus or whatever. You seem pretty shaken up. I have just the thing to calm your jangled nerves."

I hadn't heard the word jangled before, but it sounded just right for how I was feeling. This time when Samantha pulled a joint out of a little angled side pocket and lit it up I didn't say no. I had seen how happy and silly it made her and that was just how I wanted to feel at that moment.

12.

Something changed in me after that Bicentennial Independence Day—a small, but noticeable shift. Before that, even when I was angry at Momma and avoiding her, I always felt like there was an invisible force tying me to her, as if she was the lens I saw life through, no matter what. If I did something she didn't want me to do and she was angry, I felt miserable and guilty. If she was scared or worried, I'd be sad and full of regret. When she was happy and joyful, even if I was irritated with her, I couldn't help feeling happy too.

But that day, even with all my regrets, part of me was glad for what I did. For the first time, I could imagine what it would be like to be an adult and not have to answer to anyone. I knew I had hurt her, but I had done what I wanted to do anyway—crossed the bridge to meet Samantha, even gotten high for the first time—and when I went home, I expected her to be angry and cry and make a scene. Instead, she took me in her arms and said quietly, "Please don't do that again, Noor. Just tell me what you are doing next time. I was so worried."

"I'm sorry, Momma."

And I was sorry, but I also realized that I was becoming my own person and the thread that used to bind us so tightly together slipped from her hand that day and something in me was set free. I know that she felt it too.

I'd found a newsstand in the Village that carried newspapers in Arabic, including the Lebanese *an-Nahar*, so whenever I met Samantha I'd stop by and get one. At night, I'd read and reread each page, absorbing it with a near unquenchable thirst. By late July the negotiations that were supposed to accompany the Syrian "peacekeeping" presence in Lebanon fell apart and, as Momma predicted, the lull in fighting was soon over. Rockets and mortars were fired by all sides deep into residential neighborhoods in Beirut, causing massive destruction and death and immobilizing the city. For the first time I found it hard to imagine how anyone could be living there under these circumstances. I remembered the time a shell had landed close enough to our building to shatter the windows, how Baba's arm had been cut by flying glass and I was terrified for him, especially as he was alone. I realized that my instinct had been right too. How could he leave any time soon if he couldn't even drive safely to the airport? Some peacekeeping force. We tried every day to reach him, but the line would either be busy or just ring endlessly. It was he who finally managed to contact us, and his voice was strained and sounded as far away as it was.

"I'm fine," he insisted. "You know how it is—it is boring having to stay home all the time, but at least I'm making good progress on my book."

"Boring?" Momma said. "It doesn't sound boring from over here. It sounds like anything but, *habeebi.*"

"It can be hard to concentrate with the shelling, but I just put on Umm Kalthoum and her powerful voice helps to drown it out! Anyway, usually it is not nearby."

"Usually?" I said, alarmed. "Has anything happened in our neighborhood? To our house? Baba, I'm so scared for you."

"*La, la, la, Najnouj.* Don't worry. I am fine."

It was miserable having Baba stuck in the middle of the fighting, knowing we couldn't go there to be with him and he couldn't come to us either. My hopes of his joining us had already faded into wishful thinking and now I wasn't even sure if Momma and I would get back to Lebanon in time for school—or whether school would even be open.

When I couldn't bear being cooped up in the apartment reading depressing news any longer, I stopped making excuses to Samantha. I decided I could use the distraction and she was more than happy to oblige. I would pretend to be asleep when Momma and Gabbie left in the morning. Momma probably thought I would wake up at noon, have breakfast and just be hanging around when she got back at 2:30 or 3:00.

Since that July 4th I'd avoided telling her when I was meeting Samantha; it was easier than facing the disapproval behind her questions: *Where were we meeting? What were we doing? When would I be back?*

As soon I heard the *click* of the apartment door, I was on my feet, making my way to the bathroom. I'd splash some water on my face, dress quickly, eat whatever Momma had left me in the kitchen—a *man'oosheh*, or a plate of *labneh*, cheese and bread. On the days I met her, I was usually out the door by 9:00 after a quick call to Samantha.

"I'm still in bed," she'd say in sleepy protest.

"Get up! I don't have all day."

I knew she loved being my co-conspirator even more than she liked sleeping in. For my part, I lived with a strange disconnect between my private obsession with news of Lebanon and my secret adventures with Samantha, both of which I hid from Momma, but which were essential to my survival during that period.

I even started taking the train to save time, since the walk was so long. We didn't have trains or subways in Lebanon—just buses and *servees* taxis. I'd block my ears with my fingers when the train screeched around a curve, jump with every spark, my heart pounding the way it had when I'd hear gunshots back home. Once, a group of passengers all got off at the same station and I found myself alone in the train car with only one other person—a man on the opposite side of the car a few seats down. Every time I looked up he was staring at me with a smirk. It made a cold wave snake down my neck, reminding me of how easy it is to get in trouble if you're a woman alone in a deserted place with a man who thinks he can gawk at you any way he wants, or worse. That was when I realized you could walk between train cars. When I got up, I felt the blood rush down out of my head and I had to will myself not to black out so I could get to the door and away from him.

Those times I did take the train, I would try to focus on being out in the open air again where I could breathe and see Samantha, have a new adventure together. We'd meet sometimes in Brooklyn, sometimes in midtown, but our favorite place was Greenwich Village. First thing, we'd get a cup of coffee, which I knew Momma wouldn't approve of.

"You are still young," she would say. "Your bones are still growing, *habeebti*. Have tea instead."

We would sit at an outdoor table at Café Reggio or Le Figaro and if

I had enough money, I would buy an iced mocha, enjoying the rich tastes of the coffee and chocolate, licking the twist of whipped cream with my tongue. Samantha always got a plain, black espresso because *that is the only way to drink coffee*, she would say.

One day, I arrived at Le Figaro café to see two guys sitting with Samantha around a small table by the open window. Who were these boys? How could Samantha bring them along without asking me? She had told me about her boyfriend, Dylan, so I figured the one with his arm around her must be him, and I suspected she had some scheme in mind about me and this other boy. I felt a flush of heat in my face and I turned to leave, but Samantha jumped up and stopped me.

"Where are you going? Come meet my friends."

"I don't care to meet anyone," I said, jerking my arm free. "You said nothing of this to me."

"Oh come *on*, princess. Get over yourself!"

"I am leaving. *Yalla* bye."

"It's just a cup of coffee, Noor. Or, for you, *so-called* coffee. They have to go soon anyway, but I wanted you to meet Dylan."

I hesitated.

"Suit yourself," she said, walking back toward the table.

Both boys waved and I was embarrassed. Embarrassed to leave, embarrassed to stay, but the thought of getting back in that train and heading into the tunnel of doom again so soon made me shudder, so I approached the table, tried to smile. Caffe Dante did make the best iced mocha, and I'd been dreaming of one since I left the apartment.

One of them held up his hand in greeting, and the other one saluted me like a soldier, both without standing up. Back home we always get up when we meet someone, and this American habit was still strange to me. I had to remind myself they didn't mean to be rude.

"Noor, meet Brian and Dylan," Samantha said, nodding towards them.

The one who'd had his arm around Samantha said, "My friends call me Dylan 'cuz they say I look like Dylan. *Bob* that is." He paused and when I didn't react he went on. "And this turkey over here, the cool one with the shades and the leather? He's Brian. He thinks he's a British rocker," he said, putting on an English accent. Brian took a long drag on his cigarette, glanced nonchalantly outside.

Brian and Dylan were both very handsome and Samantha kept hinting with her eyes that I should do something. I don't know what, exactly—talk to him or flirt or let my arm brush against his. I narrowed my eyes at her to signal *no way.*

The two of them were talking about their band practice that evening. Dylan sang and Brian played electric bass. I wondered if Dylan *sang* like Bob Dylan or just had his name.

"We play in a rock band," Brian said, as if reading my thoughts. "Screw disco. And screw Bob Dylan too. Rock is where it's at, man."

Samantha noticed me grimacing when Brian said *man*. She knew me well enough by then.

"She's not a man, *man*," Samantha said.

"It's just an expression, man."

Brian really did look like a British rocker, with pants that hugged his skinny legs and wearing dark glasses indoors. He even had a scruffy leather jacket on the back of his chair, even though it was sweltering outside.

"But c'mon, my man," Dylan said, "You gotta admit, *Tangled up in Blue* is dynamite."

"And I couldn't get enough of *Knockin' on Heaven's Door* when I was in seventh grade," Samantha said, sticking her tongue out at Brian.

I remembered my parents talking about Bob Dylan back home. "Isn't his music political—antiwar?"

Dylan smiled. "Yeh, especially his older stuff. But *Jagger* here has no patience for protest music."

"Man, you're all living in the past. Get with it!" said Brian.

Dylan puckered up his lips as if to say *I love you, too.*

When they got up to go, Brian saluted me again and said, "See you around, man."

"OK, *woman*," I said and everyone cracked up again.

As he walked toward the door, Brian looked at me briefly, and nodded his head—a strangely intimate gesture that gave me a rush of pleasure, even though I didn't want to like him.

No boy had touched me since that terrible day near the front lines in Beirut and I was a bit nervous about seeing Brian again, but Samantha knew I liked him and she had arranged for the four of us to meet for a walk in Central Park the next day.

"It'll be fun." Samantha's voice on the other end of the telephone was cheerful—unlike her usual bored tone.

"Fine, but don't leave me alone with him."

"What are you afraid of, Noor? Never mind, don't answer that. We'll stay together, ok?"

By now I was used to Samantha's way of making everything sound like it was no big deal. She liked to tell me how I think too much about everything.

Samantha and I went to Central Park together to meet the guys and I was excited to see Brian approach from a distance. He had a slow, sauntering walk and that day he had his leather jacket slung over one shoulder, his dark shaggy hair and mustache making him seem older than most high school kids. Just a few months before in Lebanon, I probably wouldn't have been attracted to this boy at all. He was so—*American*—but, hanging out with Samantha was having an undeniable effect on me. I could almost hear Momma saying, *I'm afraid that girl is a bad influence. Be careful, Noor.*

But I didn't want to be careful. I don't think I knew exactly what I *did* want. Maybe it was to try to forget what I'd been forced to leave behind, to get back at Momma for taking me away I also think some private part of me was curious to see what it would feel like to be that generic "American" girl for a while, although my dark skin and hair—and for sure my accent—wouldn't help the experiment. Soon enough I'd be going back to my old life anyway, so this was a chance to experience new things. I always seemed to be attracted to people who were more daring than I was—Layla and Ra'ad and now Samantha and her friends who idolized Queen and the Rolling Stones. I think part of me wanted to be like them, but it never felt quite right, as if I was playing a role.

Samantha and Dylan were walking along the path in front of us with their arms around each other and Brian tried to put his arm around me, but I dodged him.

"What's up with you, fair maiden?" he said with a poetic flourish of his arm.

"Nothing," I said. "What's up with *you?*"

It was hard for me to enjoy being with this new person without panic starting to rise in me. I took a deep breath and tried to act natural—willing the echoes of that terrible day in Beirut to leave me alone.

"We're going to sit by the pond for a bit," Samantha said, peering at me over her huge sunglasses, clearly not noticing my distress. I was glad she hadn't.

"C'mon," I said, purposely bumping into Brian. "Let's go sit, too."

"Yes, ma'am," he said, saluting me the way he had when I first met him.

It was a gray day and off in the distance, the clouds were dark and threatening. It was still strange for me to see, since it was never cloudy in Lebanon in the summer. We sat against a tree away from the path and I let my arm rest against his, the hairs of his arm barely brushing mine, sending a thrill through me, but without the fear this time.

"You know, it never rains in Lebanon in the summer," I said, without thinking.

"Is that where you're from? Lebanon?"

I nodded, waiting for his reaction.

"Cool. I mean cool that it doesn't rain. And, y'know, cool that you're from there."

"Thanks." He didn't say *what* was cool about it or ask me anything about it, for that matter. It was obvious to me that he didn't really care and that I really did—so I had already failed at my first attempt to blend in.

"Sometimes I think you don't like me very much," he said, bumping me with his shoulder.

"Would I be here if I don't like you?"

"I don't know. Can I kiss you?"

His face was only a few inches from mine and he was staring into my eyes. A shiver ran through my body, and I pressed my mouth against his.

"Wow," he said, sitting back against the tree. "You went from pushing me away to practically devouring me all in five minutes!"

My cheeks reddened.

"Well, I guess you have your answer," I said.

"What was the question?"

"If it's OK to kiss me."

"I still don't know," he said, raising one eyebrow. "I'll have to try some time."

Brian reached into an inside pocket of his jacket and pulled out a joint. Even though I'd smoked once with Samantha, I still didn't really like the idea, but when he lit it, releasing its pungent, herby smoke, I was transported to the countryside in South Lebanon, the odor of burning brush thick in the air—a memory without a name, so powerful it almost made me cry. He held the joint between his thumb and forefinger, took a long, slow drag, and held his breath, squinting against the smoke. He passed it to me and I was about to say no, but the aroma tantalized me and I was still giddy from kissing him. I gripped it awkwardly between my fingers and took a *hit*, as he said. I tried to imitate the way he held the smoke in, but it made me cough.

"Whoa—easy does it!" he said.

I knew I must have seemed like the naïve foreigner trying to act cool. I could hear Antoine's annoying words in my mind again. *Fresh off the boat.*

Brian didn't seem to care though. He kissed my cheek and offered me the joint again. I giggled and took another hit, but slowly this time. The sky was darker now and a gusty wind blew around us, making the hairs stand up on my bare arms. Brian took his jacket and wrapped it around my shoulders.

"Here you go, pretty Lebanese lady."

For an instant I thought of telling him that I'm not just Lebanese—that I'm more complicated than that—but I dropped the idea just as quickly.

It started to rain and we got up and ran, shrieking, bumping into each other, my head deliciously foggy from the joint.

"Guess what?" Brian said.

"What?"

"It rains in America in the summer!"

"Yes, I see that," I said, grabbing his arm to steady myself. As we ran, water squished in my shoes. "And I hate it!"

The trains were packed with wet, grouchy passengers escaping the rain and I had to wait for more than half an hour before I was able to get onto one. By the time I got to the station and walked home, I was soaked and shivering and almost an hour late. Momma was sitting at the kitchen table, a cup of tea between her hands. Even from behind I could tell she was not happy—her shoulders rounded, her head bowed.

"Where were you, Noor?"

"I went for a walk and got caught in the rain. What's the big deal?"

"What is the big deal? *What is the big deal?* Is this how you talk to your mother now?"

I started to walk toward my room, but she stopped me.

"Were you with that girl?"

"You mean *Shamandar.*"

"Noor!"

"Do you really expect me to sit at home all day while you work? That is ridiculous!"

"Don't tell me what is ridiculous. What is ridiculous is you wandering the city like *nawar.*"

"*What?* I'm a gypsy just because I like to spend time with my friends?"

I went to my room and closed the door, Momma's voice muffled, but still charged with anger. We were arguing more and more often it seemed. I think she was troubled by my new-found independence and I usually tried to be home by the time she arrived to avoid fights, but since I'd figured out that I had the upper hand, she might yell and be upset, but in the end, I did what I wanted. A part of me liked fighting with her. It was my way of showing her that I refused to accept the life that had been chosen for me. If I was forced to live in America, at least it would be on my own terms.

⁂

Momma had a newspaper under her arm when she came home and she was pale. I was making myself a sandwich in the kitchen and when she came over to kiss me I knew something was wrong.

"What is it, Momma?"

She sat down with a sigh, placed the *an-Nahar* newspaper down on the kitchen table. "Will this never end?" she said, resting her head on her hands.

The Arabic headline jumped out at me—Maronite militiamen had besieged Tel al-Zaʿtar refugee camp and killed hundreds of Palestinians, maybe more. The news was like a punch in my stomach, filling me with a familiar heaviness, a dread so deep it mingled with my heartbeat and breath. I sat next to Momma and leaned my head against her shoulder. I knew she had suffered for being Palestinian, first having to leave her country as a young girl, sometimes facing prejudice and suspicion in Lebanon, but until Cybelle's remarks I'd never personally felt the sting of being looked down on. Now being so far away and hearing about Tel al-Zaʿtar made me feel so vulnerable and helpless.

"Did you talk to Baba? We have to go back to him somehow."

The faucet in the kitchen sink was leaking tiny droplets into a pan of water. *Drip, drip, drip.* I cracked my neck, watched to see Momma's reaction. She sat without speaking for a long moment, then shook her head, sadly.

"Don't you understand? This is why we left. We are not going back while such things are still happening, Noor."

My newfound sense of freedom and power seemed to be ebbing away. I started sobbing, knowing I could do nothing.

"But this is not right. What are we doing here when Baba and everyone else is still there? I don't *care* about being safe. I want to go back. I want to be with Baba." I breathed deep into my belly, trying to compose myself.

"Noor, I want you to understand something. I want to be back home, too. Do you really think I am happy being here when things are so terrible back home? Do you think I prefer to work at a tabloid newspaper rather than at a serious journal?"

"Why are we here, then? I don't understand you." I pulled away, suddenly angry again.

"I can't expect you to understand, *habeebti,* but someday you will when you have children of your own. There is nothing in the world more terrible for a mother than losing a child. Don't you see—that is what your father and I feared the day you went to the front lines. It was almost more than we could bear."

Until that day, I had suspected that Antoine might have been the real reason we left and went to America—that she was using the war as an excuse to leave Baba and Lebanon behind. Now I thought about how much danger I had really been in, how I had distanced myself from that danger by observing it through the viewfinder of the camera, feeling untouchable. I thought about the young fighters, barely older than I was, and of the mothers whose hearts were being shattered every day. I thought, too, of the young man who tried to force himself on me, the panic that had paralyzed me, how I'd kept it to myself all these months.

"Momma—"

"Yes, Noor," she said, stroking my hand with hers.

"Let's call Baba right now."

"*Hayaati,* all day from the office I have been trying, believe me. There are no lines whatsoever. Just, *busy, busy, busy.*"

We finally got through after midnight. Baba said he hadn't been able to get any lines from the home phone and he had gone to the *Centrale* to try to call, but by the time he got to the front of the queue it had closed. Hearing his voice brought everything rushing back—how safe I felt when his arms held me close, the smell of his aftershave mingling with hints of coffee and cigarette smoke, the light that seemed to shine from his eyes when he was laughing. Everything else, too. All the smells and sounds of Beirut came pouring through the phone receiver. I had to swallow hard before I could talk.

"Baba. *Ya allah*, how much I miss you."

"I miss you too, *ya ʿafreeteh*. So, how is *Amreeka?*"

"Honestly, I don't care about it at all. I only want Lebanon and you. Are you all right, Baba? Tell me honestly."

"I'm fine, *habeebti*. Really. It always seems much worse from the outside."

"Then can we come home?"

"*La, la, la, la*," he said, stringing the words together rapidly. "You must stay there until it is much more stable. You see what happened in Tel al-Zaʿtar? Such things can happen at any second and no one can predict what's coming next. No, no. You and Momma must stay awhile longer, but don't worry, I'll be waiting to beat you at backgammon the minute you come back!"

"Can't you at least find a way to come here so we can be together?"

"I wish, *ʿayni*, believe me, I wish, but it is complicated. Moving from place to place has become much more difficult. I must even be careful just going for groceries. Not to mention, *Uncle Sam* does not give away visas just like that. Momma was very lucky to get a work visa."

"Oh, Baba."

"Don't you worry, Najnouj. You will have a great adventure there in the *belly of the beast*," he said, exaggerating the words, "and we'll be back together before you know it. Now go and take care of your mother and don't worry about Baba. He's a tough guy."

It was just like him to make everything sound all right and be joking around, trying to make me feel better. And, to a point, it worked. Just hearing his voice soothed me, made me think that as long as he was in the world, I could handle anything.

Samantha, the boys, and I spent a lot of time together those remaining days of summer. I think we discovered every park between midtown Manhattan and Brooklyn, every bridge we could hide under. The summer was hot and sticky and the streets smelled of bus fumes and urine, soil and wet pavement when it rained, but we ignored it all. We joked, we kissed, we got high, we explored. When we needed a break from the heat we'd duck into a convenience store just to cool off, pretend to be choosing items and then slip out again, giggling. Having my new friends around me helped me get through those difficult times.

Sometimes a kind of terror would creep over me when Brian would press me hard against his body, but I had discovered that if *I* was the one to decide—when to embrace him, when to pull him toward me, to kiss him before he got the chance—somehow, I overcame my fear, and I think he got used to the pattern. If he approached me too suddenly, I'd pull back and make a joke or playfully avoid him, but when I was ready, I didn't hesitate to initiate. He didn't seem to mind, although one time he gave me a sidelong glance and said, "Do you always have to be the aggressor?"

"I'm not an aggressor!"

"Hey, it's cool. I dig it. C'mon, take me, baby!" he said, throwing his arms over his head.

One day toward the end of August, we had planned to meet at the Botanical Gardens. When I got there, I saw Samantha sitting by herself on a stone bench by the pond. She turned away when she saw me.

"Where are the guys?" I asked. "What's going on?"

The sun went behind a cloud for a moment and there was the tiniest hint of a chill in the air.

"Autumn's coming," Samantha said, pulling on the sweater she had tied around her waist. "Come on, sit."

A duck skated into the pond noisily, coming to a stop near some others, who shook their tail feathers vigorously, as if protesting.

"Are you going to talk to me? Where's Brian? Where's Dylan?"

The sun was shining into Samantha's eyes, making them seem even bluer than usual.

"Brian's not coming anymore."

"What?"

"Dylan just said Brian thought it was getting too heavy."

"What you mean, *too heavy?*"

"Noor, don't you get it? He thought it was getting too serious."

I put up my hand to tell her to stop talking.

"OK, I get it. *Khalas*," I said, without thinking.

"What you mean, *Kalas*?" she said with her monkey laugh, imitating the way I sometimes still broke such phrases from time to time.

If it wasn't bad enough that my boyfriend had dropped me without even a goodbye, now Samantha was making fun of me, too. I cracked my neck to one side and then the other, and started to walk away, angry at the sting of tears piercing my eyes.

"It means nothing. Nothing to you."

"I'm sorry. I'm upset too. I was just trying to make a joke."

"It was a stupid joke."

"I know. Sorry."

She put her hand on my shoulder. "Friends?"

I couldn't stop the tears from flowing now and I rested my head against Samantha's arm. She hesitated for a second, but then put her arms around me and squeezed.

"I didn't like him that much anyway," I said through sobs.

"I know, he is a bit of an asshole."

"Well, I didn't think he was until now."

"And guess what? Dylan told me this wasn't the first time. He did the same thing to two or three other girls."

"So, why—?

"When Dylan told me that, I started yelling at him and stuff."

"You did?"

"Yes! I was punching him on his arms and head and screaming, I was so mad. When he said, *What's wrong with you, you bitch?* I slapped him and said, *I'm a bitch? You're the bitch!* So, that was the end of that. *Nobody* talks to me like that."

She sounded so fierce I had to smile.

"To hell with the male species!" she said, punching at the air.

"Yes, to hell with them!" I echoed, amused at the idea that they were a different species, and we strode along with our arms around each other and Samantha started singing *No Woman No Cry*. I thought I heard a slight quaver in her voice, but it was gone as quickly as it came.

Not Like Americans

1976-1977

13.

John Wesley Graves High School. Brooklyn, New York, September, 1976.

After Tel al-Za'tar and the phone call with Baba, I think something inside me resigned itself to the idea that Momma and I wouldn't be going back to Lebanon that fall, even though I never consciously admitted it. Antoine's neighbors down the hall were on a sabbatical year, so Momma and I were house sitting for them, which worked well, since Antoine needed to move back in to his own apartment with Gabbie. Having our own flat made me less anxious about Antoine and Momma and it definitely made the decision to stay a bit more palatable, even though at first I couldn't accept the idea that I'd be going to high school in America.

On my first day it seemed to me there were about a hundred kids in my homeroom and one very serious homeroom teacher, Miss Downs, who liked to yell a lot.

Graves and Downs. I was off to a bad start.

At least I had gotten a bit used to Americans before school started because of Samantha and the boyfriends—*Allah yin'anhum*—may they be damned! I was sad that I wouldn't be seeing Samantha at school, but I would never forget how she was there for me during those first months. I don't know how I would have survived without her. Of course, she also introduced me to smoking pot. Funny to think that I had hated the whole idea the first day I went out onto the streets of New York with her—but those first days at GHS I was terrified and I would have given anything to meet up with her during a break to sneak off and smoke a joint together.

But, no Samantha.

Just a huge brick public school that was more like a prison, a lot of very loud students—all bumping and pushing—and a strange old woman who walked around in the hallways with a basket over her arm. I soon learned that the basket contained *demerits*—slips of paper she would pass out to kids and make them go down to the principal's office for the slightest reason. Talking in the corridor. Not having a note to go the bathroom.

Wearing a hat indoors. It was easy to get into trouble with Miss Haggard without even knowing you were doing anything wrong. No one seemed to know where *the Hag*—as she was called—came from, or what she was doing there. She did teach one class—Civics—and *everyone* despised her and her class.

My high school back in Lebanon was a private school and much smaller. We had to wear uniforms and if we did something wrong they would smack our hands with a wooden ruler, which was bad, but at least it was over quickly. We did sit at wooden desks with attached chairs, lined up in rows facing the teacher, just like at Graves, but almost everything else was different. There were so many different kinds of kids here—Black, white, Hispanic. Some Italians and even a few Arabs, though I didn't seem to have much in common with the ones I met. They seemed so eager to fit in I could hardly even tell they were Arab. This was exactly what I was afraid might happen to me here in America, but with me it would always be just acting. I did avoid revealing my identity at times because it was easier that way, not like in Lebanon where I'd sometimes *concealed* it because it could actually be dangerous to be me. But either way, I could never forget who I truly am.

One thing I couldn't get used to at my new high school was how loud the kids were—not when the Hag was around, of course—but they all sounded to me like they were yelling and shrieking all the time and not polite at all. I don't mean to say that Lebanese students are sweet and polite all the time, but somehow, they are nicer to each other. In my first week at GHS, we were changing classes so the corridors were very crowded. A bunch of white boys were coming toward me being very loud and acting like—I don't know—baboons or something, and one of them slammed right into my shoulder and didn't even apologize. Actually, they all laughed like they thought it was funny. In Lebanon that would never happen. 100% he would have put up his hand and said, "Sorry, are you ok?" or something like that. I was upset and offended for the rest of the day.

It made me painfully aware of being different—of not wanting to be like Americans. I thought about Samantha—how, even though she was a good friend to me and we had fun together, I was never completely myself with her. I was always trying so hard to be accepted. There is something that comes from deep inside a person that puts you at ease—assures you that you could say anything to them and it would be OK. That *something* was missing between Samantha and me. It's what I had with Layla and with

Baba most of the time. With Momma, too, when I wasn't annoyed with her.

Even so, it is true that the time I spent with Samantha, and even Brian and Dylan—before they did what they did—made me less upset about being in America, softened my anger at being away from home. Now, except for Momma and Gabbie and Antoine, I was on my own again and I couldn't imagine how I would get through the semester, let alone a year, if I had to stay that long. When I was feeling really down, I tried to remind myself of Baba's encouraging words.

My classes—all my classes—were way easier than back home and even though I wasn't a native speaker, I understood everything without trying. The strange thing is, that made me not *want* to try. I was bored most of the time and sometimes I'd stare out the window during class. Once, I did that in Geometry and all of a sudden the teacher, Mr. Walsh, called my name—or some horrible attempt at my name.

"Miss *Alhoosny! Hoosany*," he said, jolting me back to reality. "I'm sure you won't mind giving us the definition of the hypotenuse of a triangle?"

I wanted to ignore Mr. Walsh, pretend I had no idea who he was talking to, to make it clear that was *not* my name, but I didn't want to get into double trouble, so I cracked my neck and looked up.

Fortunately, I had learned this two years before so I was able to give him the answer. He seemed flustered, as if he'd hoped I would fail. After that, I found ways to appear to be paying attention even though my mind was usually somewhere else. For the first month or so, I just daydreamed my way through classes and during lunch break I'd sit by myself and read. I always had a book with me. I usually read in English, so I wouldn't attract attention by having a book with Arabic words on it. I just wanted to get through the day unnoticed until I could go home.

One day in late October, I was sitting in the school cafeteria reading *1984* for my English class. The cafeteria was decorated with skeletons, black cats with arched backs, huge spider webs, and scarecrows, all of which seemed very strange to me since there's no Halloween in Lebanon. There was a lot of clanking of trays and dishes, talking and laughter. As usual, I was keeping to myself, ignoring the comments and snickers from the jocks at a nearby table. It didn't seem to matter where I sat, they always found a way to make themselves known. I tried to focus on reading my book and inconspicuously eating my *kefta*—the grilled, spiced ground beef rolled in Arabic bread I loved so much. Most of the other kids bought their lunches, or brought peanut butter and jelly from home. Momma's *kefta* was delicious but it was hard to enjoy when I was the only one eating such "weird" food, as one girl had said to her friends when they passed by me in my first week and I was eating *yukhneh* and rice. I couldn't figure out what was weird about a meat stew with vegetables, but after that it was hard not to be self-conscious about my food.

"Mind if I join you?" The body that went along with the voice was a girl with a full figure about my age and height, with long, kinky, reddish-brown hair, her skin darker than most of the white kids at school. She was wearing a jean jacket, a gray plaid maxi skirt and a black beret pulled down so it halfcovered one eye. There was a button with a purple peace sign pinned to the beret.

"I don't own the table." As soon as the words came out I regretted them, tried to make it seem like I was joking. I gestured for her to sit down and said, without thinking, "*tfaddali*."

She set her tray down. "What's *tfaddali* mean?" I was startled to hear her pronounce it almost perfectly.

"I wasn't thinking! It means sit down, or go ahead, *ya'ni*, something like that. It's Arabic."

"Cool. Where you from?" she said, sliding into the bench across from me.

I decided I couldn't keep hiding myself forever—and why should I anyway? If she wanted to judge me, let it be *her* problem.

"Lebanon." There it was. Simple. Beautiful. *Lubnaan*.

"Really? Cool. I never met a Lebanese person before. I have met some Palestinians though."

"You have? How?"

"I met them in Israel—when I went there with my family." Rebecca told me she was Jewish and when she was in Israel she saw the way the soldiers treat Palestinians over there. I waited to see what she would say next, surprised a Jewish person would care about the Palestinians. She paused and took a bite of meatloaf and mashed potatoes and I noticed her cheeks reddening.

"I had an argument with my parents about it. They said the soldiers had a right to defend themselves." She took a sip of apple juice and shook her head. "I told them it wasn't defending yourself when you're the one holding all the weapons."

I couldn't believe that here in New York, where I thought no one knew or cared about what happened in the Middle East, this girl not only cared, but had even argued with her parents about it.

"You're pretty brave. I don't think I'd talk to my parents that way." As soon as I said this, I thought of how rude I'd been to Momma lately and added, "Well, *ya'ni*, I guess I haven't exactly been a perfect angel, either."

"Don't get me wrong," she said, "I have a great relationship with my parents. We just don't see eye-to-eye on this particular subject. They said I should remember what we came from, before I start criticizing Israel, and that got me upset. I don't see why Jews should treat anybody badly because of what happened to us." She pulled herself up straight, a fierce gleam in her dark eyes. "Far as I'm concerned, it should be the exact opposite."

I didn't know what to say. I had just met this girl and she was pouring out this story as if we were already friends.

As if reading my mind she said, "I can't believe I'm saying all this to you. It's just, I don't know, I haven't seen a person from the Middle East since that trip. I hope you don't think I'm a weirdo!"

"Honestly, you're the first person I've met here who even seems interested in these subjects. I usually avoid talking about them."

"That's really too bad. You should be proud of who you are! I figure if someone doesn't like what I have to say, it's their problem. I just say whatever is on my mind."

Before I could say anything, she went on. "My dad teases me, says I must be a commie like my grandfather, but I told him not to worry, I'm just a hippie who was born a decade late," she said, smiling and holding up her fingers in a *V*. "Keeping the seventies groovy."

I smiled, thinking how odd, but nice this girl was.

"I'm Rebecca, by the way."

"Hi Rebecca. I'm Noor. It's really nice talking to you."

"Seems to me, I've been doing all the talking." Her crooked smile reminded me of Layla's—playful and sassy.

"Next time it'll be my turn."

I was pretty sure we were going to be friends. Two misfits who seemed to fit each other just right. And for the first time since I'd been in New

York I didn't feel the need to conceal anything about myself. She was just fine with me being Lebanese, Palestinian, Arab, all of it.

The next day during recess, I went out to the Quad with Rebecca and three kids came running over to her and they all hugged in a big circle.

"Noor, meet *the posse*. Guys, this is Noor. She's from Lebanon."

I winced, still uncomfortable with revealing my identity to people I didn't know, but they all waved and the other girl said, "Hi, Noor."

The posse was made up of Maria, Greg and Alex—and of course, Rebecca. They seemed to me a totally mismatched group—Maria wore a stylish brown pantsuit and red neck scarf, her dark hair in a pretty shag cut. Alex, with his black, wavy hair, brown flared pants and vest almost matched her, and I wondered if they could be going out. Greg looked like he just jumped out of bed, with his mess of blond hair, baggy pants and shy manner. And Rebecca was, in her own words, *keeping the 70s groovy*.

It was still hard for me to get used to all the different styles in the U.S. As Gabbie said, *Here in New York anything goes*. Not like back home, where most people either followed tradition or fashion. No one really just made up their own style.

"Any friend of Becky's is a friend of mine," Alex said with a bow, and broke into a big smile as he straightened up.

Greg nodded and blushed. Something about his awkwardness made me smile.

"Hey, Becks," Greg said, recovering his voice. "We're heading to the cemetery for C Block. Want to join?"

The cemetery turned out to be a favorite hangout for the posse—which I seemed to have become part of without even trying. We'd walk through the grassy lanes and sit under maple trees that had gone from green at the beginning of school, to fiery red and orange, and now, in early November, were losing most of their leaves. Except for Alex, the rest of the posse loved to argue about different topics. Were politicians all corrupt? Was the universe infinite and what did that really mean? Did God exist and why did everyone think of Him as a him—and if he/she existed who created him/her?

The first time I brought Rebecca to the apartment, Momma was a bit cool to her. After she left, Momma said, "Is she Jewish?"

"Yes, is that a problem? She's not Israeli. It's not the same thing, you know."

"Of course it's not a problem, just asking, Noor."

Antoine and Gabbie were there too, and Antoine, trying to be funny, said, "Looks like we Christians are outnumbered even here."

Antoine was always making remarks like that. Usually I tried to ignore him, but that day it really got to me.

"Speak for yourself. I'm not even Christian—and why does it matter, anyway?"

"*Khalas*, Antoine, enough," Gabbie said, "And Noor—don't listen to my foolish brother!"

"Can't a person make a joke?" he said.

"I'm not anything," I said. "All religion does is make people hate each other."

In one way, I could understand Momma's reaction. Before I went to the U.S. I had never met a Jewish person and the only way I knew anything at all about them was when the Israelis flew fighter jets over Tyre—Baba's hometown near the Israeli border. They would fly so low we could see the blue Stars of David on their wings and sometimes they would dive towards earth, making a terrifying noise, followed by a powerful roar. Sometimes an explosion. Other times just a sonic boom that sounded like an explosion. All I knew was that when we heard the scream of Israeli jets approach, we all ran to the basements of our buildings.

Even so, I didn't want my friends to be judged, so after that I avoided bringing them home, and now that I was part of the posse, we usually had some kind of a plan anyway unless we were doing homework in the library.

14.

A couple weeks later, I left the school building expecting to see the posse waiting for me, joking around and talking out of range of Miss Haggard, ready to go to *Mug and Muffin* or *Angelo's Pizza* for a snack.

Instead, I was shocked to see, leaning against a phone pole across from the main steps, Brian. He wore the same aviators and leather jacket, but with an ivory-colored fringed scarf tied around his long neck. He had a cigarette gripped between two fingers, which he raised in the familiar salute when he saw me.

"Hello, Beautiful!" he said, as if nothing had happened and no time had passed.

I strode down the sidewalk, my throat tight with anger.

I heard him call me from behind, "Hey man, give me a chance. I just want to talk to you."

"Leave me alone!" I said, speeding up, but he caught up with me easily.

"After I came all this way to see you?"

"Well, you really are a hero, aren't you?" I said, pulling my arm away when he tried to touch it.

"Just get the hell away from me. I don't ever want to see you again."

"Look, Noor. I don't blame you. I know you must think I'm a jerk, but—"

"You *are* a jerk. Now, leave."

"Look—there's stuff you don't know. Can you just give me one chance? Ten minutes, then I promise to leave you alone if you still want me to."

I was tempted to slap him and walk away, but I couldn't help being curious what he could possibly have to say to me. Could there be some explanation for what he did that I hadn't thought of? That even Samantha didn't know?

"Five minutes," I said.

We sat on the steps of an apartment building and I moved all the way to one side away from him.

"See, before I met you, I, had a girlfriend? Amanda?"

I slit my eyes at him and waited.

"Her parents hated me. They thought I wasn't good enough for their little girl—being in a rock band and all. They forced her to break up with me—and at the end of last year, they moved away. I thought that was the end of that."

I looked at my watch.

"OK, OK, I'm almost finished," he said, pulling out a new cigarette and lighting it, cupping his hand around the match to shield it from the wind. "But then three months ago? Just before school started? They came back out of the blue, and she wanted to go out with me again. I was confused, man. I didn't know what to do. She was putting a lot of pressure on me."

"What you want from me, Brian?" I wanted to go home. He had broken my heart and now he was telling me about his other girlfriend?

"Nothing. I just wanted to say—I know it was fucked up and I'm, y'know—" He hesitated, tapping the long ash that had formed on his cigarette onto the ground.

"Sorry?"

"Yeh. I guess I'm wondering if we could just be friends again. I really dig you, man."

"I'm not a man, remember?"

"You certainly are not," he said, staring at me in the same intimate way he had the day I met him at Dante. "Just a dumb habit."

I was still angry, but the old ache of desire was rising up in me and I felt my resolve slipping away.

"So what happened?"

"To what?"

I frowned. "With *Amanda*. Isn't that what you came to talk about?"

"Yeah. Amanda. I basically went out with her a couple times and then said I couldn't do it."

"Did you tell her about me?"

"Of course."

"Why didn't you call me? Just tell me what was going on? You really hurt me."

As soon as I said this I regretted it, because it brought a sting of tears to my eyes. I brushed them away, irritated, but he noticed and tried to hug me.

"Don't," I said, pulling away.

He put up his hands and said, "No problem. I'll be on my way now, like I promised." He got up and stretched his skinny British rocker legs. "At least I tried."

I never would have imagined in a million years that I would be going out with Brian again after what he did to me, but there it was. Something about him made me melt like honey on warm bread. How sad he seemed when he told me about Amanda, the way he made me feel like I was the only girl in the world he cared about, the slow, sexy way he walked and turned around for one more salute with his head tipped down, gazing at me over his aviators.

I waited for Brian every day after school. Sometimes he came, sometimes not. The posse was seriously confused. The first time Greg saw me with Brian I could see he was distressed and I avoided his eyes.

"I'll see you tomorrow, guys," I said, waving as I drove off with Brian in his old, beat up convertible GTO, imagining myself like Audrey Hepburn soaring off in her Thunderbird, a striped scarf tied at my neck.

I still went to the cemetery with the posse during free blocks, but the truth was, my mind was somewhere else. Hanging out with Brian was the most exciting thing I had ever done. He had a way of finding the best hiding places for us to get high together and make out. Kissing him was like being suspended, floating above the earth. He caressed my body with hands that felt like silk ribbons, surrounding me, flowing around me, circling my neck and breasts. I ached for him every minute we were apart and every second we were together. He introduced me to hashish and it made me feel like nothing in the world could ever be wrong again.

A few days before winter break, he asked me to meet him at noon. He wanted us to go for a drive, but he had to be back in Manhattan for band practice at 3:00. I agreed, since I really didn't care about school, still convinced I wasn't learning anything. At the end of lunch period I grabbed my books and walked down the corridor past the students, past the principal's office, past Miss Haggard with her basket, and slipped out the door. It was freezing cold and a light snow was starting, a few flakes lazily spiraling to earth. The air had a clean smell to it, metallic. I had lined my eyes with *kohl* and I pulled my long, black hair to the front, feeling like Cleopatra or some princess in a Russian novel.

I ran down the block with my heart pounding. I saw the blue GTO parked by a hydrant and Brian rolled down the window. He pulled his aviators down to his nose and grinned. Devilish.

"Hello, gorgeous," he said, his voice strange in a way I couldn't identify.

I shrieked like a little girl as I jumped into the passenger side. He hugged me so tightly it pushed the breath out of me, but I felt none of the panic I sometimes had when I was first with him. I pulled his head toward me and kissed him like it was the last kiss we'd ever have.

He drove to an abandoned lot and parked behind an old garage. He pulled out a thick joint and lit it, the smell again conjuring a waft of burning vegetation in the hazy dusk of South Lebanon, the sounds of children's voices echoing in the streets. I opened my eyes to see Brian staring at me.

"Best ganja money can buy," he said, his voice low, gravelly. He drew the pungent smoke into his lungs and held it, lowering his eyelids and resting his head back on the headrest. I smoked with him until we were floating together, a familiar feeling of peace coming over me.

"I want you to see something, *wo*man" he said, trying to rake his hands through my hair, the thickness of it resisting, catching his fingers. "Let's go for a drive."

"I don't know if that's such a good idea. Maybe save it for another day," I tried my best not to sound worried.

"Naw, it's copasetic. I'm totally fine, trust me," he said, slurring his words slightly, grabbing hold of the steering wheel like a cartoon character gripping a knife and fork before a delicious meal.

Even though I wasn't convinced, I went along anyway.

"We won't be long, my Lebanese beauty," he said with a grin. "Remember, I have to be back soon."

The snow had picked up a little and it was dancing around the ground in swirls like dust. An uneasy feeling crept its way through the bliss of my high and I grabbed Brian's arm.

"I don't know, Brian," I said. "Maybe it's better, to—"

"Hey, where's your sense of adventure? You're gonna love this."

He drove down several small streets and eventually onto the onramp of the highway, picking up speed as he merged into traffic. My head spun and I closed my eyes. When I opened them again, I saw a sign ahead. I squinted against the snow that was coming at the windshield fast now and made out the words: "278 Staten Island."

"What? Are you taking me *there*?"

"Just sit back and relax, my lady."

He was driving faster now and the uneasy feeling came back.

"Slow down, Brian."

The car hit a patch of snow and skidded just slightly, then righted itself.

"You're making me nervous."

"It's totally fine, man," he said, hitting another skid.

In the mirror, I saw a blue light coming up behind us and heard the siren.

"Fuck!" Brian said, stepping on the accelerator.

"Are you crazy? Pull over!"

"I don't have a fucking license."

I gripped the armrest and felt myself freeze. The old familiar sensation in a new form. I knew I couldn't do anything. Brian was in charge and he wasn't about to slow down. He started to pass to the right of a car that had its right turn signal on.

"Watch out," I screamed, too late.

The other car had started into our lane and Brian pulled the wheel hard to the right to avoid it. The wheels slid on the snow as if it was oil, the car jerking left, then right, starting to spin, hitting the car he tried to avoid, then veering off the road.

A scream...distant...bridge askew...elbow slams...voice distorts...glass smashes...metal crumples...head crack:...siren screams...Momma where are you...this is all wrong...wrong place...wrong way... seatbelt yanks... roof below...no window...snow in my face...can you hear me, miss...are you all right...slippery wet...red...Brian...where's Brian...neck locked... leg locked...miss, if you hear me, raise your finger...sirens...red flash... blood red...saving me...stabbing me...blue flash...can't breathe...get off me...

Momma? Are you there? I'm here, alone. Don't leave me alone in this tunnel. It is so cold here. So dark. It wasn't my fault. I don't know how it happened. I couldn't help it.

"Noor? I'm right here, hayaati. Right by your side. Everything is going to be OK." Her voice wavering. "I won't leave you. I would never leave you, habeebti." Her hand cool on my forehead, like when I was little—fevered from influenza. "The nurse is getting another blanket." "Nurse?" "Yes, Noor, you were in an accident." "Accident?" "A car accident. You got a concussion." Pain in my right leg, like fire, or a blade. I scream. "What is it, Noor?" "My leg." "Yes, it is broken. You had an operation." "Operation? What are you talking about?" "They had to put pins in it." A warm blanket on my body. Lights brightening. "Excuse, me, ma'am, the doctor is here to see the patient, now." Momma's hand pulling away from mine. "No!" Me gripping her

hand.

"It's OK. You stay right there, ma'am."

My eyes try to adjust to the light and I see him. Grayish, thick hair. White lab coat. Stethoscope in his pocket. A nice face, trustworthy.

"Nice to see you awake, young lady! You've been through quite the ordeal." He held out his hand to me. "Dr. Savage," he said.

I tried to shake it, but my own hand felt rubbery, weak. He gripped it, his hand warm. *Had he really said Dr. Savage? Maybe I was dreaming.*

Dr. Savage sat on the chair next to the bed.

"I'll bet you have no idea what the heck you're doing here, do you?"

"Not really, but my leg hurts and I'm dizzy."

"How about a few sips of apple juice?"

The nurse brought over a cup of cold juice and pulled back the foil top. The cool liquid felt good in my throat.

"Well, my young friend. I have two things to tell you, ok?"

I nodded.

"First of all, flying through the air without wings is not generally recommended for the human species."

I tried my best to smile, but it felt more like a grimace.

"Second, you may be feeling some discomfort in your leg for some time. You've had surgery—and the good news is—this first operation was a success."

"First operation?"

"Yes. We'll get to that, but for now, we've got you nicely pinned together."

I saw Momma frown and draw back. Dr. Savage put his free hand on her shoulder.

"You should go home and get some rest now, Mrs. al-Husayni," he said, pronouncing the name surprisingly well.

"I'm not going anywhere," Momma said, squeezing my hand.

"I had a feeling you might say that. I'll ask the nurses to set up a cot for you right here, then, but you'd better at least get something to eat."

Momma raised her head and *tchh'd* to say no. "I'm not hungry."

After a time where I floated between waking and non-waking, the nurse came in. "Some nice folks are here to see you with some goodies, lucky girl."

Antoine followed her in, holding a vase of pink roses and a bunch of balloons. Gabbie was right behind him with a covered food tray which she set down on the tray table, and Antoine tied the balloons to the foot of the bed, putting the flowers where I could see them.

"Noor! You're awake! You look beautiful, *hayaati.*"

I knew I didn't, but somehow it made me feel better, even coming from him. It usually annoyed me when he tried to cheer me up, but that day I needed all the cheering I could get.

"Thanks, Antoine. Even though you're lying."

I let him kiss my cheeks and forehead. I thought I saw tears in his eyes, although everything was blurry so I couldn't be sure.

"*Pourquois* you want to give us all a big scare, like that, *ya polissonne?* If you needed a rest, well, it was only four more days to winter break!" he said, his typically awkward joking making me smile just a little, especially the way he mixed French, Arabic, and English together in a big mess.

"My head hurts and I'm dizzy. Can I have some Pana—Tylenol?"

The nurse brought a cool washcloth for my head. "You may feel that off and on for the next few weeks—even beyond. You've got yourself quite a concussion there, Missy."

Concussion, I thought, trying to understand.

"The most important thing is complete bed rest. Nothing stressful allowed." She looked over her glasses at me and then at Momma. "She'll be getting something a lot stronger than Tylenol in that IV, so she'll be feeling pretty woozy soon—and she'll need her rest."

Gabbie had made Lebanese chicken and rice and salad, but I had no appetite. I took a few bites and pushed the plate away. Gabbie prepared three more plates and Antoine ate hungrily, but Momma mostly moved the food around on the plate rather than actually eating it. The aroma of the Lebanese food reminded me of home and it helped to cover the smells of alcohol and bandages.

"OK, honey, time to take your vital signs."

The voice cut through the haze of my morphine-induced sleep and I half opened my eyes. The lights in the room had been dimmed and I could see that Momma was asleep on the cot that had been set up next to my bed. Antoine and Gabbie had gone. The balloons at the end of the bed bobbed as the nurse came to my side, disturbing the still air. Momma sat up and smoothed her dress and hair. The nurse came and went, her efficient motions and crisp manner angling into the hush and calm of the room, the fogginess of my head. She took my temperature, blood pressure, urine sample and drew blood, although I had no idea why she had to wake me up for these things and I was too out of it to really care. I closed my eyes and drifted again as she put her things away and cleaned up.

"I'll bet you're wondering—" she said, her voice seeming to me as crisp and white as her uniform. "—what happened to your boyfriend."

My eyes snapped open.

"I don't have a boyfriend," I said, panic cutting through the haze.

She smiled knowingly.

"Well, then, the *young man* who was driving the car?"

Fear and confusion spiked through me. When I woke up from the operation, I hadn't remembered anything. Not the crash, not the drive, not Brian, but now it all came rushing back to me. Did Momma know about him? She must know. What would I tell her? Why was I in the car with him? Who was he? I knew all these questions were coming. I lowered myself down, pulling the sheet over my nose. Was Brian alive? Where was he?

"He survived. Still unconscious, but they think he'll make it." She leaned toward the bed, continued in a whisper, "I'm not really supposed to tell you, dear, so it's just between you and me."

I bit my lower lip and glanced at Momma. I dreaded the conversation that would have to come eventually. I thought of what the nurse said. *He survived… he's unconscious…they think he'll make it.* It sounded bad. I wished I could see him. Dread flooded me. Why did I get in the car with him when I knew it was a bad idea? Why was I always doing things I knew could mean trouble? Crossing off the names on our IDs. Going out with Layla in Beirut that day. Meeting Ra'ad at an abandoned building. Taking the train to Manhattan when I was supposed to be home. If Momma knew about half the things I did, I'd be in deep trouble for the rest of my life. What if she found out somehow that Brian and I were smoking hashish? And that he was a friend of Samantha's. My head was spinning. Spinning and foggy. I rubbed my forehead with both hands. Momma reached over without getting up and patted my leg.

"You need your sleep now, *habeebti*. There will be time for thinking and talking later," she said, as if reading my mind. "Remember what the nurse said—*no stress*."

I relaxed a little, trying to push aside some of the thoughts swirling in my head. *At least I am alive. At least he is alive, too. We could so easily have died.*

Going home from the hospital was worse than I expected. Once I was off the IV painkillers, I was in pain all the time. They sent me home with Percocet, but it made me nauseous and out of it, so I tried to avoid it as long as I could and mostly took the medicine only at night, to help me sleep. I also had to get used to hobbling around on a plaster cast and crutches and the stabbing sensation in my leg that came with every step. And there was something else. Ever since the war started in Lebanon I would jump and scream whenever I heard a loud bang—a backfire or a book dropping. Now it was even worse. Once a snowplow driving down the street hit a bump and made such a noise, I ducked down and covered my head. Sometimes in my sleep, I'd dream that I was falling and landing on my head. Other times, I was in a van and men with rifles were holding me down, trying to undress me. I'd wake up drenched in sweat, shaking.

Over winter break, I was too upset and in too much pain to go anywhere, so I spent most of the time at home, reading four more books than the *one* we'd been assigned over the holidays, reading the newspapers Momma brought home even more avidly than before. Baba found a way to call me almost every day and I cherished those brief conversations, the line crackling, his voice distant, but his warmth coming through anyway, a warmth I felt, too, when I held his worry beads in my hands, pressing them to my nose, sensing some trace of him still. I tried to keep up with my journal, but some days I just didn't feel like writing anything. I remembered the days I had to stay home in Beirut and how the Rollei had both saved me and gotten me into trouble. Gabbie had taken me to a camera store to get it repaired, but nothing really inspired me to use it in New York, so it sat on my desk collecting dust, next to a photograph I took of Layla with only her eyes showing, like some feral creature.

I had plenty of time to think about Brian, too, to consider what had so attracted me—but also blinded me to his dark side that seemed so obvious to me now. True, he was very good-looking, but there are lots of good-looking guys I'm not interested in. I think it was partly what I *didn't* know that appealed to me. The time we spent together was like being suspended outside of reality. I knew almost nothing about him—who his family was, their religion, their values, if they had money, where they were from. Back home people are always taking note of such details—and in any case you wouldn't be going out alone with a boy who wasn't a family member. I think Brian was my rebellion against the traditions I'd grown up with, and the relationship was a way of exploring a different way of being in the world.

During the war, there was so much fear and trauma associated with revealing your identity that the desire for anonymity was sometimes strong. When I crossed off religion on my ID card, though, it wasn't that I wanted to be *less* me, it was to be me on my own terms, the person I decided to be—and was becoming. In the U.S. it was a little different. I knew that some people judged me out of ignorance and indifference—the opposite of Lebanon where I struggled with too *much* being known about me.

Most people I met when I was first in New York had no idea what it meant to be Lebanese or Palestinian, Christian, Muslim, Shiʿa or Sunni—they just knew I was foreign and not like them. I had hoped that if I made myself smaller and quieter, avoided standing out, maybe I wouldn't be judged or disrespected. Of course, I realized that's what the other Arab kids I'd met at school were doing, too. But I told myself that I was different because once I met Rebecca and the posse, I loved being with friends who accepted and liked me just as I was, who I didn't have anything to hide from.

The more I thought about Brian the more complicated it seemed. When I was with him, I enjoyed flirting and having fun, being admired by a handsome boy who didn't ask too many questions and who was a bit mysterious. It had been an exciting adventure that was separate from everything else—until it turned into a disaster. Maybe if I had known more about him, had paid more attention and been just a little more 'Arab,' I would have avoided this mess.

One day, about a week after I came home from the hospital, Momma came into my room, midmorning. She had taken a leave from her job after the accident, saying there was nothing in the world more important than taking care of her only daughter. I said I'd be fine, but she had refused to go back, and I'm sure she didn't mind having a break from the eye-strain and hours a day of editing the gossipy, superficial stories in *The Sun* either.

That day, she brought me a tray with a *labneh* sandwich, green olives, mint and tomatoes, a small pot of sweet tea, and a saucer with a few Digestive biscuits. My appetite had come back and it was nice to have her making all my favorite snacks and dishes. She sat on the bed while I ate.

When I'd finished, she said, "Noor *hayaati*, we cannot go on acting like nothing happened. I wanted to give you time to recover a bit, but now it is time."

I avoided her eyes and cracked my neck to both sides like I always did when I was nervous, even though I knew Momma hated it.

"How did this terrible thing happen?" she said quietly. "I suppose it's my fault for bringing you here to America."

I sighed. "Accidents happen in Lebanon too, Momma."

"He was on drugs, Noor. They found it on him. Found it in his blood. *Ya'ni*, serious drugs. We are lucky you didn't die. I will tell you one thing, if he makes it out of the hospital—and probably jail? You are forbidden to see him ever again. Do you understand?"

I pulled the blanket up over my face. She pulled it off.

"Don't ignore me, Noor. Once the break finishes, you come home right after school—every day. I will be there to pick you up, is that clear?"

"Why are you always against me? Trying to restrict me?"

"You know you are not allowed to go out alone with boys and now you've gone with one who was on drugs and got in a car with him? Not to mention your grades at school are a disaster. Here, see for yourself."

She handed me my report card that must have come in the mail. I pushed it aside.

"I don't care about school. I hate this school. You made me come here in the first place. That's the disaster."

"Excuse me? Be careful what you say, Noor," she said raising her hand.

"Go ahead! It couldn't be any worse than it is already."

Momma put her hand in her lap. We stayed like that, frowning and silent, for the longest time, but then, her shoulders shook and tears slid down her cheeks.

"Oh, Noor," she said. "*Habeebti*, I really don't want to fight, but I honestly don't know what to do with you sometimes."

She put her arms around me and I started crying, too.

"I'm sorry, Momma."

She lifted my chin up. "It's all right, *habeebti*. It's going to be all right, but we're going to have to make some agreements."

The *agreements*, as Momma called them, were actually rules that she made up and I had to follow. Just as she promised, I wouldn't be allowed to stay after school, even for study halls, unless the next report card had at least a B+ to A- average. We both knew that I was more than capable of that, but that I just hadn't been working. Next, she would be driving me to and from school every day—and to Physical Therapy once I got the cast off—so there would be no bending her rules. Lastly, I was forbidden from talking to Brian for any reason. I was sure that at some point I would break that rule if he recovered, but for now it seemed he was in no condition to be talking on the phone anyway.

One day when Momma was at the grocery store, I called Samantha. When she heard about the accident, she called me, but Momma had said I couldn't talk on the phone.

"That's *bullshit*," I said, the swear sounding unfamiliar coming out of my mouth. "She just doesn't want me talking to you."

"Forget about it, sister How *are* you? Tell me everything."

"There's not much to tell, really. Brian convinced me to get back together, we got high, drove on the highway in a snowstorm, got chased by the police, hit another car, crashed into a ditch and almost died. The End."

"Holy shit, Noor. It's like Bonnie and Clyde!"

"Who?" I said, then cringed, picturing Samantha shaking her head.

"Forget it, but that's wild. Brian's a flaming idiot. Why did you get back with him?"

"He told me about his old girlfriend, Amanda—how her parents refused to let her see him and then moved away and when they came back, she begged him to get back together. How he was confused and didn't know what to do, decided to stop seeing me. I guess I can't really blame him."

"Talk about bullshit! The only true thing in that story is that he had a girlfriend named Amanda. He dumped *her* when he met you, and then he dumped *you* when he met some other chick named Carol. Noor, you are *way* too gullible."

"Samantha, are you sure?"

"Yeah, I'm sure. And I found out he's been doing all kinds of crazy stuff—'ludes and acid, not that I'm judging anybody, but you don't do that shit and then drive!"

I was too shocked to say anything. It was Samantha who finally spoke again.

"Hey, I don't know when we can hang out again, sounds like your mom thinks everyone on my side of the bridge is, y'know, radioactive right now? But just promise me one thing—don't let him get to you again. He is super bad news."

When I got off the phone, there was a knock at the door. Gabbie had come by to see me. Even though she was still right down the hall it was different not living in the same apartment any more.

"I missed you, *ya wahsheh*," she said using one of her favorite nicknames for me. Not many people could get away with calling me a *wild beast*, but it always cracked me up the way she said it. "How are you feeling? It's good to see you up. Shall I make you something to eat?"

"*Shukran*, Gabbie I'm fine. How are you?"

"Fine, fine. Business was slow so I closed up early and decided to come say hi."

Gabbie was a seamstress and she had her own little shop nearby. I was glad to have her in my life. She knew how to cheer me up and even though she wasn't political at all, it was good to have someone from back home to talk to, someone who knew what I was talking about if I said I missed taking walks on the *Corniche al-Manara*, or was craving a pressed chicken sandwich with garlic sauce from Marrouche restaurant that you bought through the little take-out window on Sidani Street.

"Gabbie, what's gullible mean?" I said, trying to sound offhanded.

"It means you believe everything you hear."

When I thought about everything that had happened that year, and especially after what Samantha told me, I did feel pretty gullible. How could I have accepted Brian's story without checking? I should've called Samantha to ask her, but I knew she would have tried to talk me out of seeing him and I didn't want that. I had convinced myself that Brian really loved me, even though he hadn't actually said that—but I had wanted to believe—*needed* to believe it.

To my surprise, Momma let the posse come visit. I think she was worried about me because I'd started sleeping for a lot of the day, pulling the shades down to keep out sunlight, crying for the slightest reason. Alex was in Vermont on a family ski trip, so it was just Rebecca, Maria, and Greg.

Momma knocked on my bedroom door.

"Your friends are here, *habeebti. Yalla*, get out of bed and fix yourself up."

"They're just my friends. Can't they just come in here?"

"No *habeebti*, that's not nice. Just comb your hair and put these on."

She brought me a pair of shoes and a turtle-neck sweater from my closet.

I didn't have the energy to dress, but even less to argue. I was happy that the posse came to see me, but ashamed too, knowing I'd ignored them every time Brian showed up. What kind of a friend does that? I hated it when I saw other girls doing the same thing. I sat on the edge of my bed with my right leg sticking out in front of me like a tree branch and combed my hair, half-dreading having to face them. What must they think of their shallow friend who didn't deserve their loyalty after all?

I tucked the crutches under my arms and made my way slowly to the living room. When I got there I saw three figures on the sofa—but they looked more like the Marx Brothers than the posse. They all leaned in together and Groucho—Rebecca—snapped his eyebrows up and down and pulled the cigar out of his mouth to say, "Where've you been all my life, Sweetheart?" Harpo—Greg—put his hand on his heart shyly, and Chico—Maria—took his pointy cap off his head and bowed. "I've finally found my *Chica!*" he said solemnly.

I collapsed into a chair and started crying and laughing. I couldn't even speak. They all came over, pulled me up and enclosed me in their arms. Groucho pulled off his thick mustache and eyebrows and Harpo tossed his curly blonde wig into the air.

"I'm so sorry," I said, starting to sob again.

"What's this, Sweetheart?" Rebecca said, getting back in character. "We're going to have to cheer you up." She snapped her fingers. "Waiter, get the lady a martini."

And with that, I was laughing again.

Momma appeared at the door. "It's nice to see my daughter smiling. I'm making a traditional Arabic meal and you're all invited."

"Much obliged, Mrs. al-Husayni," Greg said.

Good move, I thought. Momma would love this bit of formality. Rebecca and Maria both thanked her as well, saying she really didn't have to.

"It is no trouble at all."

Momma winked at me and said, "*Mahdoomeen ashaabik.*"

I remembered the time I'd brought Rebecca home and had sworn never to bring my friends again. I didn't know if this truce would last between Momma and me, but I was glad for it.

"Momma thinks you guys are cute," I said. "*Ya'ni*, I guess you're OK."

While Momma was cooking lamb stew with green beans and rice, we sat in the living room and they took turns signing my cast in different colored pens, the smells of meat, garlic and cilantro filling the air. I asked them what they were doing over break. Maria was working at a bookstore and Greg was studying for the SAT since he was a junior and he wanted to get a head start. Rebecca told me about how she'd gotten to spend the week in Bermuda with her cousin's family.

"Poor thing, how she suffers," Maria said.

"That's what you were doing while I was lying in a hospital bed with my leg up in the air!" I pretended to pout.

"Let's hope Alex doesn't come back from New Hampshire with *his* leg in a cast, too." Rebecca said.

I avoided talking directly about the accident, instead telling them about all the attention I got in the hospital—how everyone wanted to sign my cast and Momma's friends brought food and sweets. I tried to make it sound like I was fine, and I did feel better than I had for weeks, having my friends around me again. I realized how lonely I'd been since the accident.

In spite of the fact that things had generally been quieter in Beirut since six thousand Syrian troops occupied the entire city of Beirut and beyond in November, Baba still hadn't been able to secure a visa. With my leg in a cast and possibly more surgeries to come, I couldn't imagine how our family could get back together any time soon. I couldn't believe that "just the summer" in New York had become a semester and now was becoming a year. The only good thing about getting back to school was that after two weeks at home with my leg propped up on five pillows, I was ready to get out of the apartment—but I was a mess.

I jumped when the elevator jolted to a stop. I jumped when the car door slammed. I jumped when Maria came up behind me and said *Hey, Chica!* and when Miss Downs banged her fist on her desk. I screamed when my classmate dropped his textbook on the floor; started shaking when Miss Haggard yelled, *young lady*! Then, there was my leg. I had messed it up pretty badly and although I knew that I would need more operations, for the moment I tried not to think about it. The pain was getting better as long as I didn't put too much pressure on it when I walked.

Worst of all, the independence I had before the accident evaporated. I had to depend on Momma to get everywhere. I wished I could hobble on my crutches to and from school even with snow on the ground, but that wasn't an option. I wasn't allowed to do anything by myself. I knew it was my own fault. Momma had talked about how terrible it was almost losing me in Beirut—and now I had nearly died—again. And for nothing. For a lying, cheating, reckless boy who didn't even love me.

The only way out of my "imprisonment" was to do really well at school. All I had to do was to go back to my old, studious ways. I knew I could get A's if I just made the effort, but this time, I wouldn't just get A's. I'd get A+s. I'd ace every test and ask for extra credit in every class. I wasn't going to give Momma any excuse to restrict me a day longer than necessary.

Black is Beautiful

15.

I'd been working on my new study plan for a few days and was on my way to the cafeteria to hang out with the posse—maybe even go with them for a chilly walk in the cemetery for a small break. After all, Momma couldn't stop me from leaving school during the day—and she'd never know anyway. From the window that faced the quad I saw a few dozen students walking in a circle, holding signs and raising their fists in the air, shouting something I couldn't hear. I squinted to see the handmade signs. *DIVEST FROM SOUTH AFRICA NOW! DOWN WITH APARTHEID. BLACK IS BEAUTIFUL.*

I had heard a little about what was happening in South Africa, but I think I was too busy feeling sorry for myself to pay attention—and I really didn't know what apartheid was or what they meant about divestment. I couldn't believe that right at my own school, protests were happening and I didn't know anything about them. I didn't think Americans even cared about politics.

I pulled my crutches up under my arms and hurried as best as I could down the stairs and outside, into the fierce cold, wishing I had brought my jacket. By the time I got there, the principal and some other adults were breaking it up but there were a few last chants—*Divestment yes! Apartheid No! Free, free Mandela!* The adults were speaking through a megaphone, telling the protestors *get back inside or get expelled,* and the students were scurrying around angrily, some yelling back. One even said, "Get off our backs, pigs!" Others were pulling at them, urging them to leave without getting into a fight.

I went up to a girl who was collecting signs to ask her if they were planning anything again, and just as I said *excuse me* someone folding up a banner backed into me, nearly knocking me off my crutches. I exclaimed and he turned around and caught my arm just in time.

"Whoa! You ok?" he said, helping me get the crutches back in place.

When I got my balance back, I found myself looking into the most beautiful pair of golden brown eyes I had ever seen. They were owned by a very handsome boy with a soft, light brown afro. I realized I was staring and I pulled myself upright and said I was fine.

"It's OK. Thanks," I said.

"Thanks for knocking you over?"

I was suddenly shy. "No, no. Thanks for—I don't know."

Just then, the principal came over and told everyone to hurry up and get back to class, and as the students scattered, the young man said, "I'm Jamal. See you around?"

Jamal? I thought. *Jamal? 'arabi?* But he didn't appear to be Arab. He seemed more like Black or part Black, with skin the color of the warm red-brown clay we use to make pottery back home. When I got back to the cafeteria, I had only a few minutes before class. I propelled myself along with my crutches and found Rebecca and Maria finishing their lunches.

"*Hola, Chica,*" Maria said.

"Where were you?" Rebecca said, passing me an apple and a piece of bread.

"At the protest."

"What protest?"

"The South Africa one," I said.

"I forgot it was today."

"I think they just started up a new group," Maria said.

"Who planned it?"

"Not sure, but I heard they meet in the gym after school Mondays."

"I'd go, if I weren't *grounded,*" I said, banging one crutch on the floor for emphasis.

"Where there's a will, there's a way," Rebecca said.

As I got up, I noticed the jocks at the next table gawking at me and making whooping sounds. I tried my best to ignore them, but as I passed by I swear I heard one of them say in a low voice, *nice ass, huh?* I turned around, ready to confront them, but they were talking loudly to each other as if nothing happened. Rebecca was already half way out of the room and I hurried to catch up with her.

"Hey, Rebecca."

"Yeeesss?" she said.

I got close to her and leaned on my crutches, putting my mouth near her ear.

"Do you know a kid named Jamal?"

"Noooo. Why?"

"Nothing, never mind."

I lifted one crutch up to the side like I was waving.

"See you later," I said speeding ahead of her.

I wasn't ready yet to tell Rebecca how intrigued I was with Jamal and I certainly wasn't ready to have another boyfriend any time soon. I didn't need Rebecca teasing me and encouraging me either, but I found myself thinking about him a lot, hoping I would run into him in the corridor. He was so handsome, but in a casual way—as if he wasn't aware of it. Not like Brian, who was so conscious of his image—as if he was admiring himself in a mirror all the time. I loved that Jamal cared about South Africa and was doing something about it, not like a lot of other guys who only seemed to care about sports or impressing girls. I didn't know why he had an Arabic name, but it was just one more reason to like him.

The next Monday, at the end of school, I passed by the gym on my way out. There were a few kids hanging around on the bleachers, talking. I recognized some of them from the protest, but Jamal was nowhere to be seen. I waited for a few minutes and when a couple more kids showed up, I asked one of them about the meeting. He said the idea was to meet every week and plan some kind of *meaningful actions*, but they still didn't know exactly what. I told him I might be interested and asked if I could come to a meeting.

"Far out! We can use all the help we can get."

I had to find a way to get to the organizing meetings, but I knew there was no way Momma was going to make any exceptions. She would probably think if I joined the group it would be one more excuse for doing badly at school, so I had to come up with a strategy. A good one.

It was pretty simple, really. In the first month back, I did nothing but study—and it showed. My papers and quizzes came back with mostly A+'s. But I didn't want to leave anything to chance and I figured the best way to impress Momma was to do some extra credit work, too. I asked for meetings with my Math teacher, Mr. Walsh and my English teacher, Mrs. Clark.

I knew Mr. Walsh liked me, even though he tried to act tough with all his students. I sat at the desk closest to his, the big blackboard behind him still covered with algebraic equations on one side and geometric figures on the other, some partly erased to make more room. Chalk dust filled the lip at the bottom of the board.

"Mr. Walsh, I know I messed up last semester and I'm trying so hard to make up for it. I was hoping you'd give me a few extra assignments—really hard ones."

"You're already doing great. Why do this?" He leaned back in his chair, twirling a metal compass, his bushy eyebrows raised.

"I need to prove that I can be the best—for myself, but—" I rolled the worry beads between my fingers inside my pocket, "—for my mom, too."

Once I'd said this, I realized how much I did want to make her proud—not just to convince her to loosen our "agreements," so I could go to meetings after school.

He brought his chair upright, nodded, rolled up his sleeves.

"All right, then, let's get to work."

So, I had to prove the Pythagorean Theorem, calculate the volume of a tetrahedron and the length of the diagonal of a rhombus, etc., etc. He kept me there for almost an hour. I got near perfect scores on everything he threw at me, and the best thing was, he actually wrote his comments on the sheets I used to solve the problems, so I had "evidence" to take with me.

As for Mrs. Clark, she proposed that I write a five-page essay on the importance of education. I would have one week to complete the assignment. I loved the idea. It gave me a chance to dig into a subject that was close to my heart. Before that year, I had always been an excellent, hard-working student and of course, Baba was a university professor, and Momma was always talking about the importance of education, of getting into one of the best universities. It was a given in my family.

The pages were to be hand-written, so for me to write five pages in a week was really quite easy. In fact I purposely wrote with very small handwriting, so I was able to pack in a lot of information and a good deal of my philosophy of life into those pages. I started by writing about how there are many poor and refugee children in my country, who would give anything to have the opportunity for a good education. Many of them suffer in under-funded, low quality schools and the chance of them going on to college—or in some cases even high school—was very limited.

I spoke of living through civil war, how our schools were often closed because of fighting. How it was boring and frustrating not being able to continue our studies, how we would work twice as hard once we were back in class.

I talked about being half Palestinian and how strongly we value education—that in fact, Palestinians have one of the highest education levels in the Arab World—that in my opinion one of the reasons for this is pride. Since many Palestinians live under occupation, it's a way of proving our importance and value to ourselves and to the world—while forging a path to pursue prestigious careers and advanced education all over the world.

In the last page of my essay, I admitted that when I came to the U.S., I thought that school was too easy and a waste of time, because I had gone to a very challenging school in Lebanon, and I became lazy and didn't think I had to bother. I wrote that it was the first time in my life I got bad grades, and although I hadn't really acknowledged it before, I was shocked and humiliated when Momma faced me with a terrible report card.

I wrapped up by saying that the most important thing any young person can do with his or her time is to be a great student, because there's no limit to what human beings can learn and achieve, what we can make of ourselves if we care deeply about something, and what we can contribute to society and the world as a result of what we've learned.

When Mrs. Clark handed the paper back to me with her comments, she nodded approvingly.

"Congratulations, Noor. It's good to know that at least one of my students knows what an essay is."

"Thank you, Mrs. Clark."

"It's also refreshing to read something so genuine, full of passion, energy, and honesty. This is what makes for good writing. After all, if you're not excited by what you're writing, why should anyone be excited about reading it?"

I hadn't ever really thought of it that way, but it made perfect sense. I thought about all the authors I loved, how thrilling it was to read each page. How could they write like that if they were bored or uninspired?

"You're a very promising student, Noor. Keep up the good work and I have no doubt you'll go far. Just try not to slip on any more banana peels on the way—metaphorically speaking, of course."

"I'll try not to!"

Fortunately, midterms were only a couple of weeks away. They didn't send home a formal report card, but the tests and graded papers I brought home spoke for themselves. I presented these to Momma, along with the comments on my extra assignments. She spent the next half hour reading over everything.

That night she made me *sheikh al-mihshi*, one of my favorite meals.

"Don't think this changes anything," she said, as she piled rice on my dish, the smell of eggplant, lamb and tomato filling my nostrils.

After that, Momma allowed me to stay after school two days a week to study. She said that if I kept my grades up, she'd let me start walking to and from school again, once the snow melted. She made me promise to be back by 4:30, though, because she—and all of New York, it seemed— was on edge—worried that the murders that had been happening in the Bronx and Queens were connected. At first we hadn't paid much attention. They seemed so far away. We heard about crimes in Brooklyn too, but they seemed more random. But after two incidents became three and then four—mostly women with dark, curly hair, or couples making out in their cars—everyone had the jitters. So I promised.

The next Monday, I became an official member of the *Graves High School Students Against Apartheid*. Momma thought I was working on a project in the library with other students. I convinced myself that, in a way, I *was* working on a project with other students, only not in the library, and surely not the type of project she had in mind.

I had more energy than I'd had in months. I woke up most mornings ready to jump out of bed and had to remind myself that I still had the cast on.

At my first meeting, there were six or seven other kids in the gym. We had to keep the lights out so we wouldn't draw attention, and the only light came in from the narrow windows near the ceiling.

When I saw Jamal sitting a few bleachers up, wearing a turtle-neck sweater and flared jeans, a thrill ran through me. I tried to come in quietly so I wouldn't interrupt the conversation, but everyone turned toward me.

"Hey, hey, hey, a newcomer," one said. "Cool."

Someone else said, "Don't let her escape!"

I was shy from all the attention.

A girl with tight black curly hair styled short around her head and wearing a sleek black halter-top caught my eye. She looked me up and down the same way some women do back home. I wasn't sure if she approved or disapproved of what she saw, but she had a hint of a smile when she said, "Welcome, soul sister."

I wasn't sure exactly what that meant, but I got the general idea. She was beautiful, with dark brown skin and bold eyes that fixed confidently on mine when she spoke.

"Thanks, guys," I said, glancing up at Jamal.

In the beginning, I tried just to listen while they talked about their plans for the rest of the year.

Everyone seemed to have a different idea of what to do.

"I say we meet with the principal. We should demand he write a letter to Congress pushing U.S. corporations to divest." That from Tim—the "don't let her escape" guy.

"Yeh, like that'll ever happen," someone else said.

"We should do a "die in," said a girl with a thick pony tail down her back, named Cynthia.

The *soul sister* said, "You're all full of shit, you know that? As Steve Biko says, Black South Africans need to think for themselves, advocate for themselves, liberate themselves. This is *their* struggle Best a high school student in the U.S. can do is solidarity work."

"So we sit around and twiddle our thumbs while people are dying?" said Tim.

"I didn't say that smart-ass. I said we do solidarity work and not pretend we can somehow liberate South Africa from over here in Brooklyn."

Cynthia looked across the bleachers at Tim. "And I guess we have to admit, Biko was right when he said we white liberals think we're not part of the problem since we never personally harmed a Black person. But what have we really done to help either?"

Tim scowled at Cynthia and turned away.

Jamal, who'd been quiet up to that point said, "How about we hear from the new kid?"

It took me a minute to realize he was talking about me. I didn't know any of them and I had no idea what to say. It made me even more embarrassed that it was *him* asking me to join in.

"I'm not even from here. Where I'm from it's…" I hesitated, trying to think of a way to explain. "Well—just *different*."

"Tell me about it," said the *soul sister*. "I used to live just a couple miles from here in Bed-Stuy and it's, *well, different*, too. I'm Angel, by the way."

"Hi. I'm Noor," I said shyly. "I'm from Lebanon, and back home there's a civil war going on right now."

I hadn't spoken to any other kids about the war except Rebecca and the posse. Lebanon felt like another planet sometimes. It was like trying to explain what was happening on Mars or Jupiter.

"That's tough," said Angel, "real tough."

"Lebanon. Far out," said Jake, the kid who was drawing in the dust.

That's exactly how it felt. Far out. Far away. So far. But even so, these kids seemed genuinely interested and I didn't feel any hint of judgement from them.

Jamal hopped a couple of bleachers down so he was closer to the group. "So you were an activist over there?"

"I was mostly just trying keep from getting my head blown off!"

Angel whistled through her front teeth.

"You have to understand," I continued, excited to be talking about my country. "People were dying in the streets. It was all about survival. The only time I ever went to a demonstration was at my dad's university. Nobody dared do such things in the open."

Everybody became very quiet.

"I told you it was different."

"Civil war. Bummer," said Cynthia.

"I know this isn't about Lebanon. I was just trying to say that the perspective is so different from over here. Like Angel was saying about South Africa. Maybe we should try to do something to let the people there know the world hasn't forgotten them."

"And how do you propose to do that?" Angel asked.

"I really don't have any proposals yet—it's just my first day!"

"That's cool," Jamal said. "We'll give you until next week to come up with one."

I cracked my neck and I must have seemed nervous, because he added, "Just kidding. No pressure."

The next week, I came in with a note pad.

"OK, I said. Here is my proposal."

"Here we go, comrades," Jamal said, "everybody take notes!"

I blushed, not quite sure if he was teasing me or them or both. Of course, I was kind of teasing *him* about saying I should bring a proposal.

"Don't think you can just march in here and take over, Missy. We've got our organizational structure, y'know," Angel said.

"Oh—sorry," I stammered, my cheeks getting hotter by the minute. I closed the note pad.

"Don't worry, sister," Angel said. "We're long on ideas, but we've got about as much structure as an octopus. Thank God someone's organized."

Tim side-eyed Angel. "At least we have a democratic process. Everyone's voice is equal here."

"Easy when you're only eight people," said Dan.

But I could see Angel's point about the octopus. Tim thought we should confront the *fascist* school administration and force them to let us do weekly rallies in the quad. Angel suggested meeting with South African students and activists at local universities to coordinate with them. I came up with the idea to create a divestment petition and go door-to-door to collect signatures.

After a lot of arguing and back and forth over details, Angel proposed a vote. "Enough talk. Time for action," she said. "Time to put *solidarity* to work."

I could tell Angel and I were going to be friends.

We decided to start by focusing on our school and the surrounding community, trying to get more people involved. We'd organize rallies, do leafleting, try to connect with South African students at NYU and Brooklyn College, and draft a petition to take around the neighborhood that we could send to our state reps. Everyone was relieved that we actually agreed on a plan of action by the end of the meeting.

Tim and Cynthia would organize the rallies (and Angel told Tim to *knock himself out* if he wanted to go meet with the fascists, but he'd have to do it alone).

Jake and another kid named Dan would do the leafleting. That left Angel, a quiet kid named Sam, Jamal and me.

"So who wants to do colleges with me?" Angel asked.

Jamal said, "I'll go with you. My parents work at NYU. They might even be able to help connect us with some students."

I tried not to show my disappointment that I wouldn't be working with Jamal, but, on the other hand, I was excited about the petition. Since I'm a good writer I said I'd write a draft and Sam offered to help edit it and go with me to collect signatures. Mostly I was just glad to be doing something political for the first time since I got to the U.S.

I also spent some time in the library reading up on Biko and learned that he was a grassroots anti-Apartheid activist who started the South African Student Organization. When I read that he'd said, *It is better to die for an idea that will live, than to live for an idea that will die*, it gave me chills. How can we even know which ideas will live? Which will die? But if a person could be so confident in their beliefs, so fearless, imagine the depth it gave their life.

A few days later, I was rushing through the quad, late for my biology class. I was passing through one of the arches that led to the science building when I saw the jocks from the cafeteria coming toward me. They stopped in front of me, blocking my path, and a flood of terror washed through me. For a moment, I couldn't move or think what to do.

The one directly in front of me had wide, football-player shoulders. "Late for somethin'?" he said, grinning.

"I have to get to class." I tried to sound like I wasn't intimidated, but there was a tremor in my voice that I knew gave me away.

"Maybe the Hag'll come rescue you," another one said, snickering.

I got a burst of strength and tried to move around them, but the first guy stayed put.

"Hey, boys, she's not bad for a *camel jockey*, huh?"

More snickering. I turned around and tried to make a run for it and there was Jamal, coming right toward me. I'm sure he could see from my eyes how scared I was, but he just walked up, cool and casual.

"Hey, guys, what's up?" he said.

The main guy seemed taken by surprise.

"You a Christian, man?" Jamal said.

"What the fuck? Of course I'm a Christian. What's it to you, Mocha-Java?"

"So, you must know all about, y'know, the wise men in the desert and all. I mean, if you think about it—Jesus was really a 'camel jockey,' too."

"Get the fuck out outta here, dick wad."

More snickers.

Another kid said quietly to the one with the football shoulders, "He's kinda got a point, though, y'know, Judd."

Judd pulled himself up even taller.

"You can all eat me! C'mon, let's get the fuck outta here."

He pushed past us, almost knocking me off my crutches. For the second time that year, Jamal kept me from falling. Once they were gone, I couldn't stop shaking. Jamal tried to take my hands in his to steady them, but I pulled back.

"I'm OK, but my God, what jerks!" I said, fighting back tears.

"*Racist* jerks." Jamal's eyes showed the anger that he had held back when he was talking to them. In the afternoon sun I could see their amber color. *Lion's eyes*, I thought.

"Look out for those bastards. They're bad news."

"I'm really glad you were there. How did you even know where I was?"

"I saw you from across the quad. Can you dig it? I just had a question for you and I was trying to catch up to you when I saw those *assholes*—oh, sorry."

"It's what they are. But I never heard that before—*camel jockey*."

"I'm kinda used to dealing with racist jive, y'know? When you're Black? You wouldn't believe some of the crap you hear."

"Actually, I *would* believe it."

"I guess you can relate, huh?"

We both stopped talking for a long moment. I glanced at my watch.

"*Ya Allah*. I'm fifteen minutes late for class! How am I going to walk in now without a note?" I hadn't missed a single class second semester and I was trying to keep a perfect record.

"Maybe you should go see the principal and tell him what happened."

"No way. If I get them in trouble, it will mean more trouble coming back to me. I'll just have to skip class and think of something later."

"We could take a walk and talk some more about life and stuff."

"Don't you have class? No point getting us both in trouble!"

"Just study hall with Ned Garrison. He's the coolest. The kids all call him Ned. He doesn't even take attendance—says if we don't want to come it's our loss."

"I wish my teachers were like that."

I asked him if he ever walked in the cemetery.

"What do you think I am—a zombie?"

I was getting better at not asking what every new word meant—and figuring it out for myself instead.

"Yes that *is* what I think."

He started to walk toward me, rocking from one foot to the other, his eyes still closed, and I had to step aside so he didn't run into me. My heart jumped, partly because of him almost touching me but also because somehow it was a bit scary in a little kid kind of way.

I was excited to be with Jamal and to have a chance to talk by ourselves, but I needed him to know that I just wanted to be friends. I still hadn't recovered from my terrible experience with Brian, and my first boyfriend had cheated on me, so I was beginning to question if I had the worst possible judgment about the male gender—or what Samantha had call the male *species*. For now, walking and talking with him was perfect.

"So, what's up with the cemetery?"

"If you can forget that these are all dead people for a minute—it's really beautiful here."

It was a mild, late winter day, last year's grass soggy from the melting snow, the sun shining through the still-bare branches of the maple trees, warming our faces.

"Sometimes I come here with the posse because no one knows where we are. After all, who would come to a graveyard?"

"What's the posse?"

"That's just the nickname my friends gave themselves."

As we walked along one of the long paths, I told Jamal that we liked to hang out and talk there. I told him they were the first friends I felt really comfortable with in the U.S.

"I can say anything to them. Especially Rebecca. I bet you'd like them."

"They sound cool. Hey, what happened to your leg?"

I could tell I was blushing. I really didn't want to tell Jamal about the accident. I didn't want to tell him that I had a boyfriend until recently. That he was a liar and a cheater. That he did drugs and then drove. That I had made a stupid mistake. Many stupid mistakes. That maybe I didn't dare to think I could find someone who would want to be with me because of who I really am. That maybe I wasn't even sure I deserved it.

"Noor?"

I had drifted off while all these thoughts bombarded me.

"I was in a car accident. Long story."

"How bad?"

"I might need another operation or even more, but it's OK. I'm alive, after all."

"I, for one, am very glad about that!"

This time, he was the one blushing.

"How did you even think of saying that about Jesus? I can't believe it worked. I thought for sure they were going to beat us both up."

"Honestly, I had no idea what to do. That *Jesus was a camel jockey* line came out of nowhere. Did you see Judd's face?"

"But you seemed so calm. Like it was no big deal."

"I guess I'm just a cool dude," Jamal said, drawing out the words and smoothing his hair back with his hand, which was really funny because he didn't have the kind of hair you could smooth back at all.

"Oh, really? You think you're so cool?" I said, giving his arm a push and almost losing my balance again.

"Not as cool as you are, of course."

"Of course."

"Can I ask you one thing?" I said.

"Anything."

"Why is your name Jamal? Are your parents Arab?"

"They're what we call Black Muslims here."

"You're Muslim?"

"Sort of. My dad used to pray and read the Quran, but not so much anymore. It's more about pride and having good values—stuff like that. What about you?"

"What about me?"

"Are you Muslim?"

"I hate religion."

"Whoa, okay, is your family Muslim?"

"I hate that question."

"Why?"

"Remember what I said once at a meeting about the civil war in my country? How people are killing each other?"

"But isn't that basically political? A power struggle?"

"Yes, but they use religion to separate people. To decide *who* gets power. Who gets to live and die. It's really terrible."

"No wonder you hate religion."

"But since you asked so nicely, my family is mixed. In a lot of ways. I'll tell you about it next time. Right now, I have to get back or I'll miss my *next* class, too."

16.

I could hardly believe the school year was nearly over. The past few months had been some of the happiest of my life. Strange to think of those weeks in December and January when I would lie in bed miserable and in pain, with the curtains closed, refusing to go out of my room, even to eat. I thought I would never be happy again. I would keep my eyes closed, thinking of how I'd made so many bad decisions, done things that got me into trouble, how I'd gotten into the habit of lying to Momma and never telling her what I was really doing.

Strange to think that it all started getting better when Momma grounded me. At first, it had been one more thing to be angry about, but it also made me think about how I'd been neglecting both my studies and my friends and how miserable that made me, and once I started working hard, everything began changing for the better. I joined GSAA, met Jamal, and I was getting A's in all of my classes. All that *and* I still had time for my friends.

One Friday morning in late April I was sitting with the posse in the auditorium. It was one of our new favorite hangouts, especially if it was cold outside or we didn't have a lot of time. Someone would make sure Miss Haggard wasn't around and no teachers could see us and then we'd sneak into the quiet, dark room. The only light was from the glowing red exit signs. We'd usually go to a corner far from the doors so no one could hear us and we'd sit in one of the rows of chairs as if we were at the movies. We all knew that Alex and Maria liked each other, but now it was official that they were going out together and Alex had his legs across Maria's lap. Rebecca had a tiny flashlight that she flashed on their faces.

"No funny stuff, you guys."

"Cut that out," Alex said, holding his hand in front of his face.

"Oh, leave them in peace," Greg said. "Hey, what do you guys think about Jimmy Carter so far?"

"Well, at least he's better than Ford," said Rebecca. "I would've asked Noor to take me to Lebanon if *he'd* won again!"

"I think Carter's a decent human being," said Maria.

"Who cares?" said Alex. "All I want is a cigarette."

"*Alex!*" Maria said, pushing his legs off.

"What? I think all politicians are full of shit and I couldn't care less which one wins."

I had to smile because in a way I agreed with him, but of course he couldn't see me in the dark.

"Alex, you're loco." Maria said.

"Oh, come on give me a kiss."

"Uh, uh, uh," said Rebecca, shining the light on them again.

The door at the top of the auditorium opened and a ray of light entered the room. We all lowered our heads and Maria started giggling.

"Sshhh!" someone said.

"Just me, guys. Relax."

Jamal's voice—mellow and warm as a summer breeze. My heart thumped.

Jamal was practically part of the posse by then. It was perfect, because we could hang around together without it being awkward and no pressure on either of us.

Rebecca leaned against me and whispered right in my ear, sending a shiver down my neck.

"Here comes your boyfriend."

I whispered back, "He's *not* my boyfriend."

"Oh, right. I forgot."

Jamal sat in the row behind us and leaned forward between my chair and Rebecca's. His arm brushed mine and it felt like an electric current passed between us.

"How's it hangin'," asked Alex.

"Cool, brother."

"Jamal, good sir, do you have any bets as to what Jimmy Carter will do about divestment?" Greg asked.

"I don't think that's even seriously on the table," said Jamal. I could imagine him shrugging and rearranging the pick in his soft afro. "Even if Jimmy privately thinks Apartheid is wrong, I don't see him taking on the big corporations. Not at this point anyway. What do you think, Noor?"

"I wish I knew. I guess I'm cynical but when politicians say they're studying and discussing issues, that sounds to me like an excuse to do nothing. One thing I don't like is how he's always talking about religion. That makes me nervous."

"Really? That's part of what I love about him," said Maria. "As my *abuelita* used to say, *you can always trust a man of God.*"

"Oh boy," said Rebecca, "Not sure I agree with *that*. I trust a man—or a woman—if they're *trustworthy*. I guess we'll just see."

"Well, I think Jimmy's a good guy," said Maria. "He seems honest to me."

"I concur," said Greg.

"I'm going for a fucking cigarette," said Alex. "Anyone care to join me?"

"Nobody wants to be with you while you pollute the air," said Rebecca. "You're an environmental hazard all by yourself."

"Love you, too, Ms. Rebecca. OK, you turkeys. I'm truckin'."

"Hasta luego."

"See you round, brother."

"May the force be with you, Sir Alex."

Familiar voices in the dark.

"Bye, Alex." That was me, of course.

Nothing. Just Everything.

Spring 1977

17.

Jamal and Angel met with student activists at NYU, who agreed to have GSAA co-sponsor an anti-apartheid rally they had planned for the end of May. I was thrilled to be there with so many college students, a bunch of kids from Graves, and even some NYU professors. The rally was huge and it got me thinking that if people could protest like this all over the world, maybe it really would start putting pressure on companies and the government to change their policies.

We left the rally exhilarated. We'd been able to accomplish something bigger than our own little committee and I was proud to be a part of the effort.

On the walk back, Jamal put his hand on my shoulder. He was the first one to say what was on both of our minds.

"Hey, so what's up with you for the summer?"

"I don't know. I thought we were going back to Lebanon, but now I'm not so sure. I have to see the surgeon in a couple of weeks."

"Go *back*, go back? Or go back for a visit?"

"Everything's still up in the air. What about you?"

"We're going up to our cabin in Maine for most of the summer. It's what we always do. Me, my sister, and my parents. And our dog, Malcolm."

We both fell quiet as we walked, each of us carrying a hand-written sign slung over a shoulder.

Spring had finally come and the world was bursting with life. Wherever there was a patch of dirt or grass there were purple and yellow flowers poking through, somehow thriving in the midst of so much concrete and chaos. Like me, they too had survived the bitter winter and here they were—stunningly, vibrantly alive.

If we did go back to Lebanon, these could be some of the last days I would spend with Jamal. I knew for sure that my feelings for him were more than a crush, but I hadn't acknowledged this to him, or even fully admitted it to myself. And now, what would be the point? I was so comfortable with him, like he just *got* me most of the time. Even when we disagreed, we listened to each other and I knew that over the past few months I'd grown as a person, partly because of our friendship and working together on the committee. I couldn't bear the idea of never seeing him again.

"That sounds like fun," I managed, finally.

"Well, it's very restful, for sure. I get a lot of reading done and I get to commune with the bugs and the bullfrogs, chase rabbits with Malcolm. Definitely a big change from the city."

'I…" I began.

Jamal smiled and dipped his head—one slow nod. "Yeah, me too."

He put his arm around my shoulder and I leaned into him, overcoming my shyness. We hugged, a little awkwardly since we were still holding the signs and there were cars and people passing by, but it was so good to finally acknowledge what we'd both been feeling for a long time.

Antoine was at the apartment, helping Momma core zucchini and eggplant for stuffing on a Sunday morning. *Koosa mihshi* was one of my favorites but it was hard to find the right kind of squash in America. In Lebanon the squash and eggplants are no longer than your index finger and are so tender and delicious.

"Look what I found at Suleiman's Market!" Momma could barely contain her excitement.

"Where's that?" I asked.

"Over on Atlantic Avenue, where all the Arabic stores are," Antoine said, rubbing his side. "*Akh*, my back."

"Why don't you sit, like I am, then?" said Momma.

"Oh, never mind," he said with a grimace. "It always hurts when I work bent over."

"*Ya haraam*," she said, "poor thing."

Gabbie was there, too, altering a graduation dress she'd brought home to finish that weekend. "My brother is very sensitive you know."

"You guys are ganging up on me," Antoine said. "Thanks a lot!"

"No problem," Momma said.

"Can I make the *hashweh*?" I asked.

I didn't have the patience for coring the veggies and I usually poked the corer through the skins when I tried, but I did like to mix together the meat, rice and spices for the stuffing.

"Sure, *habeebti*. Don't forget to rinse the rice in the colander—and drain it well."

Antoine said he had to make a phone call. "I'll be right back, I swear." he said.

Gabbie had gone back to their apartment to use the sewing machine, so it was just Momma and me.

"He should try having your leg for a while and see how he likes it."

"He wouldn't last a day."

"He's not tough like us Palestinians," she said quietly.

I liked that Momma was making fun of Antoine and including me in her conspiracy. She was in a good mood. We'd been getting along better lately and she loved when we cooked together on a quiet weekend day. There was an early heat wave, and our air conditioners barely made a difference. We had fans going everywhere and it reminded me of the humid heat of Lebanon in summer, when my parents and I would be together in the kitchen, the big fan turning back and forth, moving the hot air around, Baba and me snapping green beans, Momma cutting onions and tomatoes. She'd be singing and he'd hum along. It seemed like such a long time ago.

I figured Antoine would be on the phone awhile to avoid working in the kitchen, so I took the opportunity to open the subject that had been on my mind since the discussion with Jamal about the summer.

"Momma, when are we going back?"

I knew she was anticipating this question. I had the feeling that she might be in conflict too. She had gotten a new job as an editor at *Dar al-Arabi* book publishing company recently and I knew she liked it a lot, but she still talked about Lebanon often. I knew she missed it, too. But tensions were rising again back home. Kamal Jumblatt, who was a very popular figure in the LNM, had been assassinated in March and this was followed by the killing of thousands of Christians in retaliation.

"I'm honestly not sure, Noor, but *ya 'ni*, you're seeing Dr. Savage again next week. Let's see what he says."

"What if he says everything is fine?"

She circled the corer inside the squash, digging out the pulp with a few expert twists of her wrist, set it down and picked up an eggplant. The lines in her forehead deepened.

"What do *you* think?"

I was totally caught off guard. Since we had left Lebanon, I don't think she had ever consulted with me this way. She always seemed to have the answers and would just tell me what they were.

"Me?"

She set down the corer and the half-cleaned eggplant in the bowl. "Yes, you, Noor. I want to know what you are thinking. What *you* want to do."

If I said I wanted to go home, I'd be leaving behind Jamal and all my friends, all the experiences I'd had over the past year. And what would it be like to go back to a war zone—where all the conflict and hatred, the injustice, fear, and destruction were still there—but now my people were being kept apart by the Syrian army? I couldn't even imagine. At least when there were soldiers and fighters and tanks in the streets before, they were Lebanese and Palestinians.

On the other hand, if I said I wanted to stay—what did that mean? How could I bear not to see Baba after a whole year of missing him? Not to smell the salty air and see the mountains rising above Beirut? Not to open the door and find Layla and her mother there, come by to share a cup of Arabic coffee together? And, did going back mean forever? For a visit?

"I don't know, Momma. I'm confused."

She wiped her hands on her apron and stretched them out to meet mine.

"I'm confused, too, *hayaati*. I admit to you. In a way, as a Palestinian, missing home is my fate. In Lebanon, I missed Palestine every minute of every day. Here I miss Lebanon. And, even though it might sound strange, in a way I will miss New York when we go back."

I couldn't help noticing that she said *when* we go back. It was a relief to hear it, but also to know that she was feeling some of what I was. Conflicted. Confused. Sometimes overwhelmed.

"How is your leg feeling now?"

"It hurts. Some days worse than others. It's hard for me not to imagine the pins sticking into me every time I take a step."

Momma winced.

"It's OK, Momma. Remember? We Palestinians are tough."

"True, but you're half Lebanese, after all."

We both laughed until tears came, as if it was much funnier than it actually was.

Right after school ended, Jamal left with his family to Maine. We promised to write to each other and he asked me to come up for a visit. I said I would try, but I was pretty sure Momma would never agree to such a thing.

"She's a nice lady, but she can be a bit traditional when it comes to letting her only daughter stay at a boy's house." I didn't mention that Momma had never even heard of Jamal.

"I get it. Remember, my parents are Muslims, too."

"We'll just have to be happy with letters, maybe some phone calls."

"When do you get the cast off?"

"In a few days. I'll let you know what happens."

We spent a wonderful last day together, wandering through the Botanic Gardens. I had been avoiding going there because of all the memories, but it turned out to be just right. It was one of those perfect summer days when the humidity is low, the air is clean and clear and there were bees buzzing in and out of the flowering bushes, crabapple trees with their luscious pink blossoms bursting. We picked a spot under a lilac tree and Jamal spread out a blanket. He broke off a lilac cluster and tucked it behind my ear. The scent, sweet and vibrant, seemed to bring me back to something I'd known, yet was entirely new at the same time.

"They smell so beautiful I want to bathe in them!"

"And that purple is gorgeous next to your black hair."

"It's always been one of my favorite colors—and now I have one more reason to love it."

I sat by Jamal on the blanket, my shoulder against his, filled with the pleasure of the day and his presence. Everything was so perfect, I tried to live this moment without thinking about the future.

My leg was not healing as Dr. Savage had hoped. Some of the bones failed to knit properly and he said another surgery was inevitable. Two days after the operation, I came down with a fever and chills. Somehow, my leg had gotten infected during the surgery and the infection quickly spread. They put me on IV antibiotics and kept me in the ICU.

I had one of those fevers where you are there and not there, in reality and out of it again. I vaguely remember saying some strange things and someone wiping a cool washcloth on my forehead. Momma's voice, far away.

I'm right here, habeebti. Just rest now.

Even through the fog of fever, guilt crept in. I can't imagine that any other kid could possibly have put their parents through as much as I had. At one point, I remember holding Momma's hand.

"I'm sorry, Momma."

"What for, *hayaati?*"

"Nothing. Just. Everything."

"Hush, hush."

Her hand on my head was soothing, as if her touch might heal me when nothing else could. Sometimes there were strange words and voices around me, like a veil. *Septicemia. Monitoring. Relatively rare. Still in the danger zone.* Once, I heard a telephone ringing. I couldn't tell if it was a dream or real. Then, Momma's voice, as if a long way away.

"*Aloo?*"

A pause.

"Rasheed? Is it you, *habeebi?*"

An image of Antoine somewhere in the room, a skinny figure floating between Momma and me, more ghost than human, hair like cotton candy around his head, leaving the room when Momma spoke.

Rasheed. Habeebi. The words danced nebulously around my head. Then it hit me. *Baba.*

"Is it Baba? Is he here?"

"He's on the telephone, *habeebti.* Here, talk to him."

"Baba, is it really you?"

"Yes, Najnouj. *Salaamtik, ya 'afreeteh.* Are you trying to give me a heart attack once again?"

"No, Baba. I'm sorry. I don't know what is happening to me."

"Come on, *wa law?* I am just joking, *habeebti.* Don't worry about anything but healing, now."

"Can you come? I want to see you. Why aren't you here?"

I wasn't sure where I was or where he was. There was quiet on the line for a minute.

"I wish, Najnouj. More than anything. Hopefully you'll get better soon and we will see each other. Until then, just concentrate on getting well. Promise."

"Yes, Baba. I love you."

"I love you too, *ya 'afreeteh*," he said in a rough voice that sounded the way the fishermen in Tyre spoke.

Another time, voices came in and out. My ears somehow muffling them. A man's voice. *We cannot lose her. What is this disaster?* Who was it? I knew this voice, but distorted. Not Baba. *Ah, mon dieu—there must be something more we can do.* Antoine. It was Antoine. Then a higher voice. A woman. *We will not lose her. She is tough—and she has survived worse.* Momma. Only she knew how strong I was, but I didn't feel strong. I felt myself slipping away, like I, too, was part ghost, only half in this place where Momma and Antoine were discussing me as if I wasn't there. Then, Momma crying. I don't think she realized I could hear her.

I had no sense of how much time had passed. I only know that I opened my eyes and saw clearly. Saw that I was in a hospital room. That there were flowers—lots of them on a small table, and I could smell them. Neat flowers—roses and carnations with ordinary smells—and something else—a joyful fragrance that made me think of freedom and running and dancing. Of Jamal. Of our last day in the Botanic Garden when we had sat under a tree and I held his hand and the air was filled with this wild, purple smell. And now here, in this room, a big, overflowing, messy bunch of lilacs in a vase. Had he sent them? Did he know? And Momma was there, asleep in a chair. A pinch in my arm. An IV, dripping its alchemy into me. I could hear clearly, too. The *beep, beep, beep* of some hospital machine counting something about me. My heart probably, or my breathing. Steady. So, once again, it seemed—I was alive. It was as if some force in the universe wanted me dead, but I kept refusing. *No! I will not die. Damn you, Death. You are an ugly, miserable thing.*

When Momma opened her eyes she didn't move or say anything. She just smiled like she, too, understood that I refused to die—that I was here to stay for the time being.

Once the infection cleared, they put on a new cast. The doctor was optimistic, saying that the second surgery had gone well in spite of the infection. I might have a slight limp, but other than that I should be able to walk without a cast within a month or two.

"*Limp?*"

Dr. Savage put his hand gently on my shoulder.

"You did yourself quite a bit of damage, there, young lady. We're trying to get you back as best we can, but I just want you to be aware that's a possibility."

I went home from the hospital feeling very discouraged. It seemed that my foolish mistakes would haunt me for the rest of my life. Was I really going to walk with a limp? *Forever?* I felt a pang of anger at Brian for letting this happen to me. What kind of person takes his girlfriend for a ride when he's stoned? In the snow? Without a driving license? And lies to her to get what he wants? I never should have gotten in that car and I'd live with the consequences of that decision for the rest of my life. But that didn't change the fact that *he'd* been the one behind the wheel.

I had to spend two more weeks resting most of the time before I could get up and do anything. With Jamal away and most of the posse gone, Momma at her new job, which was more demanding than the old one, I was alone most of the time. I wrote a letter to Layla, one to Baba and a few long ones to Jamal, but I didn't want to worry him, so I told him what had happened but said I was fine now. I didn't tell him how miserable I was feeling or anything about a limp.

One day, out of the blue, the phone rang and it was Samantha.

"Ciao, bella. How are you?"

"*Samantha?* It is really you? It's been, y'know forever."

She laughed—that monkey laugh of hers. "Yeah, y'know, it has."

The *y'know* had somehow snuck in, replacing my usual *ya'ni.*

I told her about the surgery and the infection and how I was stuck at home, bored.

"Well, screw that! I'll come hang out with you."

Samantha came the next day while Momma was at work. Her straight blonde hair was parted perfectly down the middle. She pulled up a chair next to the bed and set a cassette recorder down on the desk.

"I brought something to cheer you up."

"A new Marley tape?"

"Not this time, sister. Since Fleetwood Mac came out with their album, *Rumours*, I've been obsessed. You're gonna love it."

Then she slyly pulled a joint out of her pocket.

"But first something to set the mood."

I bit my lip. "Oh, I don't know, Samantha. I haven't really been smoking."

"You know it'll fix what ails you. Numb your pain and soothe your soul."

Good old Samantha. She might have been a bit of a *shaytaanah* but she definitely knew how to cheer me up.

"You know me too well! But we'd better open up all the windows, because if Momma ever figures it out, I'm dead!"

It felt so good getting high with Samantha—especially listening to Fleetwood Mac. And she was right, I did love the album. We were listening to *Songbird* when she told me about her new boyfriend, Dave.

"He has a car. We have fun. He has the best little finger maneuvers," she said, wiggling her index finger.

I spewed out my lungful of smoke. "Oh, my God, Samantha. You are *so* bad!"

"Life's too short to be good."

"Life's too good to be short!"

"Hah! See, I told you it'd cure what ails you."

Samantha came to see me a few more times and once I was able to walk around again with crutches, I went out to meet her too. We went to see Star Wars. We took walks. We smoked some. We ate heroes and pizza, drank coffee. Thank god for Samantha. She was going to Italy with her family at the beginning of August, but by then Rebecca and Maria would both be back.

The first letter from Jamal was only two paragraphs, but I read it dozens of times. He was rereading the *Autobiography of Malcolm X* and he promised to lend it to me when he got back. He told me about swimming in the pond and how the bottom was squishy under your feet. At night the bullfrogs were so loud he had to close the windows so he could sleep.

Then he'd get so hot he couldn't sleep anyway. So, he'd lie awake thinking about me. About my curly black hair tickling his face when I put my head on his shoulder. On sunny days he'd lie in the hammock with his eyes closed, pretending I was next to him. *'Dad,'* he wrote, *'tells me that Noor means light. Is that true?'* It made me smile. *Yes*, I whispered to myself. *I am light and you—Jamal—are beauty.*

I kissed the letter, smelled it. It smelled vaguely smoky and I imagined him writing it next to a campfire in the woods, with the bullfrogs croaking in the pond.

I decided to tell Momma that I wanted to stay at least for fall semester. I said I probably shouldn't really travel yet, anyway. Dr. Savage had said it would be OK once the cast was off, but it couldn't hurt to wait a bit longer, could it, just in case?

When I got the second cast removed, it was both a relief and a disappointment. Dr. Savage had been right about both things. It had healed nicely and he didn't expect additional surgeries would be necessary, but, he was also right about the limp. It wasn't as bad as I'd feared, but it was there. Undeniable. I rocked to one side just slightly with every step on my right foot.

"Will it get better?"

Dr. Savage smiled sympathetically.

"It's *OK*. I just want to know," I said, bringing out my tough "Palestinian" side.

He smiled and nodded.

"Atta girl. I'm afraid to say you'll be keeping that limp as a souvenir, but pretty soon you'll learn to compensate and you'll barely even notice it."

"Fine," I said, swallowing hard. "Thank you for being such a good surgeon, Dr. Savage—and for being honest with me."

I liked saying his name. I liked that it didn't match his personality at all and it was so inappropriate for a surgeon. Over the coming weeks and months, I made it my mission to walk as normally as possible and Dr. Savage was right. With time, it was as if I just had a sore hip.

On July 31st the serial killer we now knew as *Son of Sam* assaulted a couple sitting in their car in Brooklyn, killing the woman and blinding the man. The jitters we'd all felt each time we'd heard about a new murder turned to panic. Momma made me stay home while she was at work and she took taxis to and from the office, coming home early every day that week, and double locking the door to our apartment, until he was finally arrested.

I thought about a lot of things that week—how there were many days I'd had to stay home in Beirut because it was too dangerous to go out. How this was a new kind of danger I couldn't comprehend—that someone would get a thrill out of approaching another human being—especially a woman—and killing her. For sure, some people get a thrill out of war, but I don't think it's personal so much as a matter of belief. Even if it's wrong-headed, *they* are convinced they're right.

I wondered what could have happened to this man, who called himself a "monster." How does someone become so cruel, full of hate? But we'd seen hate and cruelty in war, too, hadn't we? Maybe once we put a wall between ourselves and others, we don't see them as human any more. Maybe that is true whether the wall is against one person or a whole group. If you see yourself as superior, or as having been wronged by this person or group, then anything you do to them is justified and "right"— pleasurable even. It made me wonder if any one of us is capable of such impulses if we feel deeply wounded and wronged. How would I feel, and what would I do, if I came face to face with Janine's killer or if something happened to one of my parents?

I thought of the times I'd sat in a car with Brian in deserted areas, purposely isolating ourselves, enjoying the thrill of being alone together. Of me, with my dark, curly hair, the type that *Son of Sam* apparently sought out. Such thoughts lingered, long after the last incident that, strangely, had been in Brooklyn. For weeks I was watchful, nervous every time I went out, found myself alone on the street, heard a noise behind me or saw a dark-haired, hulking man approach.

Something else kept swirling in my head, too—the idea that it was dangerous just being a woman, that we have to constantly watch out for ourselves, avoid certain situations, be careful in ways that men never have to think about. On the other hand, if we don't take risks then what is the point of life? If I hadn't gone to the front lines that day and had stayed home like a "good girl" instead, I would have been safe, but I wouldn't have seen what was really going on outside our relatively safe neighborhood. And even though I regretted going back to Brian, the truth was I learned so much about myself and about relationships that I wouldn't have if I'd just gone home and studied every day after school.

18

Fall 1977

There was one day in late August when the temperature dropped down into the sixties—Fahrenheit that is—and I started thinking about how beautiful it would be in a couple months when the leaves turned bright orange, yellow, and red. I knew Baba would love that transformation and I even thought of dusting off the Rollei so I could take pictures to send him.

That day someone had a fire in a fireplace and it smelled cozy, warm and mapley. I pulled out the trunk where I kept my fall and winter clothes. I took out my favorite beige turtle-neck sweater and the flared jeans Momma had taken me to buy the spring before. I was surprisingly happy that I'd soon be putting away my shorts and wearing warmer clothes. I was even excited to be starting junior year in a couple of weeks.

Only one year before, I had been so miserable about everything, resentful of living in New York, of starting school at Graves, yet here I was, imagining going back to school, imagining how it would feel to put my arms around Jamal in a few short days. My strength was gradually returning and I was getting used to walking on my leg again—free from the cast. Soon I'd be seeing all my friends, going to GSAA meetings, and because I was a junior now, I'd be able to take some electives—actually have some choice over what I'd be studying.

The first day of school, I got up early, washed my hair with Aquamarine shampoo and clipped it up to one side. I ironed my pants, slipped into my brown suede platform shoes, and put on a huge pair of silver hoop earrings. I felt great walking the six blocks to my high school, my long hair fragrant against my cheek, reminding me of what Jamal had said in his letter. I worried that the platform shoes would exaggerate my limp, wondered what people would think—what Jamal would think, but I didn't care. I was standing up tall and feeling good in my body and I wasn't going to let a little limp spoil it.

Jamal's family had gotten delayed coming back, so I hadn't seen him yet. We had just talked on the phone a few times and the sound of his voice thrilled me every time. I wondered if I would see him in the hallway, if we'd have any classes together. I thought of his lion's eyes catching the sunlight, the casual way he held his body, the way he could always make me smile, with just a word or a gesture.

I got to my homeroom early and watched the students coming in. Some I knew, some not. A few of them were still sleepy-eyed, but most were chatting excitedly with their friends. The girls whispered to each other, admiring a new dress or hairstyle. The boys—spread-legged at their desks—slapped fives and watched the girls out of the corners of their eyes. When the teacher came in, everybody quieted down. The teacher wrote her name on the board, "Mrs. Whistler." A few of the boys whistled before she could turn around and a current of snickering rippled around the room.

To my surprise, she didn't get angry or yell the way Miss Downs would have last year.

"Well, that's original," she said with a smile. A couple of the guys scratched their foreheads and everyone quieted down. "Never heard that one before." Some friendly snickers.

"Now let's—," she began, but the door swung open and in came— Jamal! His clothes were rumpled and his afro was flattened on one side.

"Sorry," he said, holding up one hand.

"Pleased you could join us, Mr—?"

"Ahmed. Jamal Ahmed."

Jamal sat and gave a quick scan of the room before his eyes landed on mine, holding my gaze for a few, long seconds as we shared a secret smile.

On the way to our first classes, he waited for me outside the door and I let my hand brush his. He hooked his little finger around mine, making my heart jump.

"Pleased you could join us, Mr.—" I said, trying to imitate Mrs. Whistler's accent.

"And I'm pleased to join *you*. Couldn't ask for a better welcoming party," he said, taking advantage of the crowded corridor to bump into me.

At my first break, I went outside and saw the posse from across the quad. Alex and Greg were sparring with imaginary light sabers. As soon as they saw me they "called a truce" and we all had a big group hug.

"It feels like a year since I've seen you guys! I missed you."

"Missed you, too," they somehow managed to say all at the same time.

"*Como esta todo, Chica?*" Maria said. "*Estas muy linda!*"

"*Gracias*," I said, posturing with my hand on my hip like Miss Chiquita Banana.

Greg gave me a wistful look. I knew he liked me, but he knew about Jamal and me so he never did anything about it.

I felt lucky to have such good friends in America. Thanks to them, I didn't feel the need to hide who I was anymore. Instead I felt proud of everything I was—being Arab, having an accent, being from the Middle East, having a complicated, messy, mixed up background. I'd even started using my full name when I was introduced to someone new. I didn't care that it was cumbersome. *Hi*, I'd say, *I'm Noor Haddad al-Husayni.* When they said, *Huh?* Instead of getting flustered and embarrassed I'd calmly say, *that's N-O-O-R H-A-D-D-A-D A-L-H-U-S-A-Y-N-I.* If they thought it was weird, let it be there problem, not mine.

I thought of Layla and our adventures together, good and bad. I wondered when I would see her again. Wondered what she would be doing right now. She was a freshman in college. I could hardly believe it. I wondered if we'd remain friends and how the long separation would affect the friendship. We did still write letters to each other from time to time, but actually seeing each other was different. Would she still recognize me? I could imagine her saying, *Look at you. You're Amerkaaniyeh, now. Are you too good for your old friends?* I'd pull my eyebrows together and say, *La. Never! I will always be 'arabiyyeh first!*

"Hellooooo?" Rebecca put her hands on my shoulders and shook me. "Earth to Noor."

"I was just thinking."

"Don't think. Your brain might overheat! Now, *yalla*, it's time for class."

I loved that Rebecca was picking up Arabic phrases here and there. I realized that was one thing that made her and my other friends so special. They didn't think of me as just any other American friend. They really *liked* that I was Lebanese-Palestinian, liked my accent and that I couldn't help *salt and peppering* my sentences with Arabic, as Rebecca said—and they genuinely cared about what was going on in Lebanon. It was so different from my first days in America, when I felt like I had to hide who I was, that no one cared about Lebanon—or even if they did care, they didn't understand it, knew only that there was a long, drawn-out war going on there.

"*Yalla*, let's go," I said.

"Fare thee well, fine friends," Greg said.

I arrived home one day that week to find Momma already in the apartment.

"Congratulate your mother!"

"For what?"

"I was promoted to Senior Editor."

"Wow, *mabrook!* That's fantastic. When do you start?"

"I already started."

I was genuinely happy for Momma securing a job that she liked but it also felt like one step farther away from Lebanon. I sometimes wished Baba could come and live with us in New York, but in a way I was glad he was staying. I was convinced that we'd find our way back to Lebanon before too long and even though I was glad to be in the States for now, I didn't want it to become permanent. Not only that, but I knew that as much as he missed us, Baba didn't want to leave. He *belonged* in Lebanon.

A couple weeks after school started, Jamal asked me if he could walk me home. On the way, he said he had something for me. We sat on a park bench and he pulled out a little box tied with a neat purple ribbon.

Oh, no, I thought. *Too soon for a ring.*

My face must have shown my alarm because he set the box down on the bench. "Don't worry. I'm not asking you to marry me."

"No, of course not. I just—" I knew I was blushing.

"Just open it."

Inside there was a macramé bracelet with the Palestinian flag end-to-end with a South African one. I stretched it out and held it flat on my two palms.

"But, where did you find it?"

"I didn't find it. I made it."

"You *made* it?"

"For my foxy lady."

"I can't believe it. It's beautiful. It's perfect."

I could feel tears coming and I blinked hard to stop them.

I put my arms around him and kissed his cheek.

"Hey, don't I get a real kiss?"

"That was real."

"You know what I mean."

I kissed him quickly on the lips, still not used to the American habit of making out in public.

"But how did you know how to do it?"

"Truth is, my sister, Aisha is really into making jewelry and crafts and stuff."

"Oh, so she made it?"

"No! She just showed me how. When you're hanging out in the woods all summer, you have to get really creative to not go bonkers, y'know? I have to admit, the box and the ribbon were her idea."

"I love it."

"Does this mean you'll go out with me?"

"Go out with you? You mean like—?"

"*Officially.*"

I squeezed his hand and held up my wrist for him to help me tie on the bracelet.

"I'll think about it and let you know."

"Too late! You already put it on. Now you are mine, all mine!" he said, imitating a Count Dracula voice and rubbing his hands together.

Sometimes the things you don't say to a person are as important as the things you do say and the words that remained unspoken that day hovered between us like a candle flame—elusive and soulful but melancholic as well. Neither of us could know what the future would bring, but at some point, I would be going back to Lebanon. Maybe in a semester, maybe in a year, but for sure I would be going back. Until then, the best we could do was to savor our time together.

~~~

It was a Monday, a week or two after Labor Day. Walking to school first thing in the morning it was still cool, so I buttoned up my sweater and walked as quickly as my leg would allow. I arrived at school to find Jamal and a few other kids from GSAA talking tensely outside the school building. I knew something was wrong. When I approached, my first thought was, *who died?* I was afraid it was one of our friends. Jamal wore a somber expression. Angel was crying, Tim kicking at a mound of earth.

"What's going on?"

Jamal opened his mouth to speak but Tim jumped in.

"They *fucking* killed Biko. Fascist mother-*fuckers!*"

I covered my mouth with my hand. "Oh, God, no. How?"

We knew that Biko had been arrested and put in a South African prison for his anti-apartheid work. But killed because of it? My stomach clenched as I remembered his words. *It is better to die for an idea that will live, than to live for an idea that will die.*

Jamal put his hand on my arm. "He died in prison. God knows what they did to him."

Angel wiped her cheeks and pulled her chin upright. "Our people are still being bound and shackled, slaughtered like sheep. In the *twentieth century.*"

I tried to hug her, but she held up her hand and took a step back.

"Stripped naked and beaten for speaking the truth." She paused. "There's an emergency meeting today at NYU. Everyone should be there. Classes or no classes."

Tim pumped his fist into the air. "Power to the people!"

Angel slit her eyes at him. "This is about *Black* power."

"What do you think I mean, Angel? Power to the white man?"

"I think you're a spoiled white boy who likes to act more radical than Eldridge Cleaver."

Tim looked like he'd been slapped in the face.

"I'm not the enemy, Angel. We're on the same side, remember?"

"Yeah, it's easy to act all badass when you know you'll be going back to your nice, bougie life at the end of the day, but you have no idea what it's like to have to put your life on the line fighting for what's right."

"And you do, Angel?" Tim leaned sulkily against a telephone pole, his usual bravado sucked out of him.

Angel waved her hand dismissively.

"Let's all take a breath, guys," Jamal said. "This is no time to get at each other's throats. Tim—"

"Forget it, man. I'm outta here."

"Come on, man. Just be at the meeting. We'll sort this out."

"I'm supposed to work with *her*? Fuck that!"

"Yeah, fuck it. Go home to your mommy. She'll make it better."

"Angel," Jamal said quietly, clearly dismayed.

"OK, Jamal, you and your white girlfriend can piss off, too."

"What the hell? First of all she's not *white* and second of all, why are we fighting? How is this going to help?"

Angel turned to me. "Sorry, Noor. That wasn't called for. I'm just sick of white folks thinking they know what it means to be Black when they don't know shit about it. For us, a walk down the block could cost us our life—or at the very least our dignity—if a cop doesn't like the way we look at him, or the clothes we're wearing, or for no damn reason at all. What white person ever had to worry about jive like that?"

My throat tightened thinking about how wrong it was that anyone should have to live with that kind of fear. When I'd come to America somehow I'd assumed people would be treated more fairly than in Lebanon, but I was learning fast that that wasn't the case at all.

It was true that I didn't know what it was like to be Black, but I didn't know what it was like to be white either. I'd also been threatened because of who I am, swallowed insults and been scared for my life, but it didn't seem right to say any of that to her just then. I wanted to put my arms around her but I knew it was better to wait and listen.

"I just feel like being with other Black folks right now. People who really *get it*. Like, on a gut level, y'know?"

"I know. So many times I wish I can be with other Arabs—people who *get me*, as you say. To be with people you don't have to explain yourself to."

"You got it, sister." Angel nodded.

"Hey, I gotta get going," Jamal, said, pushing his hands into his pockets. "I have to try to get my head around all of this."

"Jamal, wait," I said, but he kept walking.

"I'll see you both at the meeting."

I could tell Jamal was upset by what I said, but I didn't mean it against him at all. I was being honest. I really did feel like I understood where Angel was coming from. How alone you can feel sometimes even when nothing is wrong and you have your friends around you, but they are not like you, haven't experienced what you have. It can be a lonely feeling. I let Jamal go. We *all* had to get our heads around what had happened and what to do next.

As I walked to homeroom, images came to my mind of all the innocent people who had died or suffered in Lebanon for standing up for what they believed in. It seems like they always go after the good guys. They're the ones the government is *really* scared of. A deep heaviness settled into my belly. It seemed I'd either be chasing death or it would be chasing me, wherever I went.

After Biko died, it was hard to imagine how any of us could focus on studies. I knew my grades would suffer for a time, but I didn't care. I'd make it up somehow, but for now, all I wanted to do was to be with activists—planning demonstrations, leafletting, writing letters to the editor.

The passion and anger inside me about Lebanon was finding its voice here in the U.S. for another cause that felt more and more like my own. I would never forget what Angel said about wanting to be with other Black people, and I knew that in some deep way this *was* more their fight than mine, or Tim's or Cynthia's. Just like the disaster in Lebanon was rooted in me in a way it couldn't be for Angel or even Jamal, no matter how much they cared, but I also knew that solidarity was important. I wished that Americans cared about Lebanon the way they cared about South Africa, but it seemed to me that it somehow was invisible. That *we* were invisible.

After the meeting at NYU, I caught up with Jamal heading into Washington Square Park.

"Hey—wait up! Why are you in such a hurry?"

"I'm not, I'm not. I'm just having a hard time honestly. How can we ever win this fight when the deck is so stacked? I mean, Biko of all people. Damn."

"I know, Jamal. It's terrible, but we have to keep trying even when it seems hopeless. I guess that's why they call it a struggle." I put my hand on his chest. "Can we sit awhile?" I knew he wasn't saying everything that was bothering him and with emotions so high already, I wanted to be sure everything was all right between us.

We found a bench under a tree and I sat close to Jamal, hooked my pinkie finger around his. The sun was warm on our bodies and I could smell the warm scent of his skin that I loved so much, fragrant with fresh air. Jamal was staring off into the distance. The silence between us felt like a tender wound. I unhooked my pinkie.

"Jamal?"

"Yeah."

"This is such a hard day for all of us but I feel like—" I searched for the right words. "—like there's something you're not saying to me."

"Not really, why?"

"It seems like you got mad this morning—about what I said to Angel."

Jamal slid his hand over so it barely touched mine.

"I wasn't mad. I just felt hurt, I guess."

"Hurt? Why?"

"The way you and Angel were talking. Now that I'm saying it, it sounds petty, but—"

"But?"

"I kinda felt excluded."

"Seriously?"

"I know. I'm an idiot."

"Well, at least you admit it!"

"But seriously. I guess I was feeling the same thing you both described, but I didn't think you'd want to hear that, and—here's the dumb part—I could never be *Arab*, so if that's what you need, I figured I should give you some space."

"Oh my goodness, Jamal. Do you really think that if I miss my Arab friends and my country I feel less for you?"

"Well kind of. I guess I was confused."

"Life's confusing. But one thing you never have to be confused about is…"

Jamal waited expectantly.

"Is what an idiot you are!"

"Hey!"

Jamal brought my hand up to his lips and kissed it. "C'mon, we should get going. Train or walk?"

"Walk. It's such a beautiful day. It doesn't seem right, somehow, does it? The weather being so nice on such a tragic day."

We started the long walk back to Brooklyn and for a while we were both quiet. Jamal spoke first.

"Can I admit something to you?"

"Of course."

"Part of what I was thinking when you and Angel were talking was how I get that lonely feeling sometimes too. Like I'm not Black enough to be really Black, and not white either. It's like I don't quite belong."

"Welcome to the club, as you Americans say."

"Gee, thanks. Thing is, my dad is definitely Black and everyone thinks of my mom as white, but I'm not really either."

"I guess we have to decide for ourselves what we are. If you let everyone else define you, you won't know who you are anymore."

"That sounds great, Noor, but in reality, they *do* define us."

"*They?*"

"Did you know that slave owners and other racist bastards used to call us *mulattos*? Do you know what that means? It's a little mule. Yours truly. A cross between a donkey and a horse. In case you were wondering."

"That's so horrible. Who do they think they are?"

"If we were a quarter Black, we were *quadroons*, an eighth Black you're an *octoroon*."

"What? How could they even know that?"

"Didn't you know racists are great scientists? They have it all figured out. And what's more—they'd treat you differently depending on how much African blood you had. The lighter your complexion the better you were treated. Let me rephrase that. The better you *are* treated."

"It's so messed up. In Lebanon there was no slavery, but there are still awful biases. The French occupation made some people think that the more western you act and dress, the lighter your skin and hair, and the less 'Arab' you are, the better. Some Lebanese even say they're not Arab at all. They claim to be direct descendants of the Phoenicians and that makes them better than us."

Jamal dug his hands into his pockets. "Colonialism, baby. That's where it starts. Modern slavery. No whips or chains. Just mind games, prisons, politics and privilege."

I was glad I'd found the courage to talk to Jamal. Even though it wasn't an easy conversation—and it felt strange discussing our feelings when such a terrible event had just occurred—but it brought us closer, made me realize that if we could trust each other and not be afraid to face problems between us, it would help us both be strong enough to face the difficult challenges we'd meet out in the world.

I thought about my conversation with him when I'd said we shouldn't let others define us and he'd said—like it or not *they do define us*. The more I considered this I realized that both things are true. If I was facing a checkpoint in Beirut I might have no choice but to be *Muslim*, but among my friends I wasn't religious at all. And calling ourselves 'Arab' might not show all the complex parts of our identity, but it was a matter of pride—a way to say colonialism can't define us—we define ourselves. And at some point Black people stopped using the word *negro* because *Afro-American* said to the world—my ancestors are from Africa and I'm proud of it.

19.

Momma decided we should do our own Thanksgiving meal. The year before, Momma, Gabbie, Antoine, and I had been invited to the *Castello* to have Thanksgiving dinner with Samantha's family.

Momma hadn't been able to stop talking about that meal for months.

"There was more food than at an Arab table!" she had exclaimed. She loved everything about the meal except the cranberry sauce.

"Why do these Americans put sweet things with their meals? It is like having dessert in the middle of dinner."

"Because it's good?" I had said with my most sarcastic, junior year attitude.

Momma had waved her hand dismissively.

"But everything else was delicious, and *I* can make it even better."

Knowing what a great cook Momma is, she was probably right, and this year she went to the library and borrowed ten different cookbooks. She read every Thanksgiving menu she could get her hands on and tried out a few recipes in the chilly weeks leading up to the day itself.

"But who are we going to invite?" I said.

"Most people will be with family, so, good question."

"Obviously, Gabbie and Antoine."

"For sure, and we'll invite our Arab friends who don't have anywhere else to go. Bilal and Mona and their kids. Salwa—she works at the magazine—and her sister, Farah. That is six, maybe seven plus us is nine."

"That's enough," I said. "We don't need more. I'll make the pies. Pumpkin and pecan."

I hadn't met a lot of Arab kids my age in New York, and although I liked Bilal and Mona's daughter Farah, she was only twelve. It occurred to me that having Rebecca and the posse, Jamal, and Samantha in my life made me feel better about not having Arab friends in New York.

Momma stuffed the turkey with a traditional *hashweh* made of rice, meat, pine nuts and almonds. She roasted butternut and acorn squash, sweet potatoes, carrots, potatoes and beets. No candied yams on Momma's table! I insisted on mashed potatoes and cranberry sauce, which I'd cook, and she made the best gravy I've ever tasted. Even though we'd have the two pies, Momma couldn't resist baking a *kunaafeh* for dessert, too. There was *hummos* and *baba ghannooj* for appetizers, so it was kind of a hybrid Thanksgiving, like everything else about us. I wished Jamal was there and Rebecca, too, but they were with their own families.

I hadn't dared tell Momma about Jamal, but I really wanted him there. When he and I had talked about Thanksgiving the week before, he'd said that his heart was with the Native Americans, who didn't have a whole lot to be thankful for on that day since the European *invaders* had stolen their land, uprooted them, tricked, ambushed and slaughtered them. But Thanksgiving was as much a tradition in the Ahmad family as it was for most Americans and Jamal knew it was futile to resist the traditional family gathering. So he would usually settle for delivering a small tribute before the meal, where he made his feelings on the subject known.

After the meal, everyone was stuffed, and tipsy from the Lebanese wine Antoine and Gabbie had brought; the best vintages of Chateau Musar and Ksara—a red and a white of each, and Momma let me sample them. Everyone needed a break before dessert, so Momma made a big pot of Arabic coffee and we all sat in the living room, listening to Arabic music, some people smoking cigarettes. Momma would never tell them not to, but she opened up the window to let the smoke out until the guests complained they were cold.

I slipped out to use the telephone in the corridor and dialed Jamal's house.

"Ahmad residence," he said when he answered.

It made me smile. His whole family answered in this formal way, not to mention that they pronounced the name all wrong, with the accent on the second syllable and leaving off the "h" sound, so it sounded more like *Amen* except with a "d."

"Haddad-al-Husayni residence speaking." Since I'd started using both last names I liked hearing it.

"You goof! Everything ok?"

"I just wanted to say hi and, well, can you sneak away and come have dessert with us? I miss you."

"Miss you too. But the tradition here is we do the meal early? So we finished like three hours ago?"

"Well we're Arab, ok? Everything we do takes at least three hours longer!"

"Well I guess I never have to worry about being late then."

"Very funny."

"Did you tell your mother you're inviting me?"

"She'll be fine."

Silence on the line.

"It'll be fine. Just come!"

After I hung up, I waved to Momma, pantomiming that I needed to talk to her, so she came out to the corridor.

"My friend Jamal is coming by to have dessert with us."

"Jamal? Who is this Jamal?"

"Just a friend from school."

"A *friend?*" she said, raising her eyebrows.

"Yes, Momma. A friend."

"Is he Arab?"

"Not exactly."

"Not exactly? Approximately then?"

"*Khalas*, Momma, please? You don't mind, do you?"

"No, of course not. It's just—"

"Thanks, Momma," I said giving her a quick kiss on the cheek.

I went back to sit with our guests, but I hardly noticed what they were saying. All I could think about was that Jamal was coming over and Momma hadn't even really objected. When the doorbell rang, I jumped to answer it. You couldn't see the door from the living room, but I kissed him on both cheeks Arab style to be on the safe side anyway. I'd never kissed him like that before and he was puzzled.

"You should get used to it. That's how we always kiss! *Yalla*, come in."

I led Jamal to the living room where everyone was still sitting, having multiple conversations in Arabic.

"Excuse me," I said, "This is Jamal."

Everyone stopped talking at the same time. It was like a conductor had signaled the orchestra to stop playing. Jamal was a bit pale, but he managed a little Jamal-style bow.

Momma was the first to speak.

"Jamal. Welcome. *Ahlan wa sahlan*," she said, a bit stiffly.

"Thank you, Mrs. al-Husayni."

Momma smiled faintly, clearly appreciating being addressed this way. She disapproved of the recent trend of teenagers calling adults and teachers by their first names. She'd *tcch* and say, *Akh, these American kids. No respect.*

"Jamal, these are our friends," I said pushing him into the room, introducing him to the guests. None of them stood, but Antoine sat forward in his chair and surveyed Jamal from head to toe.

"Jamal? What sort of name is that?"

"Antoine!" I said.

"I just wondered. Do your people hail from Sudan? Or, maybe Egypt?"

Jamal bowed his head ceremoniously—in a way probably only I knew was sarcastic—and reached his hand out to Antoine, which Antoine shook limply.

"My *people*," he said, "hail from Brooklyn."

Antoine opened his mouth, clearly ready to pursue the interrogation, so I was relieved when Momma stepped in.

"Well, I'd say it's time for dessert. Jamal, please join us in the dining room," she said, leading the way and narrowing her eyes at Antoine as she passed him.

I hadn't known what to expect, but I guess I should have known better than to anticipate an enthusiastic reception for Jamal. I'd thought it was a good time to introduce him when there were lots of people around and I had avoided thinking about the fact that Jamal had three or four strikes against him.

First, he was a boy, and a good Arab girl does not bring home boys.

Second, he was Black. And even though Momma and some of her friends would never admit to being prejudiced, when it came to one of their daughters bringing a Black boy home? That was a whole different matter. Even if I did say he was "just a friend."

Third, even though he had an Arab/Muslim name, somehow it was worse because they probably saw him as an imposter, a fake. *Why would a Black boy have an Arab name?* I could almost hear them asking.

Fourth, whatever he was, he wasn't *one of us*. He was different, other, whatever you want to call it. I sat down heavily in my chair at the dining table. Jamal kicked my foot under the table, trying to cheer me up, but I was not in a mood to be cheered. I regretted the moment I picked up the phone to invite him. He deserved better.

I glanced around the table at all the faces there. Bilal was much darker than Jamal, with thick, black eyebrows. Mona was pale, with gray-green eyes. Their daughter was dark like Bilal, but with Mona's eyes, and the boy was a carbon copy of his father. Salwa and her sister had medium colored skin, with dark hair and eyes. Antoine, of course, was Phoenician.

"Noor? Jamal? *Yalla* the desserts are delicious," Momma said, pushing two plates piled with pie, *kunaafeh* and ice cream toward us.

I shook my head.

"A few bites," she insisted.

I couldn't eat. I was too upset by how dry and unwelcoming they were with Jamal, how rude Antoine was. The worst part was not being able to say anything because I would never insult our friends even though I felt insulted. And, I didn't want to ruin my first—and possibly only— Thanksgiving with Jamal. I tried to smile for his sake, but I think he knew how I was feeling and he squeezed my hand under the table. I pushed the plate toward him with my free hand.

"*Yalla*, try some, Jamal."

"They do look delicious." Jamal let my hand go and sampled a little of each pie, finished every bite of the *kunaafeh*, Momma's specialty, with its melting sweet cheese and sweet syrup. I was relieved that everyone was busy eating desserts and not watching us anymore, except for a few side glances here and there. I wanted to be anywhere else, but I waited until dessert was over, helped clear the dishes and then told Momma I'd be right back.

Jamal, as polite as always, excused himself with a bow. "Good meeting all of you. Happy Thanksgiving."

The guests mumbled *Happy Thanksgiving*. Momma stood up and walked after us, pulling at my elbow so I had to slow down.

"Five minutes, Noor," she whispered in my ear. She let go of me and turned to Jamal.

"It was a pleasure meeting you, Jamal. Please give your family my best."

I knew Momma was trying, but it didn't feel completely genuine. She certainly didn't give him the warm welcome I had naively hoped for. I walked with Jamal down the long six flights and outside.

"I'm *so* sorry, so mad, I don't even know what to say." I started to cry.

"It's cool," he said wiping my cheeks with his thumbs. "Believe me, I've experienced worse. I dated an Irish Catholic girl for about five minutes freshman year. Compared to her family, this was a red carpet welcome!"

I couldn't help smiling. "You dated an Irish Catholic girl?"

"Yeah, I don't know what I was thinking," Jamal said, digging his hands into his pockets.

The November air was chilly and there was a faint smell of smoke in the air. I pulled my sweater closer around my middle.

"I don't know what to say, Jamal. That was awful."

"C'mon, *Foxy Lady*. It's not a big deal."

"Yes, it *is* a big deal. It's not OK for them to act like that. It makes me ashamed."

"Ashamed? It's not you doing it."

"No, but they're my—" I fished for the right word—family? clan? tribe? "—people."

We hugged and said goodbye, but I needed time to think before going back home. I ended up at the park near school and sat on a bench. I was only wearing a cardigan and the air was cold, the sky darkening quickly. Purple-gray clouds churned like waves in the November ocean. I pulled the sweater close, wrapping my arms around my middle. I couldn't see anyone. Only a squirrel scavenging around the wastebasket.

"Hello, little *sinjaab*. You and I are the only lonely ones tonight. Everyone else is cozy at home, suffering from too much food. I wish I could give you the piecrust that's still sitting on my plate. Homemade. And a pecan, too. You would love it."

The squirrel sat up on its miniature back feet, turning its head this way and that, as if listening to my every word.

"You are so quiet and peaceful, little *sanjoob*. I wish I could be more like you—not always analyzing everything."

The squirrel noticed an acorn nearby and hopped off, snapping its thick tail. A gust of wind curled around me, sweeping a cluster of sad, brown leaves around my feet, the vivid colors of autumn long gone. I got up, suddenly frightened. I couldn't stay here anymore, but where could I go? I couldn't bring myself to go home and face them all at that moment. I wished I could go to Rebecca's, but of course she and her family were in Boston at her grandparents' house, and everyone else was having family time.

I walked past a small gazebo, peered into its shadowy interior. Inside was a small concrete table and two benches. It was dark and unwelcoming, reeked of urine. A cold shiver ran from my scalp to my feet. I wanted to run from this place, but I became aware of a faint sound of music in the distance growing louder. Voices. I suddenly felt isolated and terrified in the deserted park and I ducked inside the gazebo, gripping the concrete bench, keeping my head down. I lay there frozen, and out of nowhere, images of the young soldier who'd held me down rushed at me from the gloom of the gazebo, as if he was really there.

Then, laughter. A man's. Then a woman's. Closer now. Out of the opening in the gazebo from my lowered position I could see them. He, holding a boombox on his shoulder. She, moving to the sound of the music. Bumping into each other. When they passed, I stood up and ran out into the night toward home, the chill air causing a stabbing pain in my bad leg every time I came down on it. When I got home I would give apologies. I would tell them I'd gotten sick, needed to go to bed. I would deal with Momma in the morning, but I had the night to figure it out.

I lay in bed shivering, partly from the chill of the night, partly from the terror of my, *what*? Not a nightmare, because I was awake. Not just a memory either—it was too real for that. Delusion? Hallucination? Brian had told me about bad trips people had on LSD, where they were convinced something dreadful was really happening to them. I'd also heard about soldiers coming back from Vietnam and having nightmares, being plagued by bad memories. I hadn't been in combat exactly, but I'd lived through a war, experienced what people do and say under cover of war.

I thought about the little boy hit by a sniper bullet on Hamra Street, his wounded body on the pavement, his mother screaming, the sirens wailing. I knew it could easily have been me. I could have lain bleeding on the street while the crowd closed in, Layla screaming at me to open my eyes. It could have been any one of us, because in war you no longer matter. You're no longer a person, really. You're just an obstacle or an asset.

I put on a nightlight the way I had for months after the incident in Beirut, but I couldn't sleep anyway. Every little creak of the floorboards made me jump. The rushing sound in my head from my own blood pumping made me think of how we can die at any moment. Every time I started to drift, images of that day returned, jolting me awake again. I remembered how powerless I had felt, how vulnerable, held down by someone who didn't care at all how I was feeling, oblivious to my fear, to the fact that I might die of suffocation under his weight. I wondered if I would ever be free of these ghosts that I kept hidden inside, or if they would torment me forever.

It wasn't until the first hint of light snuck around the window shade that I finally slept. The last thing I remember thinking about was Jamal. We were so comfortable together, as if we'd known each other all our lives. I was sure I could say anything to him and he'd understand. But it mattered to me to have my family like him too, for Momma to like him. With Ra'ad and Brian I'd kept them as far away from my family as possible. But with Jamal it was different. It was *important*. Important enough that I needed them to accept him. I could almost hear Layla saying, *Relax, Noor. You're not marrying him. He's just a high school boyfriend after all. Stop taking it so seriously.* That comforted me and I finally drifted off.

Momma had the day after Thanksgiving off. She let me sleep in, but I sensed her opening the door once or twice and then quietly reclosing it. I knew she was worried about me, but angry, as well.

When I got up, she was reading the newspaper in the kitchen with a cup of milky Nescafe next to her. She had always loved the kitchen. Even in Beirut it was her favorite place in the house. This one wasn't as nice as our kitchen in Lebanon, but bigger than Antoine's, and it had a window overlooking a neat row of small garden plots that had been planted behind the attached brick apartment buildings neighboring ours. It had a big gas stove with a long, new Formica counter next to it, and a small table and chairs. It smelled of cardamom, cinnamon, and onions. She ignored me when I walked in, kept the newspaper in front of her face, noisily turning the pages.

"*Sabaah al-khayr, Momma.*"

"Morning." Her reply in English. Flat. "I hope you've slept off whatever was bothering you last night."

"Slept off? Actually, I didn't sleep until dawn." My voice harsher than I intended.

"All right, Noor," she said, clattering her coffee cup on the saucer. "What's going on?"

I knew I should apologize for being rude but I also wanted her to apologize, or at least to understand how I felt. Adrenaline rushed through me as I started to speak.

"Why did everyone treat my friend like that?"

"Like what?"

"Like he's the enemy. If I'd brought anyone else here it would have been a different story."

"I don't know what you're talking about. You invited him, he came, I welcomed him in, offered him dessert and then *you* decided to pout."

"Momma, that's not fair. The first second he walked in, everyone acted like Son of Sam had come in the house. You must have seen the looks on their faces just like I did, and then Antoine interrogating him. *Do your people hail from Sudan?*" I said, mocking Antoine's body language and accent.

"So you're blaming me for Antoine's behavior?

"No, but you know you were cool to him. It was so *obvious!*"

"What are you implying?"

"I'm saying y—your friends are racists."

Before I knew what was happening, my cheek was stinging and Momma was standing next to me, her open-palmed hand still next to my face and the newspaper in disarray on the floor. Momma never hit me and I put my hand to my burning cheek, suddenly full of shame. Although I hadn't quite included her in the accusation, it was implied. I had blurted out the most hurtful thing I could have, when really I had meant something a bit different.

"I'm sorry, Momma. I didn't mean it to come out like that."

"And how did you mean it?"

I took a moment to think through my answer this time. "I felt you didn't like him because he's Black. Because he's not like *us*."

To my surprise, Momma sat down at the table and took a slow sip of coffee, rested her chin on her knuckles, the two lines in her forehead deepening. The smell of coffee lingered in the air. The radiators in the apartment clanked like an angry symphony. I fidgeted with a napkin, glanced at her out of the corner of my eye.

"I hope you know how hard it is to have your own daughter suggest that you are a racist. It is something I hope you never experience."

I opened my mouth to answer, to deny that I'd called *her* a racist, but she held up her hand to quiet me.

"As a Palestinian, I've been fighting racist attitudes all my life, wherever I've lived. I'm still haunted by the memory of being kicked out of our family home by people who thought they had more of a right to it than we did. What kind of message do you think that sends to a child?"

"That they were better than you?"

"Not just better." Momma's eyes were full of fire. "That we were worthless. That our lives didn't count for anything, and that was reinforced when Baba died from asthma when we had to flee our land on foot. We were still miles from the Lebanese border."

My chest tightened.

"I've spent my whole adult life trying to remind myself that I—that *we*—do have value."

I wished I could tell her how I'd struggled after I was attacked—and still struggle every day—to believe in myself, but I couldn't bring myself to tell her, or anyone else, the truth about that day. I doubted I ever would.

"You have more value than most people will ever dream to have, Momma!" I surprised myself with this outburst. I don't think I even knew I felt this way about her before I said it.

"Really, *hayaati*? I'm not a terrible racist?" She let me sit with that before continuing. "Now I have something else to say. Maybe our society isn't the most tolerant. Maybe we do sometimes judge people unfairly even though we've suffered from being judged ourselves. Honestly, I don't think anyone—in any society—is really free from prejudice, including me. I mean in an unconscious way."

"That's what I was trying to say, but it came out wrong because I was upset."

"To be honest, I'm proud to have a daughter who cares enough to make me stop and think about the things that matter so much."

"Oh, Momma. I feel the same about you. I really do."

"When you brought Jamal home, what was really going through my head, was not *why is my daughter bringing home a Black boy?* It was more *why is my daughter bringing a boy home at all? Who is he? Is she dating him? More than dating him?* My mind was racing, and I admit, maybe it did make me a little anxious that he is Black. *And* I was confused by his name. Why an Arab name? So now you know my whole thought process. I'll leave the psychiatrist's fee on the table when we're done."

She closed her hand around mine.

"It means so much to me that you were honest, Momma, and talked to me about your feelings."

"Don't get used to it. It might be another ten or fifteen years before it happens again!"

We hugged and tears dribbled down my face.

"Now tell me the truth. Are you dating him? And why *does* he have an Arab name?"

"Can we talk about this later?"

"Fine. Just give me a yes or no answer to the first question. You can explain the rest after."

I wished I could have lied and said no, he was just a friend, but after she had been so honest with me, I'd never be able to live with myself.

"Yes, Momma, but don't worry, I only see him at school. And his parents are Black Muslims. It's a thing here. That's why they named him Jamal."

Momma didn't speak much about Jamal after that. She only asked two things of me. That I not be alone with him at his house and that I not sleep with him. The second was easy, because I knew I wasn't ready for that. *Momma!* I'd said, *I'm still in high school for god's sake.* As to not going to his house, I promised her not to, but I wasn't entirely sure I'd keep that promise.

My hope— unrealistic I know—was that Momma would give her blessing to the relationship, tell me that if it made me happy, then she was happy for me. She didn't, but she didn't forbid me from seeing him either, so that was something. Forbidding wasn't really her style, though. She relied more on guilttripping, and on *innuendo*, as Greg would say. And somehow those things hurt me more than outright refusal. It was as if she was leaving it up to me to do the "right" thing. As rebellious as I had been since we'd been in America I was surprised by how much Momma's approval meant to me now.

I was a bit shy about approaching Jamal after that. For sure I was upset about what happened at Thanksgiving and I wanted to be certain he knew how sorry I was, but how could I explain to him that my family's acceptance was also important to me—because *he* was important to me? I knew I couldn't say that to him yet, though. At least not in so many words. I remembered Samantha saying Brian broke up with me because it was *getting too heavy*, and that had stuck with me. The last thing I needed was for Jamal to feel *our* relationship was getting too heavy.

I wished I could talk to Layla. She understood me better than anyone. She was the one I could talk to about anything. I wouldn't even have minded if she acted older and wiser, as she always had, because just then I needed that—needed someone who could be more objective than I could be at the moment. It made me ache, thinking about lying on my bed with her, putting on makeup and talking about boys. I missed her so much, I wished I could get on the next plane to Beirut. I couldn't call her because it would cost too much, and even if I could get a phone line—which was doubtful—I wouldn't want Momma to hear me talking about Jamal, so I called another good friend instead.

"Rebecca? How was your Thanksgiving? I'm so jealous you got to go to Boston."

"It was nice, except for the usual *dynamics*." I could imagine Rebecca gesticulating for emphasis as she said this. "How was yours?"

"It was a *disaster*."

"Why? What happened, Noor?"

"I was stupid enough to invite Jamal."

"Why stupid?"

"Long story, but they all treated him like an outsider, and I ended up having an argument with my mom afterwards."

"I go away for two days and your whole life falls apart?"

"Exactly. Hey, I can only talk for a minute while Momma's in the shower. Can we meet up?"

I hadn't talked to Rebecca or the others much that fall, because I'd been so involved with committee work. I knew Maria and Alex had broken up, and I'd talked briefly to Maria about it, but I didn't know all the details. In truth, I'd been so busy with my own problems that I'd avoided theirs. But it was sad that there was no more posse. They had been there for me through *thick and thin*, as Americans like to say, through all my bad decisions, dramas, accidents, even when I ignored them to be with Brian. But they were also there to talk about life, love, take walks, give hugs. And it all fell apart over a breakup.

If romantic relationships caused such misery, maybe it was best to avoid them in the first place. That was my mindset when I went to meet Rebecca. If I'd never met Brian, I wouldn't have had the accident. If Jamal and I had remained just good friends, maybe I could have spared him being humiliated. If Maria and Alex hadn't gone out, there'd still be a posse.

Rebecca ran towards me, her mess of tangled hair flying. She picked me up and twirled me around. Just like old times. Minus Greg and Alex and Maria. Still, that hug filled me up and made me want to laugh and shout and dance and cry. She smelled of the Herbal Essence shampoo and sandalwood that had become so familiar to me since we'd been friends.

"I love you, Rebecca!"

"I love you, too, girl! I missed you."

"I miss *you*. And everyone. And every*thing*," I said.

"Me, too, but life will limp along somehow."

I hugged her again. "For sure it will. But it's still sad."

I thought of Beirut and how people carried on the best they could even with a war disrupting every aspect of life.

Rebecca had suggested meeting at the graveyard *for old times' sake*. The air felt more like late December than late November and the sun kept sliding under the clouds, making it feel even colder. I put up the hood of my winter coat and looped my arm around Rebecca's. Brown leaves had been raked into piles, pushed to the side—forgotten and ignored—like the graves that no one put flowers on any more. It made me so sad I almost told Rebecca I wanted to leave, but it seemed to fit my mood, so I clung to her, as we strolled through the alleys and lanes of the dead.

Rebecca squeezed my arm close to her side. "So, what's going on?"

I sighed. "It's complicated. When my mom and I first got to New York, I would've happily taken the first plane right back to Lebanon if I could have. But now everything is different. I miss Baba and my friends and being home, but New York is home, too. I have you and my other friends—and Jamal. When I first knew him I thought it was just a crush. I had no idea how much I'd come to care for him."

"So far so good," she said. "I'm pretty sure he feels the same."

"I know, but I'm so ashamed of how they treated him. It's bad enough that he's had to live with discrimination all his life. How could I ever take him back home—or even face him after this?

"But it's not your fault."

"I invited him over even though I knew it was risky."

"I doubt he blames you, Noor. You were trying to do something nice."

"I know."

"And by the way, was it your mother or other people?"

"Honestly, mostly Antoine. But you could tell Momma and the others didn't really approve."

"Hah! That reminds me of the one and only time I took Alex to my house."

I stopped walking. "Alex?"

"Yup. I went out with him for a couple months Freshman year. After we broke up he ended up going out with Maria. That's how I first met her."

"*Wallah*? I mean really?"

"One day I brought him over to "do homework" together but Mom figured it out immediately. She didn't kick him out but she gave him a good dose of the silent treatment."

"But why?" I asked.

"Because he's a *goy*! A non-Jew. My parents would never admit to thinking that way, but deep down they do. She never brought it up with me, but I never brought him home again, either. Dad is always joking about me going to college and meeting a nice Jewish boy—preferably one who's on track to be a lawyer or doctor."

"Exactly! Actually, I think my parents would secretly like me to marry a professor—and definitely an Arab. But just like you, they would never admit it because they're too liberal."

"Maybe all parents are the same, the world over," Rebecca said.

"Except the ones who don't pay attention to what their kids are doing. So I guess we're the lucky ones. At least they care, even if they are misguided!"

Rebecca held my hand, the way friends do in Lebanon. I'd missed that.

"There's one more thing," I said. Jamal is such a great guy, but—"

"But?"

"I don't know. Did you ever feel like you just want someone to be stronger? More—what is the right word—*assertive*?"

"Well, I know what you mean," she said, "but Alex is the exact opposite. He was so assertive I used to have to remember to stick up for myself or I'd get my socks knocked off. Honestly, it's one reason we broke up. He didn't really pay that much attention to what *I* wanted. That's why Maria broke up with him too. He started pressuring her to sleep with him even though she kept saying no. Even though he knows she's Catholic—not a very committed one, but still, she feels very conflicted about abortion and she's even a bit traditional when it comes to sex before marriage and birth control, stuff like that."

"That's terrible about Alex. I don't think Jamal would ever do that."

"Exactly," she said. So where's the problem?"

"I don't know." I hesitated. "Remember the time I told you about those kids who cornered me and called me a "camel jockey" and Jamal came to the rescue?"

"Yeah?"

"And he outsmarted them by saying *Jesus was a "camel jockey" too.*"

"That was a stroke of *genius.*"

"I know, I know," I said, aware of my cheeks reddening. "But there was part of me that wished he'd confronted them somehow. Maybe it's because of the war, but back home we're all so assertive and argumentative about everything." I smiled thinking about it. "Sometimes Jamal just seems so passive to me."

"So what—you wanted him to get in a fight with them?"

"Well no—of course not."

Rebecca grabbed her beret as a wind gust threatened to carry it away. "Have you ever heard the expression *the grass is always greener on the other side?*"

"That's a good one!"

"And *you've* got a good one. Now go get him, girl!"

I knew I had to have a talk with Jamal, tell him at least some of what was on my mind. I hadn't seen him or called him over the weekend and I didn't want him to think I was avoiding him. I just needed time to think. He must have come in late Monday because I didn't see him in homeroom, so in the afternoon I went to find him. I checked all the familiar places— outside the cafeteria, at his locker, in front of the school. Each time I approached a new place, my heart raced with excitement, even though I tried to stay cool. Finally, I decided to check the gym steps at the back of the building, where we sometimes met.

As I approached, I recognized his shape, the soft afro, the relaxed way he stood. I smiled. I was about to call his name, when I saw someone approach him. A girl. I could see she was Black, too, slim and feminine. She was wearing a wide-legged, yellow pantsuit and she walked toward him, rocking from side to side, arms spread wide. I ducked behind one of the pine trees that grew along the side the building. He grabbed her and lifted her up in the air, then let her slide back to the ground, kissed her nose.

I felt like my heart was bursting. I walked away as fast as I could, trying to make sense of what I'd seen. I'd been upset the last time I saw him, but not at him. Could he have felt insulted and even angry because I didn't stand up for him at Thanksgiving? Maybe it made him question if it's too difficult to manage a cross-cultural relationship. But start a new relationship or rekindle an old one so soon? That didn't seem like Jamal. I didn't know what to make of it.

I'd often wondered why he didn't have a Black girlfriend, and now I was miserable at the thought that he might. I remembered how left out he'd felt when I talked about wanting to be with other Arabs; remembered, too, what Angel had said about Black power, how annoyed she was at Tim for trying to be "more Black than Eldridge Cleaver." How she had called me Jamal's "white girlfriend." Maybe he'd decided that Angel was right. I couldn't get these thoughts and images out of my head and I started to breathe so fast I couldn't catch my breath.

The next thing I knew, I opened my eyes and I saw an older woman standing over me.

"What happened, dear?" she said, reaching down, helping me to my feet.

"I think I must have fainted."

"I'll wait here until you feel better. I'll call you a cab."

"No, no. You're so kind, but I'm close to home."

She put both her hands on my cheeks the way Baba's mother—my tata—used to. "You're burning up," she said and I burst out crying.

"I'm so sorry," I said, wiping my tears. "and so embarrassed."

"No need for apologies, dear. We all have bad days. Now, no argument. Just wait one minute while I hail a taxi."

When it arrived, I sat in the back and waved goodbye to this woman whose name I didn't know, overcome by sadness, as if I'd known her all my life, as if she was Momma and Janine, my aunties, and Tata, there to comfort me when I needed them most.

For a few days after that, I buried myself in my studies, and it felt good to be using my head for something other than going over and over all the negative thoughts that kept flooding in. I decided to take a break from

GSAA and turn into a hermit, secluded in my room when I was home, a book in my hands. I would put a cassette into the player, the music acting as a kind of hypnosis. One afternoon, when I was hibernating like this, and Momma was still at work, the phone rang.

I was too nervous to speak when I answered and heard Jamal's voice.

"How are you, Noor?"

"I'm OK."

"You don't sound OK."

"I'm fine," I said.

"Noor I know you were upset on Thanksgiving, but it seems like you're upset with *me*."

"It's not that." I hesitated. "I saw you with that girl."

Silence. I pictured Jamal with one hand deep in his pocket, pacing, the phone cord stretching behind him. It was raining and with only my desk light on, the apartment seemed dismal, the smell of last night's dinner lingering disagreeably.

"What girl? When?"

"Monday. At the gym steps."

"That was Aisha!"

As if that explained everything.

"My *sister*."

Now it was my turn to be silent, taking a moment to process. When I did, I was so embarrassed I just stood with my hand over my mouth. Finally, he spoke again.

"I can't believe you thought I'd go with someone else. It seems you don't know me at all!"

"But it really *looked* that way.

"Noor, we need to talk. Could we meet for coffee?

Morrie and Minna's Soda Fountain—or, M&M's as Jamal called it— was about halfway between our houses. Their doughnuts and coffee were way better than Chock Full O' Nuts, and Morrie and Minna didn't care if you hung around *as long as you're a paying customer*, as Morrie had said, leaning over the counter with a hairy arm to pass us our doughnuts—Jamal, a chocolate covered one, and me, a plain cake cruller.

I loved the swiveling stools at the counter with their red leather seats, but today we sat at a small table at the back of the shop, hoping for a little privacy. Even then, a couple times I noticed Minna lingering at nearby tables, rag in hand, well after they were wiped clean. It reminded me of back home, how you never really have any privacy. Everyone is your aunt or uncle and they don't see why you'd want to keep anything from them, for any reason, ever.

Jamal leaned across the table and spoke in a low voice. "Noor, I need you to know that as long we're together I will never go with someone else."

"That means so much to me and I promise the same thing to you. But when I saw you with Aisha—and I didn't know who she was—my mind was racing, to be honest. I couldn't help wondering if the Thanksgiving disaster made you think it couldn't work between us, if that's how you'd be treated in my home. I felt so guilty and responsible."

"But that's your family, not you. I would never judge you based on their behavior."

"I was so frustrated that night I admit that one part of me wished you had stood up to them, told them what you *really* thought instead of being so polite. I should have done that, too."

"If you want us to be together you have to accept me for who I am, even if you don't always like it. Just the way I accept you, even when I get annoyed."

"You get annoyed at me?"

"Oh because Noor is perfect. What could possibly bother me?"

"Well, what could?"

Minna had gone to wait on a group of customers who came in, and now the smells of hamburgers and French fries mixed with the dark aroma of brewing coffee.

"Sometimes all you seem to care about is meetings and organizing and homework."

"I thought you liked that."

"I *do*. I love that you're so passionate about everything, but sometimes I feel like you don't have time for *us*."

I had to stop and think what he meant. I knew I had a tendency to throw myself completely into things that mattered to me, but I thought I was like that with our relationship too.

"It's just that I care so much. Especially with something as important as the South Africa work. I thought you felt the same."

"Of course I do, but *we're* important too, and it seems like sometimes you forget that."

I sighed. "Maybe it's coming from a war zone. Or maybe it's just who I am."

"Or some of each?"

"Probably. Back home your choices could mean the difference between life and death. Sometimes I just feel so responsible for everything."

"I can dig it, I really can. I'm just saying there should be a balance."

"So what do we do?"

"I'm not sure, but I bet the chocolate milkshakes those guys just got are delicious."

I turned around as they were being set down at a table up front.

"Wanna share one?" Jamal said, snapping his eyebrows up.

"Ice cream in December?"

"You should talk. Drinking hot tea in the desert."

"There's no desert in Lebanon, Jamal!" I said, indignant.

"I know, I know. Anyway, do you want one or not?"

"Sure—coffee ice cream and chocolate syrup."

"OK, boss."

"I'm not bossy! Well, maybe I am just a little. Fine. You order."

Jamal ordered a coffee milkshake with chocolate syrup and I grinned at him.

"Happy, your majesty?"

"Sure, but you still didn't answer my question."

"Which one?"

"What do we do?"

"Keep doing what we've been doing?"

"But all these things you don't like…"

"It's not *all these things*, Noor. It doesn't mean I don't want to be with you, but maybe my faults *are* a big deal to you."

I thought about Momma and her reluctance about Jamal, how disappointed I'd felt, but sitting there with Jamal I realized that maybe it was OK. After all, she'd accepted that I keep seeing him, just on certain terms. And I had no idea what the future would bring. Maybe next year I'd be in Lebanon, so why not just enjoy being with him while I could? Again I thought of Layla. *Relax, Noor.* I reached across the table and cupped my hands over his.

20.

Not long after I met Jamal at Morrie and Minna's, Momma took me Christmas shopping in Manhattan. As we walked along Fifth Avenue, big, dry snowflakes started to fall, swirling silently at our feet like fog, gathering on trees and light posts, on our hair and our shoulders. Christmas lights and angels, stars and Santas, wound around trees and stretched across streets. Department store windows were framed in tinsel and red velvet, cotton-snow blanketing miniature landscapes, golden bells tilted in mid-ring. I felt a thrill of cold and excitement and I grabbed Momma's arm and kissed her cheek. After all our ups and downs, it was nice just to be happy in her company. We bought scarves, colognes, and handbags to send to Lebanon with Salwa and Farah, who were going home for the holidays. I dragged Momma to the window of Saks Fifth Avenue to look at a pair of shoes. They were burgundy-colored suede with a three-inch heel.

"They'd be perfect for the holiday dance!"

I wasn't even sure I was going, but the shoes were so beautiful. I gasped when I saw the price tag. "OK, *khalas*, never mind."

I tugged at Momma's arm. "Let's go have coffee in the Village on the way home." In that moment, I felt like the little girl I was before the war in Lebanon—before *everything*—when I loved Momma completely, loved to stroke the soft skin under her arm, loved to listen to her voice when she read to me.

"Say yes."

I could see the pleasure in her face. So much of the time since we left Lebanon I had kept myself distant, blaming her and picking fights, but on this day I let myself feel all of the old warmth.

"Yes, *hayaati*—let's go, why not?"

Momma's eyes were watery as she reached out and touched my frozen cheek with her gloved hand for just a second before bending down to gather up our bags filled with gold-and silver-wrapped boxes, tied with huge red and green velvet ribbons.

We caught the D train to Greenwich Village. I'd always loved the Village—even the names thrilled me. Bleecker and MacDougal Streets. Le Figaro and Dante Cafe, with their heavy wood bars and smoky air. We decided on Caffe Reggio, brushing snow off our coats and settling into a small marble table in the corner of the dark café near the old-fashioned espresso maker.

While we were sipping our cappuccinos, Momma leaned forward, the lines in her brow deepening for a second. "I have something I need to say to you."

She set down her cup and leaned back in the chair, rubbing her knuckles with her thumb. I had a feeling this was about Jamal.

"Of course you know I want you to be happy, Noor, but…"

The noise from the espresso machine almost swallowed her voice. I turned to watch the handsome barista, the brisk grace of his hands as he steamed milk and brewed coffee, letting it drip into tiny cups, then slid the steaming espressos and cappuccinos across the counter for the waitress to pick up.

I was dreading what would follow the *'but.'* I couldn't believe she might spoil this moment, with the smell of coffee in the air, snow piling up in slanting drifts outside the window, the lingering feeling of Momma's hand—warm against my cheek.

"Noor?"

"*Na'am?*"

That quick frown again.

"I just can't help worrying."

"Worrying about *what?*"

"I know how much you like Jamal, but you have to be careful he doesn't take advantage of you. Not just him—any boy."

I rested my forehead on my hand, thinking what I would never say aloud. *Where were you when I had my first boyfriend at fourteen, and the two more since then? Where were you when I was held down by that militiaman? Where were you when I went back to Brian like a zombie?*

"I'm not a child anymore. I can take care of myself."

She smiled and put her hand on top of mine. "Of course you can, *habeebti*. It's just that I was hoping that when you got interested in boys, it would be somehow *different*."

I pulled my hand away. "What do you mean, different? Because he's not Arab? Because he's American? I really hope you don't mean because he's Black."

I paused, feeling the old potion rising up—one part of me badly wanting to avoid a confrontation, the other part indignant. I cracked my neck and Momma winced like she always did.

"We've already had this conversation, and anyway, I don't care about such things anymore. He is nice to me, he cares about real things and that's what matters to me."

"My daughter is becoming a real American now." Her eyes softened. "But I know you miss Lebanon, *habeebti*. I do, too."

Why was she saying this now?

"I never wanted to leave in the first place, but now that I am here I'm trying to *be* here."

Momma pulled her slim frame upright. There was classical music playing and I felt as if we'd been transported to Europe. I *wished* something would transport me at that moment.

"Yes, but America or no America, you are still an Arab girl. Here they do what they want before marriage, but we are different. Just don't be in a hurry."

"I don't know why we're talking about this again, but since you brought it up, here's what I think. I'm not in a hurry, but it's not just because I'm Arab, or a girl, or Muslim, or Lebanese, or Palestinian—or any of that! It's because I'm not ready."

I let out my breath and softened my voice. "Because *I'm* not ready, Momma. Can't you see?" I paused and fixed my eyes on hers. "Don't worry. I won't do anything foolish, but I really do like him a lot."

Momma sipped her coffee. "You are young, *habeebti*. So young. But you are strong and smart and I know you'll be fine."

I was disappointed she didn't ask me more about Jamal, ask why I cared so much for him, but at least it was a start. The conversation unsettled me, though, left me feeling somehow alone. Society puts so much pressure on us to behave a certain way—to be that "good girl" who doesn't see boys alone, doesn't have sex before marriage, marries the *right* guy—meaning the one your family approves of. And of course, how we dress and behave is under the microscope—and it's not just our society—it seems it's every society. It makes it so hard to figure out for yourself what kind of person you want to be, who you want to be with, how you want to be with them. At the same time, it was important to me that my family accept and respect my choices. I couldn't help wondering what would happen if Jamal and I somehow found a way to be together in the future. What if my parents didn't accept him? What if I was forced to choose between him and them—what would I do?

For Christmas, Momma surprised me with the burgundy heels we saw in the window of Saks that snowy night and also an album of Marcel Khalife singing and playing the ʿoud. My friends and I had mostly listened to rock music and western pop when I was younger, but now I found myself playing the album all the time. Marcel's soulful voice tugged at me, as if drawing me into a secret passage back home, stirring up my longing, my memories. Sometimes it made me happy, but other times it triggered intense images of war—ones that I thought were buried or forgotten. I thought it was strange that although Momma had made me leave Lebanon, now she gave me something that made me yearn for it all again. I took down the big brass key to our lost home in Shefa ʿAmr that hung from a nail in the wall of my bedroom. I clasped it in my hand, eyes closed, listening to Marcel.

I didn't tell Momma that Jamal's parents were flying to Montreal over Christmas break to visit friends. I didn't want her to know he would be on his own for two days.

As soon as their taxi sped off toward the airport he called me. "Meet me at 10:00 in front of M&M's," he whispered as if we were in a conspiracy, which, in a way, I suppose we were.

Momma came into the living room, fragrant from showering, twisting her damp hair in a towel. "Who is calling so early in the morning?"

"Just one of those stupid sales calls," I said, the lie catching in my throat, like dust.

"*Tcchh*, typical. What are you up to today, *habeebti*?" she said cheerfully, oblivious to how the words *up to* rang in my head like an accusation. I thought about telling her I was meeting Jamal for a cup of coffee, but decided to avoid the inevitable discussion that would follow.

"Probably just reading," I said. "It's too cold to go out anyway," I added, unnecessarily.

"Good idea, 'ayni, it really is freezing! Since you'll be here, you won't mind preparing the green beans and carrots for yakhneh, then. I'll do the rest when I get home."

"Sh-sure."

"That's a good girl. And fold the laundry when it comes out of the dryer too, ya shaatra."

My annoyance must have showed and she seemed startled.

"We are on our own, Noor and I'm going to work. You have to do your share—especially when you're not in school!"

"I didn't say anything, did I?"

The opportunity to spend the day with Jamal was ebbing away like the tide, with each new chore she listed. It was almost as if she could read my mind. But I dutifully kissed her goodbye as she went out the door and rushed to get dressed, not wanting to lose another minute until I would see Jamal.

I stood under the *Morrie and Minna's Soda Fountain* sign, anonymous in my ugly down-filled parka, the fur-trimmed hood pulled tight around my face. I tucked my hands into my pockets, since they were numb, even through the thick wool of the Guatemalan gloves Rebecca had gotten me for Christmas from a street vendor.

Baba would die here with this cold! I thought, as I kicked at a gray-frosted chunk of snow at the edge of the sidewalk.

He was only five minutes late, but by that time I was freezing.

Jamal rubbed his hands vigorously on my back to warm me up. "Sorry!"

"It's OK, habeebi," I said, embarrassing myself by using this word I'd never said to him before.

"What's habeebi mean?" Jamal said, messing up the "h" sound.

"You have to say the h sound in your throat, like you're breathing out fire."

"That sounds good on a day like today, but you still didn't tell me what it means. Yalla!" he added, urging me on, using one of the few Arabic words he'd learned.

I was too embarrassed to tell him it really means "my love," so I just told him it's something you say to a good friend. "*Ya'ni*, kind of like *honey* or *dear*."

"OK, *dear*. We'd better figure out what to do before my hair turns into, y'know, ice dreadlocks!"

We sat at our favorite table at the back of Morrie and Minna's. Jamal got coffee and I ordered tea. They brought it to me with two sugar cubes on the saucer. The sweet black tea reminded me of home, except it was in a cup instead of a glass. I remembered one of the last mornings we spent with Baba, when my parents made a typical Lebanese breakfast with cheeses, *labneh*, olives, a little *za'tar* in oil, fruit preserves, Arabic bread heated over the gas flame until it puffed up, and strong, sweet black tea in little gold-rimmed glasses set on matching saucers. Even when the weather was hot, we drank our tea steaming, drawing air over the surface of the liquid as we sipped it, to cool it slightly before swallowing. *In the desert*, as Jamal had said.

"What's on the agenda, *Venda*?" Jamal asked, interrupting my memory.

"Venda?"

"Hmm, OK, what's the plan, wo-*man*?"

"Always joking!"

"Isn't it better than always frowning? Like Ms. Haggard?"

"Oh!" I shuddered. "Yes, when you put it like that, but I have no idea what to do. I guess we could stay here where it's warm."

"What if we go to my house?"

I looked at him skeptically.

"I just meant we could have lunch there. My parents made me all this food before they left. They think I'll starve if they don't."

"Hah! And maybe you would."

"Not me. I'd eat grubs and leaves to keep from starving."

"Ekkh. Shut *up*!"

"Mmm, grubs," Jamal teased, eating yellow custard from the doughnut he'd ordered.

I was avoiding answering him because I wasn't sure what to do. On the one hand, it was a chance to be truly alone for the first time. On the other hand, I couldn't help thinking of Momma and the promises she coaxed from me when we talked about Jamal that day. And I'd have to be back in a few hours to do all my chores anyway. In the end, I decided that actually, this would make it possible, because I'd have the excuse that I could only stay a little while and still get back home in time to do them. Somehow I convinced myself that this made it less of a crime and more of a misdemeanor—and I'd certainly committed plenty of those in my life already.

"Sure," I said, trying to act casual.

Jamal's apartment had a long corridor with African masks and brightly colored Nicaraguan paintings on the walls. He led me to the kitchen, which was full of enticing smells of garlic and a fragrant mix of spices I didn't recognize. He offered to warm up some food, but I was suddenly nervous and couldn't imagine eating, so I said I wasn't hungry. He told me he wasn't either, which was probably a lie. We went into the living room and he clicked the button on the cassette player and sat down on the sofa. Sun was streaming in through the oak-framed window. I sat next to him and folded my hands in my lap. Woven baskets and ceramics decorated the walls and there was a colorful tribal rug on the floor. Something about the apartment reminded me of our house in Beirut, which Momma and Baba had decorated with original drawings and some very old Middle Eastern handcrafts and carpets.

Jamal kicked off his sneakers. "You ok?"

"Sure. Why?"

He kissed my forehead. "Maybe it's the way you're sitting on the edge of the sofa with your hands folded?"

"OK, I guess I *am* a little nervous."

"*I* make you nervous?"

"Not *you*. The situation. If Momma knew I was here she'd kill me."

"But how would she know?"

"She made me promise not to be alone with you. I mean not *you*, but *ya'ni*, any boy."

"Do you want to leave?"

Just his offering this made me feel better, made me want to stay, actually. I could see he was confused and I was confused too. There were so many times I had done things Momma didn't want me to do, but this seemed to matter more.

I touched his hand. "I love this music. What is it?"

"Al Green. "Let's Stay Together." I mean, that's the name of the song."

Jamal's expression became suddenly serious, contemplative.

"Is this the first time you've been alone—," he hesitated, "—with a guy?"

"No," I said, blushing. I felt like whatever I said was the wrong thing.

"You don't have to tell me if you don't want to."

"It's the first time I've been alone at *home* with a boy, but, *ya 'ni*, I had a boyfriend in Lebanon and one time he took me to this abandoned building."

"Were you nervous then?"

"Yes! Suddenly he was all over me and I had to make him stop."

"Well, scouts honor." He held up two fingers. "That will never happen with me."

I touched his hand. "Honestly, Jamal? Before I knew you, I started thinking all guys were jerks. Sorry, but it's true."

"Did you have other bad experiences?"

I opened my mouth to say *no* but I suddenly started crying. It was as if Jamal's question flipped a switch inside me and I couldn't stop. He put his arms around me and didn't say anything, just stroked my head gently.

When I'd stopped sobbing, he put both hands on my shoulders. "Don't go away! I'll get some tissues."

I tried to smile, dabbing at my cheeks and eyes with the sleeve of my sweater. After I'd used a pile of tissues and drunk the water Jamal brought me, I rested my head on his shoulder.

"Do you want to talk about it?"

Even though I had decided never to tell anyone about my experience in downtown Beirut, it just poured out of me, like the tears had. I told him everything. How bored we were staying at home those days. How Layla had convinced me to go out. How we got lost and ended up near the chaos of the front lines. Me snapping one picture after another of bullet-scarred hotels and buildings, feeling invincible, young men firing RPGs and rifles in every direction, the rooftop sniper with the binoculars. Layla panicking and running away. Me following, tripping on a piece of rubble. Being grabbed, pinned down, suffocated by a young man barely older than me. The panic and confusion I felt afterwards. Jumping and screaming with every sudden sound. Fearing every man who spoke to me. Falling into a tunnel of fear with every mortar blast or gunshot. Resenting Momma for taking me away, but resenting her for not protecting me, too.

How could I be saying all of this to a boy I was just getting to know?

I was sure he'd run the other way as quickly as possible—and maybe he'd think that what happened to me was nothing—I hadn't been raped, after all. I couldn't imagine he'd be able to understand why it left such a deep scar in me.

"I can't believe that happened to you, Noor. Damn. I wish I could get a time machine and go back there with you and shoot that motherfucker. Oops. Sorry."

I couldn't help smiling. I touched his lips.

Jamal folded me in his arms and I relaxed against his chest, the rhythmic beating of his heart and warmth of his breath against my head calming me until I felt like I was melting into him, the mellow sounds of Al Green lulling me.

A church bell ringing nearby jolted me back to reality and I jumped up, startling Jamal. "I have to go! I promised Momma I'd start dinner before she gets home."

"C'mon, I'll walk you."

We were quiet most of the way back to my building, but as we rounded the corner to my street he stopped. "Hey, before the vacation is over we should do something fun."

"You don't think it's fun sitting around listening to my past traumas, *Dr. Ahmed?*"

"It's totally cool, Ms. H-H. Any time. But, there's this *outasite* gig that happens at the Village Gate called "Salsa Meets Jazz." Do you like jazz?"

"Sure." In truth, I really wasn't sure.

"There's these two dynamite musicians playing together Saturday night. Dizzy Gillespie and Tito Puente. I think my mom and dad are going. Would you go with me? You could even ask your mom to come if you want."

"I can do things without her watching over me."

"Are you sure?"

"Yes! But anyway, I'll let you know if I can go."

Jamal was right. The evening was *dynamite*, as he'd said. I'd never experienced anything like it. Seeing these thrilling musicians at a little club in the Village for a few dollars. I actually asked Momma, but she said no, she was tired—but I knew it made her feel better that Jamal's parents were there.

As I was dressing to go, it occurred to me that this was the first real date I had ever been on and even Momma was fine with it, especially knowing that Jamal's parents would be there. I didn't really know what people wore at a jazz club, so I put on my dressiest pair of brown flared pants and a nice sweater, along with my favorite hoop earrings. I was tempted to wear the burgundy heels, but I was afraid they would be too much, especially with my limp and most sidewalks still packed with snow and ice, so I ended up wearing a pair of tan boots with chunky heels. The outfit turned out to be perfect.

Jamal and I sat at a table by ourselves, but not before he introduced me to his parents. His father was wearing a white skullcap like the Druze in Lebanon wear and his mother was wearing a simple headscarf. I had kind of forgotten they were Muslims, and it made me feel happy, like they were somehow familiar even though they weren't Arab. I automatically reached out to kiss his mother on both cheeks and she kissed me back, but a little awkwardly, like she wasn't expecting it.

His father was on the other side of the cocktail table and he put his hand to his chest and said, "*As-salaamu 'alaykum.*"

Now *I* was the one not expecting it. I hadn't ever heard the traditional Muslim greeting come out of an American's mouth before and it made me smile. I couldn't figure out if he was avoiding shaking hands with me because of religion or if it was just a bit far to reach, but it didn't bother me.

"*Wa-'alaykumu as-saalam.* I'm so happy to meet you both. Thank you for inviting me."

"Oh, no," his father said, in the deep voice I recognized from the phone. "Jamal is inviting you. He's the one who bought the ticket. We're just bystanders," he added with a smile that seemed to light up his whole face. "You're in for a real treat tonight, my dear, especially if you've never heard these characters before."

Mr. Ahmed was right. The whole evening was a treat. Sitting at the little table next to Jamal, drinking our Cokes from nice glasses, our arms bumping from time to time, the passion of both musicians and the playful way they blended their styles. It felt like an experience I would tell my children and grandchildren about one day.

Jamal and me. Dizzy Gillespie and Tito Puente at the Village Gate. What else can I say?

Shiti

Spring 1978

21.

Junior year was flying by. Momma and I hadn't spoken in a long time about going home. It seemed that we were both getting used to our life in New York and there were so many uncertainties about going back—what it would be like returning to a war-ravaged Beirut, whether we would find it hard to live there after being away from the stress and hardship for two years. And maybe I would miss Jamal too much if I left. We had such a good time together and he understood me in a way I don't think anyone else in the world could, even Layla, because he understood both the old and the new Noor. On top of all of that, Momma had finally secured a really good job in New York.

I'd started thinking that maybe I should finish high school at Graves and then go home for college for sure. Just one more year. Momma and I decided to call Baba to discuss it.

"I don't know what to think," Baba said. "Is my family abandoning me?"

I felt a terrible pang in my heart, because that really was how it seemed. We had been apart all this time and now we might stay away another year.

"Oh, Baba, please don't say that. You know it's not true."

"Just joking, Najnouj."

"What if we come spend the whole summer in Lebanon and then next Christmas break you come stay with us here? And then, *khalas*, the year will be over before we know it!"

"Great idea, Noor," Momma said, taking the phone from me. "What do you think, Rasheed?"

I put my ear next to the receiver so I could hear Baba's voice.

"Honestly it's a clever idea. Nothing would make me happier, but how can you leave your job for the whole summer?"

"I'll talk to them and we'll call again soon."

Momma opened the discussion with her boss and he was open to the idea of her being gone for at least a month, maybe more. *Dar al-ʿArabi* had a small office in Beirut and they had a Telex machine, which she could use to send her edits back and forth, since her work was really all on paper, anyway. She said that even if she couldn't stay the whole summer, there was no reason I couldn't. I was really excited about going back, seeing Baba and Layla and all my friends again, seeing our old house and the sea and all the smells and sights that had begun to fade in my memory. It was already the beginning of March, so it would be only a few months more. I imagined myself in the airplane, flying low over the city, seeing the mountains to one side, the Mediterranean to the other, the blocky buildings of Beirut in between.

I'd never call myself superstitious, but I'd started to think that whenever things were going really well for me and I dared to be happy, something would happen. So, in mid-March when I heard the news from Momma that Israel had invaded South Lebanon, where Baba is from, I cried most of the night. In the morning my eyes were so swollen I stayed home from school. I dreaded what this meant for our country, but also for the summer visit.

"Could it be any worse than what you already lived through?" Rebecca said.

I thought carefully before answering. "Probably not, but whether Momma will allow us to still go is another question."

I sighed and linked arms with her as we walked to Physics together. My leg was acting up from the cold and I leaned against her.

"Not to mention, we have been away so long, we're not used to guns and bombs anymore."

"Kinda nuts to think you ever *were* used to it."

"True, but I think we are somehow proud of being resilient and tough. We duck when the shells are flying and when they stop we smooth our clothes and keep moving along."

Rebecca pulled me close to her side. "You're a trip, girl. I don't think I'll ever have another friend as outasite as you!"

"You're more out of sight. I'm so lucky to have you too."

"OK, OK, enough of the mutual admiration society. Let's change the subject before we both float away in a cloud of rainbows and fairy dust."

"OK, let's talk about who'll get a better grade on the Physics test."

"That's easy. You'll win hands down. Let's talk about boys instead."

Unfortunately, my predictions came true. No one knew just how long the invasion would last or what the repercussions would be afterwards and Momma said the situation was too volatile and unpredictable for us to go.

It is the things we have the least control over that make us the angriest. If I got a bad grade I knew it was my own fault for not working hard enough. If I was annoyed with Jamal, we might argue, but we'd figure it out in the end. Even the car accident. It wasn't exactly my fault, but I knew deep inside I should never have gotten into that car—that I had a *choice*.

But a foreign army invading my country, another occupying it, macho men in Jeeps, careening through town with rifles aimed, militiamen kidnapping innocent people at checkpoints, rival militias competing to cause the most destruction in each other's neighborhoods—*these* I had no control over.

Then there was Momma. I had convinced myself that she couldn't really control me; that when I was out in the world I could do what I wanted and she couldn't do anything about it. But the truth I had to face over the next weeks until school ended is that without her I'd have nowhere to live, no way to get food or clothing. Worst of all, I couldn't go back home to Lebanon unless she agreed. How was I going to pick up the phone and call Lufthansa or Air France and order a ticket with the hundred and twenty dollars I had managed to save up?

I spent a lot of time imagining how I would convince Momma to change her mind, or how to persuade Baba to send me a plane ticket. Or just run away. I remembered how I'd fantasized in Lebanon about running away from home and living in a refugee camp. I knew it was childish, but it made me feel less helpless imagining that I could run free and take charge of my own life.

22.

The last day of school it rained hard. I cleared out my locker and said goodbye to classmates and teachers. I had forgotten my umbrella and as I stepped outside, a bolt of lightning streaked through the sky—a vast white nerve cluster with jagged branches reaching in all directions. I saw Jamal's old VW Bug coming down the street with headlights on. He flashed the high beams and I made a run for it, trying to hold on to all my notebooks and papers. I ran to the street, landing right in a river of water that had formed in the gutter. When I got in the car my feet squished around in my shoes and goose bumps gathered on my skin. Jamal pulled up the hand brake, took off his denim jacket and put it around my shoulders.

"This is winter in Beirut. Actually, the word for *winter* is the same as for *rain*. Guess what is it?"

Even after all this time, when I was agitated I still sometimes made grammatical mistakes but Jamal didn't seem to notice. He was driving at a crawl through curtains of rain.

"Hmmm. I dunno. What is it?"

"It's *shit*!"

He snorted. "It really is shitty!"

I could see Jamal was upset despite our joking and my mind raced. *Is he breaking up with me? Did he fail a class? What?*

"I have something to tell you. I, my—." His voice was unsteady. "Dad got a history chair at UC Berkeley. We're moving, Noor. Next month."

He pulled over, and out of the corner of my eye I saw him wipe his face with the sleeve of his sweatshirt. Lightning struck close by and I jumped. The rain was coming so fast that the wipers on high barely did anything.

"*Shiti*," he said quietly. "How appropriate."

Right when I thought nothing could get any worse, the one thing that was still good in my life was about to dissolve. "You're leaving? In a month? I can't believe this."

Tears pooled in my eyes and I wiped them on the sleeve of Jamal's jacket as I reached for the door.

"Noor, wait! It's not safe." Jamal sounded almost desperate. "At least let me take you home."

"No, Jamal. I need to be alone." I grabbed my pile of soaked papers, got out of the car and ran down the street. Rain engulfed me instantly, plastering my hair against my head. Jamal honked the horn of the old car, a feeble bleat, and I ran faster, screaming into the deluge.

"Why? Why this? Why now?" I ran through flooded streets and soggy grass. I ran with the roar of thunder echoing in my chest and wished it would take me away—away from him, away from Momma, away from here.

In the elevator, I wondered how I would bear living in the U.S. now that Jamal was leaving. He was the main reason I wanted to stay. Jamal, who always seemed to understand me without my having to explain myself. Jamal, who didn't see me as a mongrel who couldn't be fit into any category. He just saw Noor. Once he said I was like a mosaic, made up of all the broken pieces of the world coming together in a beautiful whole. I had teased him and told him he should be a poet, but in truth, his words described exactly what I saw in him, too. Having Jamal by my side had helped me see that in a way, this whole country was like a mosaic, but you had to discover the parts you could love, even if you didn't love the whole. And now he was leaving.

Suddenly it felt more urgent than ever for me to find my way back to Lebanon and I was determined to do that with or without Momma, somehow.

My last attempt to convince Momma we should go back home was just three days after school ended. It was a cool June day, still cloudy after the big storm, as if the clouds couldn't figure out how to move along. They swirled, dark and ominous, threatening to rain again. I pulled my sweater around me thinking how it was never cold in June in Lebanon. I had a picture of Jamal in my wallet and I pulled it out and kissed it.

"I'm sorry Jamal. I miss you already."

I heard the door handle click and I slid the photo back in its place.

"Noor? I'm home."

"Hello, Momma," I said.

I knew my only chance was to be convincing, yet diplomatic. She sat next to me, shawl wrapped around her head and neck for warmth, reminding me of women in the countryside back home.

"*Inshallah* we don't have to turn on the heat in June!" she said.

I adjusted her shawl and kissed her cheeks. "You look like a *hajjeh*, Momma, with your scarf wrapped around your head. It's freezing! In Lebanon we could be at AUB beach or Summerland getting a tan right now."

"*Habeebti.*"

I held her hands in mine. "Please let's go. It will be fine. We'll stay in

Beirut and I promise not to take risks. I won't go anywhere without you, I swear."

"*Ya* Noor, *ya ʿayni*. I wish. I really do, and I promise we will as soon as it's quiet again."

"When will it ever be quiet? Only god knows, but I can't take this anymore, Momma. I want to be home with Baba. With you and Baba."

"Noor," she said firmly. "I will not take you there while things are so unstable. Period."

"Sometimes I get the feeling you don't want to go back."

"Why would you say such a thing?"

"Because sometimes I think you had another reason for wanting to come here." I felt my face redden, felt an invisible force goading me on to speak when I knew I should stop.

"What other reason?"

"It's because of *him*, isn't it? Because of Antoine." The feelings I'd buried for so long started surfacing, my old suspicions rising up. "Ever since Antoine appeared in Beirut I could tell something wasn't right. How upset Baba was. Antoine arranging to bring us here. Why would he do that?"

Momma seemed more uncomfortable than angry, weaving and unweaving her fingers, avoiding my eyes.

"I've told you already, I came here to protect *you*, and Antoine was kind enough to help. He was going to bring us all, or have you forgotten?"

I felt a familiar boldness that seemed to emerge out of nowhere from time to time, empowering me to say and do things I never would if I stepped back and thought for a minute.

"I saw the way he looked at you that night at our party. I even saw you get out of a car with him one day near our house when I came home early."

Momma sighed. "Noor, it's not what you think and you have no right—"

"Then tell me. If it's not what I think, tell me what it *is*."

Her cheeks turned deep red and she cleared her throat nervously. "All right, Noor. But you have to keep an open mind because this is not easy."

I kept my eyes on hers, without speaking.

"First of all, I did not cheat on your father. I know that's what you're thinking, but I would never do that to him. Second of all, I did not come here to be with Antoine."

I was relieved but still skeptical.

"But we did know each other a long time before the night he came to the party with Yusuf."

Momma touched her hair, got that faraway look of hers.

"You see, Noor, we were in college together at AUB, Antoine and me. We were both studying journalism. I met your Baba during those years too, but he was already starting graduate school when Antoine and I were still freshmen. In junior year, I took a Poli Sci class and Rasheed was the Teaching Assistant. That was how we met, but there was nothing between us, at least not as far as I was concerned. Then, in senior year, I started writing for the school newspaper and Antoine was the student editor. I have to admit, I did have a bit of a crush on him."

She seemed so young, as if remembering her college days turned her back into a girl in her early twenties. "He was so handsome, with his sandy hair and blue eyes. He always took care of his appearance and he was carefree and funny. Not to mention he was editor of the paper, so to my young eyes he seemed very important. From time to time, he'd smile at me from across the room and wink and my legs would go weak."

Hearing her experience reminded me of how I felt when I met Jamal. How one glance from him from a distance sent a tingle of pleasure down my body. But I still wasn't sure what all of this had to do with us coming to America.

"That was how it went, until one day I came to the newspaper office late. He could see I was distressed. I had gotten a bad grade on one of my midterms and I was crushed. I was always a straight *A* student, like you, Noor, and I couldn't believe it. A *B-* seemed like a disaster. Antoine could see I was devastated and after work he walked with me, asked what was wrong. He put his arm around me and comforted me and, well," she paused. "Well, no more details, Noor, except to say we became, *ya'ni*, too close." Momma shifted uncomfortably in her chair and paused as if she wanted to be sure I understood what she was saying. "Close in a way I knew we shouldn't—that my family would never accept if they knew, but I was so young—and I was crazy about him. I was so sure he felt the same and we'd graduate and get married and then I wouldn't have to feel shame about what we'd done."

I had to turn away, embarrassed that my own mother—who'd given me so many warnings about boys—seemed to be admitting she'd slept with someone before marriage, before Baba. I'd barely even thought about having sex myself, but to learn about Momma that way was almost unimaginable. She took her time before continuing.

"I'm sorry, *habeebti*. This is not easy for either of us."

Her face was so serious, the lines in her forehead as deep as I'd ever seen them. I knew it must be even harder for her to tell her daughter such things than it was for me to hear them.

"It's OK, Momma."

The windows were closed and the air was stale and heavy, smelled like yesterday's onions and fish. Momma breathed deeply before continuing.

"Before Antoine graduated, he had already been offered a job in New York through his uncle who was living here at the time and had arranged the whole thing. It wasn't the best opportunity, but it was a job and he was thrilled to be going to America. He never said one word about me going with him, or about marriage, or coming back for me. I was devastated—and afraid."

"Afraid?"

"Before I knew it, he graduated and disappeared from my life—forever as far as I knew. So, there I was, twenty-two years old with no one to turn to. Momma was long dead and I'd never felt comfortable confiding in my aunt and uncle, *especially* about something like this. I felt that no man would want to marry me anymore, you understand, *hayaati?*"

I nodded, suddenly understanding Momma's warnings about boys and sex in a new way. I thought, too, about Maria breaking up with Alex because he pressured her for sex. It shocked me to think that Momma could have gotten pregnant that day. One mistake like that could change your life forever, especially for a girl.

"I know times have changed and it might seem strange to you, but in a way I felt my life was over, that I was destined to be alone and lonely and ashamed forever."

She told me that when Baba was her TA he had fallen in love with her but he didn't have the courage to ask her out—how in those days it was really difficult to act on such feelings in our society, so he just waited and pined for her and on graduation day they met again. He was graduating with his PhD the same day and somehow they crossed paths and ended up talking. He asked her how she was, what her plans were, her next steps in life. She said he was so kind, she suddenly found herself crying and confessing her situation to him.

"A few weeks later he asked me to marry him. *Antoine was a fool to abandon you*, he said, holding my hand. *He doesn't deserve you.* I couldn't believe that any man could be so loving and supportive in that situation, especially in those days in our society."

Momma said that nothing seemed to dissuade him. Not that she'd been with another man. Not that they would be starting their life together when they barely knew each other and neither of them had a job yet. He said he loved her and that was all that mattered—that if she would have him, he would be happy and he promised to do everything in his power to make her happy too.

"Even though I wasn't in love with him yet, his caring and kindness stole my heart. I knew I would grow to love such a man in time." She sighed and smiled, visibly relieved to be done with such a difficult admission. "So now you know why Baba and I were so shocked when Antoine appeared at our flat unexpectedly after all those years, why Baba was so angry."

"I'm glad you told me, Momma. I've been so confused."

There were so many things I still didn't understand—why Antoine came back, what his true motives were, why he'd brought us to New York, but for the moment I needed time to be alone, to absorb everything she'd told me.

Lying on my bed, those questions and more kept coming to me. How could Antoine abandon Momma like that? And what did he want now? Did he feel guilty? Did he think he could win Momma back? Did she love him? Did she ever really love Baba? I wished I could call Baba and get his side of the story, but that was impossible. Suddenly I felt overcome by the desire to leave New York and Momma and Antoine behind, especially with Jamal leaving soon. I just wanted to be with Baba. He always spoke the truth, never thought of himself. He was the most caring, loving person I'd ever known. I couldn't understand how Momma had been anything other than completely in love with him.

When Momma called me for dinner, I pretended to be asleep, needing time to devise a plan.

I dragged a chair over to the tall closet and pulled my big suitcase down. I'd fill it with all my clothing and worldly possessions, which were few, slip out while Momma was in the shower. I'd call Jamal from a pay phone, apologize for my impulsive behavior, ask his forgiveness and his help in planning my escape. We'd drive to Aisha's dorm at Wesleyan where I'd spend the night, she'd help figure out how to borrow enough money for me to buy an airline ticket the next day, he'd drive me to the airport where we'd say our emotional goodbyes and I'd wave from the tiny airplane window, hoping he'd see me from the departure lounge, and off I'd soar to freedom on my own terms.

I punched my pillow. I could just imagine what Jamal would say if I could talk to him. *What are you thinking, Noor? This is so jive. How could you do that to your mother? Not to mention, you'll never get away with it. Let's sit and talk this through.*

I sighed and replaced the suitcase. Instead, I pulled out the bag with the bamboo-chewing panda and put in a pair of pajamas, change of underwear, jeans, and a clean t-shirt, Baba's worry beads, the Malcolm X diary from Jamal, the gloves from Rebecca. I took the Key down from the wall and put it in my purse along with my jewelry and the envelope containing my $120 of savings. I waited until I heard Momma get in the shower, grabbed my umbrella, put the panda bag over my shoulder and tiptoed to the living room, where I called Rebecca.

"Rebecca? I'll explain everything later, but can I come stay over tonight?"

I replaced the phone receiver in its cradle and started for the apartment door. In my haste, the bag slid off my shoulder and whacked into the bookcase, sending a small decorative plate with a Quranic verse praising *Allah* in three metals, clattering to the floor.

"Noor?" Momma's muffled voice from behind the bathroom door. "Are you OK, *'ayni*?"

I pressed my fingertips against my closed eyelids. "Yes, Momma, fine. I'm going to stay over at Rebecca's." I slipped out of the door with her worried voice trailing after me.

"Noor, wait!"

Running toward Rebecca's apartment, the two bags hugged to my sides, I saw the faint light of a payphone ahead of me. I stopped, balancing the umbrella while I dug out a dime. Maybe I could still persuade Jamal—if he'd even listen to me after I'd run off like that. It was worth a try. Momma thought I was staying with Rebecca so I had time. I'd tell Jamal how sorry I was, that I couldn't bear to stay in New York without him, that I really needed his help to get back to Beirut. I'd say not to worry, that I'd make it up to Momma in the future, that first thing in the morning I'd buy the ticket and be on my way and he could hand deliver a letter from me before she even realized I was missing. I'd say I was determined to do it with or without his help and he'd relent, drive me through the night to Aisha's where I'd share her little bed and he'd sleep on the floor, our fingertips touching.

The dial tone patiently awaited my orders, humming monotonously in my ear. *Shit.* I'd left my address book in my desk drawer. I knew Jamal's number by heart, but I could see Momma, one towel wrapped around her warm, fragrant body, another wound around her wet hair, rushing to the front door, then to my bedroom, where she'd notice that the Key was missing from the wall, then all the other items that were gone, too. She'd open the desk drawer, find the address book and call Rebecca's mother, who would tell her that I hadn't arrived. She'd call Jamal's house. Jamal's father would tell her that Jamal had left abruptly, saying he was going to visit friends. He would then call Aisha's dorm, where a student would summon a barefoot Aisha to answer the phone in the hallway and by the time Jamal and I arrived, Middletown police would be waiting for us. I smacked the payphone receiver back down in its holder and made my way through the chilly, drizzly night to Rebecca's house.

Rebecca and I sat cross-legged on her bed, she in a tie-dyed night dress, me in the pajamas with a Lebanese cedar tree design that Baba had sent back with Salwa and Farah after Christmas. I told her Momma's story, how at first it had made me feel better, but the more I thought, the worse I felt. I told her about my secret decision to go to Lebanon on my own, and how I needed her help to figure it out. I thought of the day my friends and I sat in my bedroom defacing our ID cards; how our misdeed was discovered by Momma when Layla's ID card fell out of her backpack on the way out the front door of another apartment in another city, so long ago. I thought, too, of Layla on our last day together in Beirut saying, *Honestly, I'm kind of glad you'll be where you'll stay out of trouble!* How I'd quipped, *I'm not sure I know how.*

Rebecca told me that of course she'd do anything to help me, but she couldn't see my plan working. "First of all, would they even let you fly overseas alone? And even if they do, how could you possibly get enough money for the ticket? And let's say you somehow manage all of that, it just isn't *right*. You know, girl, a major reason I admire you so much is because, unlike a lot of kids, you have *integrity*, which might just be compromised if you go through with your evil plan."

"Oh, Rebecca, I just don't know what to do. This weird situation between Momma and Antoine, Jamal leaving, being stuck, unable to go back home."

"Listen to me. If Jews and Arabs have one thing in common it's how much we value family? How loyal we are to our parents? And in spite of you being a rebel and me being a hippie, we both know there's nothing more important than family, right?"

Of course she was right. I had let my frustration and confusion blind me to the obvious. I could never walk away from Momma and leave her behind just because I was angry, even if I did spend a lot of time fantasizing about doing just that.

"Noor, I really do admire your *chutzpah*, but I think we need to come up with a new plan."

That new plan presented itself, without much effort on our part, when Rebecca's mother summoned us to the living room. Momma was already sitting, a bit primly, on the edge of the avocado colored velour sofa, her hair disheveled from rain and wind. Her lips were pursed tightly, whether from anger or to keep from crying, I couldn't be sure. I sat close to her in a swirl of fear, remorse, and dread.

Thankfully, Rebecca's mother broke the tension. "I'll make us some tea. Please feel at home." She had a no-nonsense style that I could see a hint of in Rebecca, and she, too, had pretty, dark auburn hair, but wavy and carefully styled, unlike Rebecca's wild mess of curls. I liked the straightforward way she spoke, balancing the somber tone in the room.

I was struggling for words, knowing that the big, empowering, juicy balloon that was my fantasy, had been popped and lay deflated in my lap. What could I possibly say?

Momma put her hand on mine. "Oh Noor, my dearest daughter. When I realized you had left, possibly not intending to return, not knowing where you were going, I cannot tell you how wounded I felt, but also how guilty. All this time I have kept you here, trying to keep you from danger and harm back home, but if you felt the need to run away, then I have failed as a mother. What do I have if not the love and trust of my only child?"

"Momma—"

"It's all right, Noor. What I need right now is not for you to make me feel better. I need somehow to make this situation right. What I told you earlier," she said, casting a sideways glance at Rebecca, "I'd never imagined sharing with you, but it was a naïve hope, because the truth always comes out in life."

"I know Momma, but I'm still confused about our family. Confused about how *you* think of our family."

"I know, and I hope what I'm about to say will help you feel less confused."

Momma said that when I left and she saw the Key missing she knew I might not come back. She said that after her immediate panic, something changed in her. She realized that she'd allowed her fears to guide the decisions she made for years, that when she saw me so *determined*, acting so fearlessly for what I believed was right, she was moved.

"I'm not saying what you did was right, Noor, because it wasn't, but I know that it was driven by your passion for your family, your country, by the fact that we have been separate from your father for far too long."

When she mentioned Baba, I slumped against her, sobbing. I missed him so much and I felt so bad for him now that I knew about Momma and Antoine. How could he not be worried about what might happen when he was too far away to do anything about it? I just wanted to hug him, tell him how much I loved him. Rebecca's mother stopped at the door with the tea tray in her hands and started to turn back when she saw Momma and me red-eyed and hugging.

"It's OK," Momma said. "I think we could all use a cup of tea. Not to mention it is *your* home after all."

Everyone relaxed and we had tea with milk and homemade chocolate chip cookies. Even Momma had her tea with milk, so it seems it was truly a day for open-mindedness.

Momma thanked Rebecca's mother for her hospitality and for letting us *have a drama in your living room*, as she put it.

"Any time," Rebecca's mother said, "but hopefully next time it will be for a happier occasion!"

"Yes, *inshallah*, but, next time you will come to our home for a traditional Middle Eastern meal. I'll have Noor call Rebecca to arrange a time with you."

Momma made good on everything she said and implied that night— made it clear she was not interested in Antoine romantically, that she'd never intended to be with him that way. *Except in college, that is*, she said. I was a bit shocked, but happy she was able to joke about such a serious subject. She had let me in on a secret and it had brought us closer, made everything less mysterious and confusing.

It felt good to be planning together, not one of my reckless, spur-of-the-moment plans for a dramatic getaway, but one that accounted for everyone's needs and wishes. She promised we would go back before the start of the next school year—my senior year—but said that it made sense to take part of the summer to get everything in order, and I had to agree. I'd have time to reconcile with Jamal and leave on good terms, have a couple more months with Rebecca and my other friends, Momma would figure out next steps with her job and how to transition back to life—and possibly a new position—in Beirut. To say proper goodbyes to Antoine and Gabbie, to thank them for everything they had done for us over the past two years.

A couple days later, I was coming home after a *for old time's sake* day at the Botanic Gardens with Samantha, as she called it, and when I opened the door I overheard Momma talking with Antoine. They hadn't noticed me coming in and I heard him say, a bit sadly, "But what about us?"

"There is no *us*, Antoine. You're a dear friend and you've been so good to us, and I'm truly grateful for that, but that is all."

"*C'est dommage, ma chérie.* I've never stopped thinking of you all these years, hoping—"

"Antoine," Momma said in the gentle but firm way she had. "You made your choice the day you left—and left me to fend for myself. You gave up your right to be anything other than a friend that day—and you have been a good friend, so let's just leave it at that."

"Well you can't blame me for trying."

"No, Antoine, I don't blame you anymore, but Rasheed has been waiting a very long time to have his family back and that time has come."

That eavesdropped conversation erased any lingering doubt I might have had about the nature of our family, Antoine's place in it, and Momma's feelings about it. It went a long way to repairing our relationship, which had so been rocky since we left Beirut. I was able to see her as a flawed person, like I was, but with far more *integrity*, to use Rebecca's word, than I'd given her credit for.

23.

The most important thing I needed to do before we left was to make things right with Jamal. When I called him to apologize for the way I'd acted—for storming off when he was just as devastated as I was—I could tell he was crying. He said he hadn't been sure he'd ever see me again—even if I did survive that lightning storm.

It was a beautiful day when we met at Morrie and Minna's—the heavens seemed to have used up all the water they had available. Jamal was already sitting in a booth and had ordered two milkshakes that were ready when I arrived. I approached shyly and he got up and hugged me.

"I missed you, Noor."

"Missed you more."

He smiled sadly. "I guess we're going to have to get used to that."

Jamal pointed at my milkshake. "Yours is mocha, but mine is different. It's mocha."

I gave him a puzzled look and he said, "Yours is coffee ice cream and chocolate syrup and mine is chocolate ice cream and coffee syrup."

"Perfect."

I moved to his side of the table and sat in the booth next to him, held his hand under the table. I told him how heartbroken I'd been when he said he was leaving for California, that, on top of learning that we wouldn't be going to Lebanon for the summer, it was too much for me to handle.

"I know I was being melodramatic, but I couldn't help it. I felt so hopeless. Like nothing would ever be right again. I couldn't bear that you were leaving. Now it sounds crazy but I almost *wished* I'd be hit by lightning."

Jamal squeezed my hand. "I'm very glad you weren't."

"Me too. I never would have gotten to have this milkshake!"

After we finished, we went to his apartment. We lay together on the same sofa where I'd confided in him and he'd held me while I cried and poured out my story for the first time. On this day though, there were no stories, no confessions, just the warm, gentle feeling of his body surrounding mine, our lips together, our hands caressing each other's bodies. At one point, he raised up and rested his head on his hand.

"Noor?"

"Yes?"

"Do you—want to?"

"Yes I want to, but I'm not going to. Not yet."

"But this could be our only chance."

"Then, what's the point?"

"The point is to know that you're the first girl I ever gave myself to. Ever really wanted to."

"Oh, Jamal. I so badly want you to be the first, too, but I just can't."

"It's OK," he said, "Just lie with me here awhile and promise you'll never forget me."

I pressed my face into his chest, breathed in the slight woodiness of his scent that I loved—his hair and skin holding the greenness of the summer air, a faint funkiness from his bare feet.

"I will never forget you, Jamal Ahmad. The first and only boy I've given my heart to."

The last time I saw Jamal, he came over for dinner and Momma was on her best behavior. She made *maqlouba* which seemed fitting, since *maqlouba* means upside down, like everything else in our lives at the time, and it was nice that she prepared a traditional Palestinian dish for him. He said he loved it because it was so nice of her to make it for him and because he loved all the ingredients; the rice that ended up at the bottom when it was flipped over, the lamb and eggplant and finally on the top—that had been the bottom—almonds and pine nuts. I was pleased they had a chance to see each other so that awful Thanksgiving wasn't the last, lingering memory. Momma even left us alone in the living room after dinner, busied herself with cleaning up and putting away the dishes.

I pulled a photo album down from the bookshelf and opened it on our laps. He studied picture after picture, asking about each one. Photos of Baba, Layla, of AUB and Hamra, pictures in our apartment, of us having fish at the beach in Tyre with a big bunch of cousins, aunts and uncles, grandparents. There was one of a ski trip we'd taken to Faraya before the war when I was ten. When he'd studied every picture I closed the album.

"Lebanon seems pretty cool. You'll see, someday I'll come—if you're not with some other guy, that is!"

It was hard to know what to say to each other that last night. We'd be more than 5,000 miles apart, separated by a very large ocean, another continent and at least one sea. It was surreal saying goodbye, because even though we were still kids, it felt completely right being together, so we promised to write and I said this wasn't really goodbye, since I believed that he would come to Lebanon someday.

The Way Things Change

Summer 1978

24.

As the jet climbed skyward, I strained for a final glimpse of the skyscrapers, rivers, bridges, parks, the well-ordered streets and avenues of the city that had become my uneasy home, still shimmering in the low sun. It was tiny now and tenuous, as if it might slide into the sea from its island platform.

I remembered what Baba had said to me when I left Beirut—that when you depart you dwell on everything you're leaving behind, but as you approach a new place you start thinking of everything you're going to. As we crossed the ocean, I began wondering what it would be like returning to Lebanon after two years in which so much had happened. I wondered how I'd feel the first time I saw Baba, knowing what I knew. Wondered what Beirut would be like now that it was divided into East and West, occupied by a foreign army. Maybe my friends would reject me, feel that I'd betrayed them, left them at the worst time. I'd even mostly lost my accent and they'd probably think of me as an American now, even though I knew I would always be 'arabiyyeh first.

How could I even begin to explain how I'd changed? How the old, fearless Noor was now terrified that I'd walk in the wrong part of Beirut and get caught by sniper fire. Or that I had given my heart to an American boy with an Arab name and that I would miss New York terribly.

I was wearing Jamal's sweater and I pulled it closer around my body. I had asked him for it on our last day, and he'd apologized that he didn't have a proper gift for me, but if only he knew that this was the best thing he could have given me. It was soft and cozy against my skin and it smelled like him. I ran my finger around the macramé bracelet with the two flags, that Jamal had made for me in Maine. I'd never taken it off since the day he tied it around my wrist and declared, *Now you are mine, all mine!*

I remembered how I felt the only other time I'd been in an airplane— how the Middle East Airlines jet had risen from Beirut airport first to the south, then out to sea, the village of Bchamoun off to the left, tiny lines of laundry waving in the wind in silent farewell to their friend, Noor.

Now as we approached Beirut I was filled with longing and anticipation.

So many things had happened to me that I wished hadn't—the war, the assault, the accident, my injury, but these were as much a part of me now as all the good things—New York, Jamal, learning the truth about Momma and Antoine. Each hurt, each scar had taught me something about myself and the world and now I could see that painful experiences can't just be buried and forgotten. They were also part of who I'd become, adding layers, like new bark growing to strengthen the strong core that had always been there.

I was on the left side of the aircraft and when we dipped south on the approach to the airport, my heart opened at the sight of the blocky buildings of Beirut, the sensual curve of the shoreline, the mountains rising beyond the city. From the air it appeared exactly the same, but I knew that Lebanon would be as changed as I was—strong and vulnerable, wounded yet still whole, grounded in the past, but ready for whatever might come.

I didn't expect to be face to face with a Syrian soldier as soon as we walked off the plane. I knew the Syrian Army was occupying Beirut but I hadn't thought much about what it would mean other than seeing their checkpoints and tanks in the streets, yet it became a reality very suddenly when they interrogated Momma.

Why were you in America? What did you do there? Where is your husband? Why are you coming back now? Who is meeting you? Where are you staying?

I could see resentment and a hint of worry on Momma's face but she answered straightforwardly, without an argument.

"To escape the fighting. I worked at a newspaper. He couldn't get a visa so he stayed. It's safer now. My husband is meeting us. Home in Ras Beirut."

Baba came in a taxi because the car was having engine trouble. He had to wait outside where they had erected metal security barriers. He waved wildly and threw kisses from a distance and we embraced and cried across the barrier and when we exited we embraced and kissed and cried some more. Baba squeezed Momma and me so hard I think I stopped breathing for a minute.

"*Da'faan habeebi,*" Momma said looking Baba up and down. "You are too skinny. *Haraam!*"

We piled our luggage into the trunk and as we sped away from the terminal, Arabic music was blaring from the cassette player, worry beads swinging from the rearview mirror, dust swirling in through the open windows. I couldn't help smiling. We really had been away a long time.

The whole ride along the coastal route to Ras Beirut I stared out the windows as we passed sandbagged checkpoints, sand piles taller than a man and one Syrian Army tank after another. Like an abandoned city. Not a single building was free of scars, char from mortar blasts fanning out like giant inkblots, gaping holes of every size and shape imaginable marring the walls. Some balconies were so badly damaged they sagged toward the ground like a Dali painting, chairs and potted plants threatening to topple down to the street below. The majestic palm trees that lined the *Corniche al-Manara* drooping as if they'd been scorched by a relentless Saharan wind, brown fronds swaying sadly in the breeze that blew in hotly from the Mediterranean. Only the sea was unchanged, gentle and blue, that and the harsh sun above, ferocious as ever.

As we approached Ras Beirut, the damage was less extreme and I was relieved to see that our building was still standing, but somehow older and shabbier now. The wide balcony of our second floor apartment seemed smaller to me. It was covered with ivy, the potted fig and lemon trees unpruned, the wildflowers wilder than I remembered, overgrown in their boxes.

Once inside, Momma walked through the kitchen and living room, ran her hands over the inlaid backgammon board, Baba's *darbakkeh* drum, pictures of the family standing dustily on the hutch. I ran to my room, threw open the window, fell onto my bed, and breathed in all the scents of home that had faded in memory—the humid, smoky air, salty sea breeze, baking bread, wafts of garbage and exhaust, roasting meat.

That night the electricity went out, like it often did in those days. We lit the kerosene lantern and made a late dinner over the gas fire—a stew of chicken and peas over rice—the *yakhneh* that had always been a family favorite. Momma refused to accept help, so Baba brought the backgammon board into the kitchen, like the old days, and he and I played while Momma cooked. It felt almost normal. Almost.

That night I collapsed from exhaustion around midnight, and the next day I slept until almost one in the afternoon, my confused body still operating on New York time, seven hours earlier. Through my partially opened door, I heard my parents talking, Momma insisting that he was too skinny, that something wasn't right with him. It was true that Baba had changed shockingly in two years. His face was pale and lined, with dark circles under his eyes, hair grayer than before. His *karsh* was gone, but not in a healthy way. Instead he looked drawn and old, his shoulders pulled forward.

"What is it, *habeebi*? I can see something is wrong."

"You see what happens when my wife is not here to cook for me?" The joke sounded forced.

"Have you been ill, Rasheed? Tell me what's going on."

There was a long silence before he spoke again.

"I'm sorry, Nadine. I just found out. I kept thinking it was from all the stress and I didn't want to believe I was sick, didn't want to worry you."

Now that we were finally back together, it was almost more than I could bear learning that Baba had liver cancer. He'd always hated doctors and had waited much too long to see one and by the time he was diagnosed it had spread, undetected, throughout his body. Now all we could do was comfort him, take care of him, try to make up for some of the time we had lost as a family.

Momma and I promised to cook him a healthy dinner every night. Stuffed cabbage, squash and eggplants, artichoke hearts, stews with fresh okra or green beans or broad beans, the freshest fish and leanest meats available. I worked side-by-side with her in the kitchen with new-found passion. One day, we were sitting at the kitchen table eating *mulookhiyyah* with chicken, one of his favorites. He didn't have much of an appetite any more, but that day he happily slurped up the dark green leaves that made a thick, lemony sauce when cooked, and told us how delicious it was.

"You are becoming a great cook like your Momma," Baba said, squeezing my shoulders.

Once we'd settled in, I made a plan to see Layla. Momma hadn't adjusted to driving in Beirut yet, and since Baba had gotten the car back, he insisted on driving me even though I could see he was tired.

"Baba, I'm seventeen now. I can take a *servees*. Stay here and relax, please," I told him, handing him a cup of the bitter, black Turkish coffee with cardamom he loved so much, his hand trembling when he reached for it. He sighed with the first sip, his eyes closing with the pleasure of it. It amazed me how such a small thing could make him so happy, even now.

"*Sallim dayaatik*," he said, thanking "my hands," his smile as warm as ever.

He finished the coffee in a few sips and pushed himself up out of his chair.

"I will take you to town. It's not the way you remember it though, Najnouj. *Ya'ni*, Syrian checkpoints everywhere, snipers, clashes here and there. You have to be careful."

Momma insisted on driving with us to be with Baba, and even though Layla lived far from the *Green Line* that now separated Beirut into east and west, I asked if we could drive that way, just so I could see what it was like now. Baba agreed reluctantly and as we approached the area, the gutted Holiday Inn building loomed in the distance, the 26-story structure like a gruesome memorial, its walls scarred by artillery burns and gaping holes, worse than anything I'd seen on the ride from the airport. Not a single window remained. The elegant, ancient buildings of downtown, with their graceful arched windows, now stood empty, some reduced to piles of stone, twisted metal and glass. Tires, crumpled cars, a single shoe, even a toilet, lay amid the rubble. Goose flesh rose on my bare arms as if it was winter, as Baba navigated streets deserted and sandbagged, the separation of the city into east and west as complete and forbidding as if it had been marked by a concrete wall.

The image I had in my mind—lively souks, crowded sidewalk cafes, people strolling arm-in-arm—it all bubbled and crumpled in front of my eyes like a happy family photo thrust into a bonfire.

We drove in silence, no words able to express the grief pushing on our chests. I was so glad we all went together. I don't think I could have handled the sight of so much destruction alone.

When we got to Layla's house, she was waiting outside for me. I fell into her arms and suddenly I was sobbing so hard I couldn't stop. It was as if all the loss and sadness of my life came out right then.

Layla held me quietly for a time and I felt so safe and accepted that all my fears about coming back melted in her embrace.

"What is this?" she asked softly.

"It's just all so, *ya'ni*—," I stopped and sighed, wiping my eyes.

"I know, Noor, I know. *Yalla, khalas*, let's go get a coffee and catch up on the last two years. I want to know all about America and Jamal *al-jameel*," she said, playing on the real meaning of Jamal's name, *beauty*.

"What's it like living there? *Ya'ni* does everyone have big houses and fancy cars?" Layla teased, knowing that couldn't really be true.

"No, no, in New York everyone lives in apartments like here, but there we don't have balconies."

I winced when I used the word *we*.

I told Layla that Beirut would always be my first love, but that I had come to love New York, too, and that I couldn't help missing it a little already. "Especially Jamal."

"What's he like? Tell me *everything*."

Layla had that impish look, just like the old days. I grinned. How I'd missed my old friend.

"He's—my god Layla, he's so nice and handsome and kind, you can't imagine."

"*Yi, yi, yi*, Noor's in love! Did you…?" She arched her eyebrow at me and I knew exactly what she meant.

I blushed. "No, not everything, but enough." In truth, we had just cuddled and kissed and touched a little, but I was embarrassed to discuss details, even with Layla.

We both giggled and it felt almost like the old days, except that we were both noticeably older now, she a college student already. She'd loved her first year at AUB, couldn't wait to go back.

I gave her the 'Cliff Notes' to my two years in America—my anger at Momma for uprooting me and making me leave Lebanon, how distant and dry people had seemed to me at first, how I missed everything a person could miss the whole time I was there, but how I had gradually gotten used to big department stores, towering buildings, freezing winters, the greener, less earthy smells of the vegetation, the way people avoided talking about politics, having to plan visits with friends. It had all felt so alien and heartless in the beginning, but that had changed over time.

She asked me what it had been like living in Antoine's apartment before Momma and I got our own place and when I blushed and stammered she narrowed her eyes at me, cat-like.

"Out with it. Why did you get shy?"

I hadn't planned to tell Layla about Momma and Antoine but when she asked this I blurted out the whole story. Afterwards I felt guilty for betraying Momma's confidence, but Layla hugged me and promised she'd never tell. I appreciated that she didn't make a joke about how scandalous the story was and how daring Momma had been, even though I knew she'd be thinking just that. Instead, she said, "You have the best mom. I can't imagine my mother ever sharing something like that with me—or *doing* anything like that. Anyway, I'm just so glad you're back, Noor, and that your family's back together."

"Me too, but now it's too late for everything. I wish we'd never left."

"Never mind, *habeebti*. Just enjoy the time you have together."

I hadn't been back to Hamra Street yet, so we went to meet friends and have a snack, but even Hamra was changed—the mood subdued, people's faces pulled into permanent frowns, Syrian checkpoints here and there— enforcing the peace, but in an ominous, menacing way. I wondered where the carefree Beirut I grew up in had gone. It was as if there was a gray pall over everything, and everyone. Even our friends measured every word they said, speaking in low, guarded tones.

Layla suggested a walk on the AUB campus and I was comforted to find it nearly unchanged—the bursting vegetation, elegant stone buildings with red tiled roofs and arched windows, the "adopted" stray cats stretched out on paths, benches, and walls. The banyan tree. When Layla saw some friends waving from a distance, I said I'd catch up with her.

Whenever I'd thought of the tree before, it was the memory of Ra'ad and me hiding inside the narrow spaces between the clustered vertical roots, the thrill of being hidden—or partially hidden—in that tangled thicket.

Looking at it now, from outside, I noticed what I hadn't before. Root structures so often give trees their stability and longevity through their hidden, underground life, steadfast, but concealed.

The banyan's roots are fully exposed, while anchored in the soil, as if welcoming whatever might come, secure in its position, open to the world.

The rest of the summer passed quickly and it was with a heavy heart that I went back to high school to finish senior year, wishing I could stay home instead to be close to Baba. That fall and winter my parents were practically inseparable. Baba's deteriorating health required nearly constant attention and I know it was healing for both of them that Momma acted as nurse, housekeeper and caretaker for him, as well as partner. She fed him spoonfuls of her chicken soup when he had no appetite left, and read to him when he was too fatigued to hold the book for himself.

One evening, in late spring, I came in from school to find Momma curled up next to Baba on the sofa, both fast asleep, an open book still in her grip, her other hand resting on his back. I put my hand over my mouth and thought, *We lost so much time. So much precious time.* Even though I had seen horrible things in war, had been, in a way, violated, and had almost died in a car crash, this was the first time I ever really felt that it is impossible to stop time or slow it down—that we have only our one life and we can never get back what we have lost. A deep ache overtook me and I wished I could curl up with them like I had as a little girl, when I'd crawl into bed with them too early in the morning and listen to them breathing, Baba snoring. Instead, I went quietly into my room to study, trying to hold on to this image of tenderness between my parents that I knew would be one of the last.

Baba died a week later. We rushed him to the hospital in the middle of the night after Momma was unable to rouse him, but he never woke.

He died three weeks before my high school graduation, so even though it was he who had convinced me to complete my last year and not delay it because of him or *any other crazy ideas in that head of yours*, as he had said, he couldn't be there. I told Momma I didn't want to go to graduation, but she said he would have wanted me to and I think she was right.

I carried a big photograph of Baba—one that I had taken— from when he still had round cheeks, eyes that shined like there were lights inside and that big, warm smile I will never forget. I wore a garland around my head that Momma wove out of flowers from his garden, which he had started tending again when we came back, and took care of until he was too weak and exhausted. I accepted my diploma with tightness in my chest, but also a sense of peace. I knew how important it was that Momma and I had been next to him in the months before he died, giving him the love he had been deprived of for too long.

Several families of graduating seniors organized a lunch at Marrouche Restaurant, but it was too soon after Baba's death for me to be doing any celebrating, so I kissed and congratulated my friends and descended the long International College staircase, diploma in hand. Ironically, the warm, muggy air reminded me of New York now, my walks with Samantha in the Botanic Gardens, the wonderful, warm days spent discussing the universe with the posse, the exhilaration of discovering the love of my life, my soul mate, in that faraway city.

In my bedroom I pulled off my clothes and tossed them carelessly on the chair, slipped a nightgown on and opened my dresser drawer. Pushing aside my underclothes, I pulled out the blue Aerogramme airmail letter that I had read and re-read tens, maybe hundreds of times already, since it arrived a few weeks earlier. I pressed it to my chest, where the satiny material draped softly over my breasts. I smiled, brought the folded paper to my nose, hoping for a hint of him. There was the faint oily smell of the ink and as I closed my eyes and breathed deeper, I thought I might have caught a slight woodiness underneath.

In the morning, I walked barefoot down the cool terrazzo corridor, still yawning. I paused before reaching the kitchen. Momma was at the sink. From behind, I sensed that she was gazing out the window. I imagined her faraway look, the way her eyes would soften, her hair tied loosely at her neck. There was a *rakweh* of Turkish coffee, still steaming, on the inlaid tray my parents always used. Two cups, a bowl of sugar, a tiny spoon resting on the tray. The dark soil smell of the coffee stung with the brightness of cardamom. I breathed in slowly, hoping she wouldn't turn around just yet. I whispered the words.

I am home.

Acknowledgements

I am forever grateful for the generosity of devoted friends, family, and colleagues who have read, edited, offered commentaries and critiques, advised, and otherwise supported me and made the novel possible, including:

Francesca Bell, Marti Farha, Mona Fayad, Ena Fox, Nasser Hajo, Alia Haju, Ann Hood, Nada Awar Jarrar, Gish Jen, Kelley McKenna, Elias Muhanna, Dima Nasser, Stewart O'Nan, Rima Rantisi, Joanne Reynolds, Ali Saklawi, Ghada Sayegh, Liyana Silver, Beverly Pollock-Silver, Randa Azkoul Soubaih.

To Grub Street Writers, Matthew Salesses, and Adam Stumacher in whose workshops *Roots of The Banyan Tree* got its start, originally under the title *Four Swirls of Ink*.

To Joanne Reynolds and Ali Saklawi who supported me in countless ways through the many years it took to create the novel and who never let me doubt that it would find its way out into the world one day.

To dear friends Beshara, Issmat, Tala, and Yara Doumani, Lisa Goldfarb, Mark Levitan, Susan McCarthy, and Gina Zizza, who nourish me body and soul and believe in me always.

To my parents who aren't here to celebrate publication of the book, but who I know would have been proud. To my grandparents, Helen and Joseph Silver, who brought out the rebel in me and taught me to challenge authority.

To my sons, Bassil and Naseem, whose creative journeys have been as life-affirming, thrilling, challenging, and wild as my own and whose constant love brings me joy every day.

To my dearest Nasser, who has been with me on every twist and turn of the journey, and has walked hand-in-hand with me through every one of our incredible adventures together.

To my big, robust Lebanese family who have helped me grow in countless ways, taught me to see the joy in life even during times of hardship, and who keep me laughing, dancing, and drinking Turkish coffee in good times and bad.

To my small, but lovely American family who have been there since the beginning.

To Edward Vidaurre and the team at FlowerSong/Juventud Press who enthusiastically embraced the novel and brought it into the light of day.

With deep gratitude to the people who wrote such beautiful blurbs for *Roots of the Banyan Tree*: Gish Jen, Elias Muhanna, Stewart O'Nan, and Rima Rantisi.

And to all the dear people in my life who have encouraged me and kept me going through it all.

About the Author

Kathryn Silver-Hajo is a Pushcart Prize, Best Small Fictions, and Best American Food Writing nominee. Her flash fiction, poetry, and CNF appears in *Atticus Review, The Citron Review, CRAFT, Emerge Literary Journal, New York Times-Tiny Love Stories, Pithead Chapel, Ruby Literary, Rusted Radishes: Beirut Literary and Art Journal, and other lovely places.* Kathryn's flash collection *"Wolfsong"* was published in 2023 by ELJ Editions. Her work has been anthologized in *"Flare: An Anthology of Chronic Illness Told in Flash Narratives"* and *"Potato Soup Journal: Best of 2022."* Kathryn lives in Providence, Rhode Island with her husband and sassy, curly-tailed pup, Kaya.

More at:
kathrynsilverhajo.com
Twitter: KSilverHajo
Instagram: kathrynsilverhajo
Facebook: kathryn.silverhajo

Author's Note

In 1981, I moved to Beirut with my future husband after studying Arabic language, literature, and history in college and graduating with a degree in Middle Eastern studies. We lived there for several years during the second half of the Lebanese civil war and the 1982 Israeli invasion. Nothing in my readings, studies or friendships could have prepared me for the realities of life in the midst of war. In particular, I was profoundly affected by the drastic effects on children and families. I knew that someday I would write about those years in a way that transcended my subjective experience and reflected the far-reaching calamity that befell the country at the time.

My life in Lebanon, along with stories of loved ones there, provided the inspiration for *Roots of the Banyan Tree* and I am blessed to have a robust family and social network there to this day. That said, I want to acknowledge the challenges of writing about a country as a non-native resident and to express my gratitude to the many friends and acquaintances who helped me appreciate the realities that impacted Lebanese-born people in ways I could only begin to understand. In addition to conducting dozens of interviews and doing extensive research, I reached out to a number of people who lived through the entirety of the civil war for help with fact-checking and accuracy but also with opinions on whether I was accurately portraying what it might have felt like to be a teenage girl growing up in such circumstances.

I hope that *Roots of the Banyan Tree* will offer readers not only a glimpse of a culture they may be unfamiliar with, but also a sense of the complexities of living in times of war. In addition to trauma, fear, and uncertainty, profound bonds are often formed as well—some of which last a lifetime. It is the greatest honor of my life to have known so many courageous souls who lived through those difficult times, and to have had the opportunity to put into words some of what it means to survive a war, to lose loved ones to it, and to rebuild once it's over.

—*Kathryn Silver-Hajo*

Study Guide

1. What did you learn about Lebanon and the Middle East by reading *Roots of The Banyan Tree*? If you didn't know about the Lebanese Civil War before, what did you find most interesting or surprising?

2. The story is set in the mid-to-late 1970s, in both Lebanon and New York City. What differences do you notice from today's attitudes, interests, activities, and styles? What similarities?

3. What do you notice about clothing styles in the novel? Look at some pictures of 1970s fashion on the internet. How does it compare to today's styles?

4. Did any of the slang expressions and language used in the novel stand out to you? How does it compare to how you communicate with your friends?

5. Have you listened to music—especially R&B—from the mid to late 70's? Does it sound outdated to you or do you think it still holds up? Why?

6. Is Noor a character you can relate to in your own life? How is she similar to you or friends of yours? How different?

7. If you are a person of color do Noor's experiences reflect or resemble any of your own? How?

   If not, how are they different? If you are white, do Noor's experiences reflect or resemble any of your own? How and how not?

8. When Noor arrives in New York City, her first impressions of the U.S. are through the window of the taxi as they drive home from

the airport. If your family immigrated from another country, what were your very first impressions? Why do you think those things stood out?

9. Throughout the novel Noor's identity is evolving and she seeks friends and groups where she has a sense of belonging. What does it mean to be your authentic self—to become comfortable with who you are? Did being accepted in a certain group(s) help you strengthen your sense of self and your identity? Did you ever feel you were hiding part of yourself? Did you ever feel afraid to reveal your true self?

10. There's a scene at the front lines/battle zone where Noor photographs the action. Why do you think she takes this risk? What impact does the experience have on her—immediately and long term? Do you think it was worth it?

11. What is special about Noor's relationship with Layla? How would you compare it to her relationship with Rebecca and others?

12. How do you see Noor's relationship with Momma and Baba? In what ways do they influence her? In what ways does she influence them? How is she similar and/or different from each?

13. Food features throughout the novel, sometimes almost like another character. What role does food play in the novel? Why do you think the writer included such detailed food descriptions?

14. How are issues of race, ethnicity and otherness explored in the novel both in Lebanon and in New York? What does Noor learn from her friendships with Angel and Jamal in terms of her awareness of racism and how it affects people of color?

15. What does Noor's experience tell us about the world we live in?

16. What do you see as the most compelling challenges Noor faces? How does she deal with them? Do you think you'd act similarly in such circumstances? Differently? How and why? Have you faced

similar challenges in your own life? If so, did reading *Roots of the Banyan Tree* speak to you in ways other novels might not?

17. Why do you think Jamal pushes Noor away at one point? How does that experience affect both of them? What do they learn about their relationship and themselves as a result?

18. What is the significance of the Thanksgiving dinner scene to the story? How do you think it changes the characters and why?

19. If you've never lived in a war zone, how were you able to relate to Noor's experience in Beirut? What did you learn about war and how it affects relationships and daily lives? What coping mechanisms did Noor and other characters use during times of crisis? Have you ever experienced situations where you had to devise similar—or different—strategies to get through a crisis or difficult time?

20. What differences do you see in Noor's relationship with Raʿad vs. Jamal? Why does it matter?

21. What do you think is the significance of the final scenes of the novel? How has Noor changed by the end?

FLOWERSONG
PRESS

FlowerSong Press nurtures essential verse
from, about, and throughout the borderlands.
Literary. Lyrical. Boundless.

Sign up for announcements about
new and upcoming titles at:

www.flowersongpress.com

Printed in the USA
CPSIA information can be obtained
at www.ICGtesting.com
LVHW042020290724
786821LV00009B/20